DONNA LEON

BLOOD FROM A STONE

arrow books

Reissued by Arrow Books 2009

5 7 9 10 8 6

First published in Great Britain in 2005 by William Heinemann
First published in paperback in 2006 by Arrow Books

This edition published in 2009 by
Arrow Books
The Random House Group Limited
20 Vauxhall Bridge Road, London, SW1V 2SA

www.randomhouse.co.uk

Addresses for companies within The Random House Group Limited can be
found at: www.randomhouse.co.uk/offices.htm

The Random House Group Limited Reg. No. 954009

A CIP catalogue record for this book
is available from the British Library

ISBN 9780099536543

Typeset by SX Composing DTP, Rayleigh, Essex

The Random House Group Limited supports The Forest Stewardship
Council® (FSC®), the leading international forest-certification organisation.
Our books carrying the FSC label are printed on FSC®-certified paper.
FSC is the only forest-certification scheme supported by the leading
environmental organisations, including Greenpeace. Our
paper procurement policy can be found at
www.randomhouse.co.uk/environment

Printed and bound in Great Britain by Clays Ltd, St Ives PLC

for Gesine Lübben

Weil ein Schwarzer hässlich ist.
Ist mir denn kein Herz gegeben?
Bin ich nicht von Fleisch und Blut?

Thus a Blackmoor is considered ugly.
Didn't I receive a heart as well?
Aren't I made of flesh and blood?

—Mozart, *Die Zauberflöte*

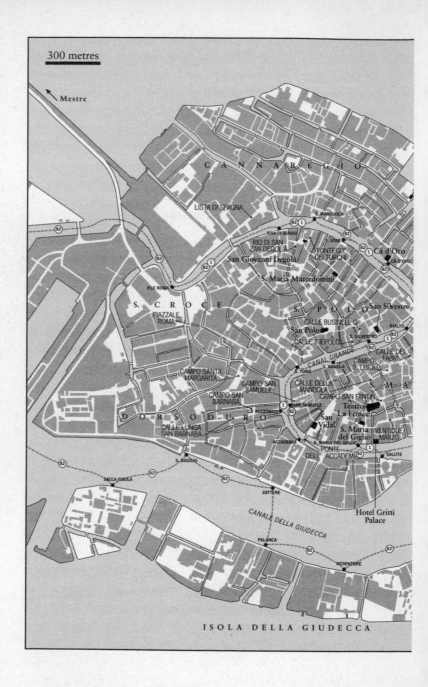

300 metres

Mestre

CANNAREGIO

LISTA DI SPAGNA

S. MARCUOLA

RIVA DI BIASIO

RIO DI SAN
ZAN DEGOLÀ

San Giovanni Degolà

S. STAE

FONTEGO
DEI TURCHI

Cà d'Oro

CÀ D'ORO

S. Maria Materdomini

P.LE ROMA

S. CROCE

S. POLO

San Silvestro

PIAZZALE
ROMA

CALLE BUSINELLO

San Polo

RIALTO

CALLE TIEPOLO

S. SILVESTRO

CALLE DEI
FABRI

CAMPO SANTA
MARGARITA

CANAL GRANDE

CAMPO
S. LUCA

S. TOMA

S. ANGELO

CAMPO SAN
SAMUELE

CALLE DELLA
MANDOLA

S. M A

CAMPO SAN
BARNABA

CA' REZZONICO

D O R S O D U R O

SAN SAMUELE

CAMPO SAN FANTIN

CALLE LUNGA
SAN BARNABA

San
Vidal

Teatro
La Fenice

ACCADEMIA

S. Maria
del Giglio

VENTIDUE
MARZO

S. BASILIO

S. MARIA DEL GIGLIO

PONTE
DELL' ACCADEMIA

SALUTE

SACCA FISOLA

ZATTERE

Hotel Gritti
Palace

CANALE DELLA GIUDECCA

PALANCA

REDENTORE

I S O L A   D E L L A   G I U D E C C A

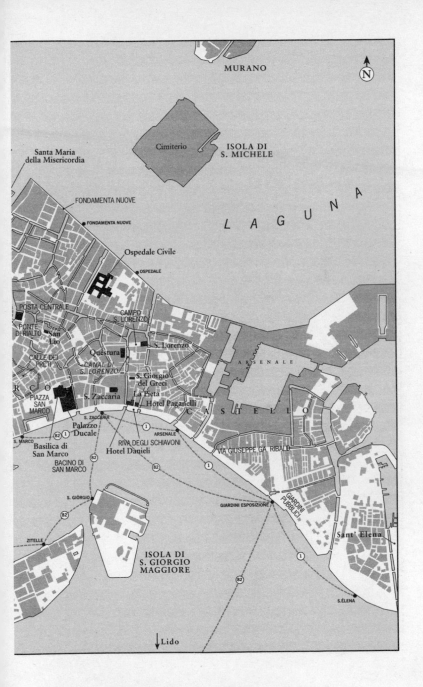

1

Two men passed under the wooden arch that led into Campo Santo Stefano, their bodies harlequined by the coloured Christmas lights suspended above them. Brighter light splashed from the stalls of the Christmas market, where vendors and producers from different regions of Italy tempted shoppers with their local specialities: dark-skinned cheeses and packages of paper-thin bread from Sardinia, olives in varying shape and colour from the entire length of the peninsula; oil and cheese from Tuscany; salami of all lengths, compositions, and diameters from Reggio Emilia. Occasionally one of the men behind the counters shouted out a brief hymn to the quality of his wares: 'Signori, taste this cheese and taste heaven'; 'It's late and

I want to go to dinner: only nine Euros a kilo until they're gone'; 'Taste this pecorino, signori, best in the world'.

The two men passed the stalls, deaf to the blandishments of the merchants, blind to the pyramids of salami stacked on the counters on either side. Last-minute buyers, their number reduced by the cold, requested products they all suspected could be found at better prices and of more reliable quality at their local shops. But how better to celebrate the season than by taking advantage of shops that were open even on this Sunday, and how better to assert one's independence and character than by buying something unnecessary?

At the far end of the *campo*, beyond the last of the prefabricated wooden stalls, the men paused. The taller of them glanced at his watch, though they had both checked the time on the clock on the wall of the church. The official closing time, seven-thirty, had passed more than a quarter of an hour before, but it was unlikely that anyone would be out in this cold to check that the stalls ceased trading at the correct time. '*Allora?*' the short one asked, glancing at his companion.

The taller man took off his gloves, folded them and put them in the left pocket of his overcoat, then jammed his hands into his pockets. The other did the same. Both of them wore hats, the tall one a dark grey Borsalino and the other a fur cap with ear flaps. Both had woollen scarves wrapped around their necks, and as they stepped beyond the circle of light from the last stand, they pulled them a bit higher, up around their ears, no strange thing to do in the face of the wind that came at them from the direction of the Grand Canal, just around the corner of the church of San Vidal.

The wind forced them to lower their faces as they started forward, shoulders hunched, hands kept warm in their pockets. Twenty metres from the last stall, on either side of the way, small groups of tall black men busied themselves spreading sheets on the ground, anchoring them at each corner with a woman's bag. As soon as the sheets were in place, they began to pull samples of various shapes and sizes from enormous sausage-shaped bags that sat on the ground all around them.

Here a Prada, there a Gucci, between them a Louis Vuitton: the bags huddled together in a promiscuity usually seen only in stores large enough to offer franchises to all of the competing designers. Quickly, with the speed that comes of long experience, the men bent or knelt to place their wares on the sheets. Some arranged them in triangles; others preferred ordered rows of neatly aligned bags. One whimsically arranged his in a circle, but when he stepped back to inspect the result and saw the way an outsized dark brown Prada shoulder bag disturbed the general symmetry, he quickly re-formed them into straight lines, where the Prada could anchor their ranks from the back left corner.

Occasionally the black men spoke to one another, saying those things that men who work together say to pass the time: how one hadn't slept well the night before, how cold it was, how another hoped his son had passed the entrance exam for the private school, how much they missed their wives. When each was satisfied with the arrangement of his bags, he rose to his feet and moved back behind his sheet, usually to one corner or the other so that he could continue to talk to the man who worked next to him. Most of them were tall, and all of them were slender. What could be seen of their skin, their faces and their hands, was the glossy black of Africans whose ancestry had not been diluted by contact with whites. Whether moving or motionless, they exuded an atmosphere not only of good health but of good spirits, as if the idea of standing around in freezing temperatures, trying to sell counterfeit bags to tourists, was the greatest fun they could think of to have that evening.

Opposite them a small group was gathered around three buskers, two violinists and a cellist, who were playing a piece that sounded both baroque and out of tune. Because the musicians played with enthusiasm and were young, the small crowd that had gathered was pleased with them, and not a few of them stepped forward to drop coins into the violin case that lay open in front of the trio.

It was still early, probably too early for there to be much business, but the street vendors were

4

always punctual and started work as soon as the shops closed. By ten minutes to eight, therefore, just as the two men approached, all of the Africans were standing behind their sheets, prepared for their first customers. They shifted from foot to foot, occasionally breathing on to their clasped hands in a futile attempt to warm them.

The two white men paused just at the end of the row of sheets, appearing to talk to one another, though neither spoke. They kept their heads lowered and their faces out of the wind, but now and then one of them raised his eyes to study the line of black men. The tall man placed his hand on the other's arm, pointed with his chin towards one of the Africans, and said something. As he spoke, a large group of elderly people wearing gym shoes and thick down parkas, a combination that made them look like wrinkled toddlers, flowed around the corner of the church and into the funnel created by the buskers on one side, the Africans on the other. The first few stopped, waiting for those behind to catch up, and when the group was again a unit, they started forward, laughing and talking, calling to one another to come and look at the bags. Without pushing or jostling, they assembled themselves three-deep in front of the line of Black men and their exposed wares.

The taller of the two men started towards the group of tourists, his companion following close behind. They halted on the same side as the church, careful to stand behind two elderly couples who were pointing at some of the bags and asking prices. At first the man whose sheet it was did not notice the two, since he was attending to the questions of his potential customers. But suddenly he stopped talking and grew tense, like an animal scenting menace on the wind.

The black man at the next sheet, aware of his colleague's distraction, turned his attention to the tourists and decided instantly that he would have good luck with them. Their shoes told him to speak English, and he began: 'Gucci, Missoni, Armani, Trussardi. I have them all, ladies and gentlemen. Right from factory.' In the dimmer light here, his teeth glowed with Cheshire cat brilliance.

Three more of the tourist group insinuated their way past the two men to stand with their friends, all excitedly commenting on the bags, their attention now evenly divided between the items on both sheets. The taller man nodded, and as he did, both moved forward until they were standing just a half-step behind the Americans. Seeing them advance, the first trader pivoted on his right foot and started to arch himself away from the sheet, the tourists, and the two men. As he moved, the men took their right hands from their pockets with a smooth, practised ease that called no attention to itself. Each held a pistol, their barrels extended by tubular silencers. The taller of the two was the first to fire, though the only sound the gun made was a dull thwack, thwack, thwack, accom-

6

panied by two similar noises from the pistol of his companion. The buskers had worked their way towards the end of the allegro, and their music plus the shouts and squeals of the encircling crowd all but covered the sound of the shots, though the Africans to either side turned instantly towards them.

Momentum continued to carry the bag seller away from the people in front of his sheet; then gradually his motion slowed. The men, their guns now in their pockets, backed through the crowd of tourists, who politely moved out of their way. The men separated, one moving towards the Accademia bridge and the other towards Santo Stefano and Rialto. Quickly they disappeared among the people hurrying in both directions.

The bag seller cried out and threw one arm out in front of him. His body completed its half-circle, then sprawled to the ground beside his bags.

Like gazelles who panic and take flight at the first sign of danger, the other black men froze for an instant and then exploded with frightening energy. Four of them abandoned their wares and took off, running for the *calle* that led towards San Marco; two paused long enough to grab four or five bags in each hand, then disappeared over the bridge that led towards Campo San Samuele; the four remaining men left everything and fled towards the Grand Canal, where they alerted the men whose sheets were spread at the bottom of the bridge, over

7

which they all ran, separating at the bottom and disappearing into the *calli* of Dorsoduro.

A white-haired woman was standing in front of the trader's sheet when he collapsed. When she saw him fall, she called out to her husband, who had been separated from her, and knelt beside the fallen man.

She saw the blood that seeped out from under him, staining the sheet red. Her husband, alarmed by her cry and her sudden sinking to the ground, pushed roughly through their friends and knelt beside her. He moved to put a protective arm around her shoulder, but then he saw the man on the sheet. He placed his hand at the man's throat, kept it there for long seconds, then removed it and got to his feet awkwardly, his knees reluctant with age. He bent and helped his wife to stand.

They looked around and saw only the people in their group, all gaping back and forth between each other's confused faces and the man who lay at their feet. On either side of the broad street extended the rows of outspread sheets, most still covered with neatly positioned bags. As the crowd in front of them turned away one by one, the buskers stopped playing.

It was another few minutes before the first Italian approached, and when he saw the black man, the sheet, and the blood, he pulled his *telefonino* from the pocket of his coat and dialled 113.

2

The police arrived with a speed that astonished the Italian bystanders as much as it scandalized the Americans. To Venetians, half an hour did not seem a long time for the police to organize a boat and a squad of technicians and officers and reach Campo Santo Stefano, but by that time most of the Americans had drifted away in exasperation, telling one another that they would meet back at the hotel. No one bothered to keep an eye on the crime scene, so by the time the police finally did arrive, most of the bags had disappeared from the sheets, even from the one on which the body lay. Some of those who stole the dead man's bags left red footprints on his sheet; one set disappeared towards Rialto in a bloody trail.

The first officer on the scene, Alvise, approached the small crowd that still stood near the dead man and ordered them to move back. He walked over to the man's body and stood, looking down at him as if confused as to what to do now that he could see the victim. Finally, a lab technician asked him to move aside while he set up a wooden stanchion, and then another, and then another until they ringed the sheet. From one of the boxes the technicians had brought to the scene he took a roll of red and white striped tape and ran it through slots in the tops of the wooden stanchions until a clear demarcation had been created between the body and the rest of the world.

Alvise went over to a man who was standing by the steps of the church and demanded, 'Who are you?'

'Riccardo Lombardi,' the man answered. He was tall, about fifty, well-dressed, the sort of person who sat behind a desk and gave orders, or so thought Alvise.

'What are you doing here?'

Surprised at the policeman's tone, the man answered, 'I was walking by, and I saw this crowd, so I stopped.'

'Did you see who did it?'

'Did what?'

It occurred to Alvise only then that he had no idea what had been done, only that the Questura had received a call, saying that a black man was dead in Campo Santo Stefano. 'Can you show me some identification?' Alvise demanded.

The man took out his wallet and extracted his *carta d'identità*. Silently, he handed it to Alvise, who glanced at it before handing it back. 'Did you see anything?' he asked in the same voice.

'I told you, officer. I was walking by, and I saw these people standing around here, so I stopped to look. Nothing more.'

'All right. You can go,' Alvise said in a tone that suggested the man really had no choice. Alvise turned away from him and went back to the crime team, where the photographers were already packing up their equipment.

'Find anything?' he asked one of the technicians.

Santini, who was on his knees, running his gloved hands over the paving stones in search of shell casings, looked up at Alvise and said, 'A dead man,' before returning to his search.

Not deterred by the answer, Alvise pulled out a notebook from the inside pocket of his uniform parka. He flipped it open, took out a pen, and wrote 'Campo Santo Stefano'. He studied what he had written, glanced at his watch, added '20.58', capped the pen, and returned both notebook and pen to his pocket.

From his right, he heard a familiar voice ask, 'What's going on, Alvise?'

Alvise raised a languid hand in something that resembled a salute and said, 'I'm not sure, Commissario. We had a call, saying there was a dead man here, so we came over.'

His superior, Commissario Guido Brunetti,

said, 'I can see that, Alvise. What happened to cause the man to be dead?'

'I don't know, sir. We're waiting for the doctor to get here.'

'Who's coming?' Brunetti asked.

'Who's coming where, sir?' Alvise asked, utterly at a loss.

'Which doctor is coming? Do you know?'

'I don't know, sir. I was in such a hurry to get the team here that I told them at the Questura to call and have one of the doctors sent.'

Brunetti's question was answered by the arrival of Dottor Ettore Rizzardi, *medico legale* of the city of Venice.

'*Ciao*, Guido,' Rizzardi said, shifting his bag to his left hand and offering his right. 'What have we got?'

'A dead man,' Brunetti said. 'I got the call at home, saying someone had been killed here, but nothing more than that. I just got here myself.'

'Better have a look, then,' Rizzardi said, turning towards the taped-off area. 'You speak to anyone?' he asked Brunetti.

'No. Nothing.' Talking to Alvise never counted.

Rizzardi bent and slipped under the tape, placing one hand on the pavement to do so, then held the tape up to make it easier for Brunetti to join him. The doctor turned to one of the technicians. 'You've taken pictures?'

'*Sì*, Dottore,' the man answered. 'From every side.'

'All right, then,' Rizzardi said, setting down

his bag. He turned away, took out two pairs of thin plastic gloves and gave one pair to Brunetti. As they slipped them on, the doctor asked, 'Give me a hand?'

They knelt on either side of the dead man. All that was visible was the right side of his face and his hands. Brunetti was struck by the very blackness of the man's skin, then bemused by his own surprise: what other colour did he expect an African to be? Unlike the black Americans Brunetti had seen, with their shading from cocoa to copper, this man was the colour of ebony buffed to a high gloss.

Together, they reached under the body and turned the man on to his back. The intense cold had caused the blood to congeal. Their knees anchored the sheet, so when they moved him, his jacket stuck to the cloth and pulled away from both his body and the pavement with a sharp sucking sound. Hearing it, Rizzardi let the man's shoulder fall back on to the ground; Brunetti lowered his side, saying nothing.

Points of blood-stiffened cloth stood up on the man's chest, looking like the whorls a pastry chef's fantasy might create on a birthday cake.

'Sorry,' Rizzardi said, either to Brunetti or the dead man. Still kneeling, he bent over and used a gloved finger to touch each of the holes in his parka. 'Five of them,' he said. 'Looks like they really wanted to kill him.'

Brunetti saw that the dead man's eyes were open; so too was his mouth, frozen in the panic that must have filled him at the first shot. He was a handsome young man, his teeth gleaming in striking contrast to that burnished skin. Brunetti slipped one hand into the right-hand pocket of the man's parka, then the left. He found some small change and a used handkerchief. The inside pocket contained a pair of keys and a few Euro bills in small denominations. There was a *ricevuta fiscale* from a bar with a San Marco address, probably one of the bars in the *campo*. Nothing else.

'Who'd want to kill a *vu cumprà*?' Rizzardi asked, getting to his feet. 'As if the poor devils don't have enough as it is.' He studied the man on the ground. 'I can't tell, looking at him like this, where they got him, but three of the holes are grouped pretty near the heart. One would have been enough to kill him.' Stuffing his gloves into his pocket, Rizzardi asked, 'Professional, you think?'

'Looks like it to me,' Brunetti answered, aware that this made the death even more confusing. He had never had to trouble himself with the *vu cumprà* because few of them were ever involved in serious crime, and those few cases had always fallen to other commissarios. Like most of the police, indeed, like most residents, Brunetti had always assumed that the men from Senegal were under the control of organized crime, the reason most often offered to explain their politeness in dealing with the public: so long as their manner did not call attention to them, few people would trouble to ask how they so successfully managed to remain invisible to and undisturbed by the authorities. Brunetti had come over the years no longer to notice them nor to remember when they had displaced the original French-speaking Algerian and Moroccan *vu cumprà*.

Though there was an occasional round-up and examination of documents, the *vu cumprà* had never attracted sufficient official attention to become the subject of one of Vice-Questore Patta's 'crime alerts', which meant there had never been a serious attempt to address the patent illegality of their presence and their profession. They were left to ply their trade virtually untroubled by the forces of order, thus avoiding the bureaucratic nightmare that would surely result from any serious attempt to expel hundreds of undocumented aliens and return them to Senegal, the country from which most of them were believed to come.

Why then a killing like this, one that had the stamp of the professional all over it?

'How old do you think he was?' Brunetti asked for want of anything else to say.

'I don't know,' Rizzardi answered with a puzzled shake of his head. 'It's hard for me to tell with blacks, not until I get inside them, but I'd guess in his early thirties, maybe younger.'

'Do you have time?' Brunetti asked.

'Tomorrow afternoon, first thing. All right?' Brunetti nodded.

Rizzardi leaned over and picked up his bag. Hefting it, he said, 'I don't know why I always bring this with me. It's not as if I'm ever going to have to use it to save anyone.' He thought about this, shrugged, and said, 'Habit, I suppose.' He put out his hand, shook Brunetti's, and turned away.

Brunetti called to the technician who had taken the photos, 'When you get him to the hospital, would you take a couple of shots of his face from different angles and get them to me as soon as you've got them developed?'

'How many prints, sir?'

'A dozen of each.'

'Right. By tomorrow morning.'

Brunetti thanked him and waved over Alvise, who lurked just within earshot. 'Did anyone see what happened?' he asked.

'No, sir.'

'Who did you speak to?'

'A man,' Alvise answered, pointing in the direction of the church.

'What was his name?' Brunetti asked.

Alvise's eyes widened in surprise he could not disguise. After a pause so long that anyone else would have found it embarrassing, the officer finally said, 'I don't remember, sir.' At Brunetti's silence, he protested, 'He said he didn't see anything, Commissario, so I didn't need to take his name, did I?'

Brunetti turned to two white-coated attendants who were just arriving. 'You can take him to the Ospedale, Mauro,' he said. Then he added, 'Officer Alvise will go with you.'

Alvise opened his mouth to protest, but Brunetti forestalled him by saying, 'This way you can see if the hospital has admitted anyone with bullet wounds.' It was unlikely, given the apparent accuracy of the five shots that had killed the African, but at least it would free him of Alvise's presence.

'Of course, Commissario,' Alvise said, repeating his semi-salute. The officer watched as the two attendants stooped to pick up the body and place it on the stretcher, then led them back to their boat, walking purposefully, as though it was only through his intervention that they were sure of reaching it.

Turning, Brunetti called to a technician, who was now outside the taped circle, taking a close-up photo of the heel prints that led towards Rialto. 'Is Alvise the only one who came?'

'I think so, sir,' the man answered. 'Riverre was out on a domestic.'

'Has anyone tried to find out if there were any witnesses?' Brunetti asked.

The technician gave him a long look. 'Alvise?' was all he said before returning to his photos.

A group of teenagers stood against the wall of the garden. Brunetti approached them and asked, 'Did any of you see what happened here?'

'No, sir,' one of them said, 'we just got here now.'

Brunetti moved back to the cordoned area, where he saw three or four people. 'Were any of you here when it happened?' he asked.

Heads turned away, eyes glanced at the ground. 'Did you see anything at all?' he added, asking, not pleading.

A man at the back peeled himself away and started across the *campo*. Brunetti made no effort to stop him. As he stood there, the others dissolved until there was just one person left, an old woman who held herself upright only with the help of two canes. He knew her by sight, though she was usually in the company of two mangy old dogs. She balanced her right cane against her hip and beckoned him towards her. As he approached, he saw the wrinkled face, the dark eyes, the white bristles on her chin.

'Yes, Signora?' he asked. 'Did you see something?' Without thinking, he addressed her in Veneziano rather than Italian.

'There were some Americans here when it happened.'

'How did you know they were Americans, Signora?' he asked.

'They had white shoes and they were very loud,' she answered.

'When it happened?' he insisted. 'Were you here? Did you see?'

She took her right cane and lifted it to point in the direction of the pharmacy on the corner, about twenty metres away. 'No, I was over there. Just coming in. I saw them, the Americans. They were walking this way, from the bridge, and then they all stopped to look at the stuff the *vu cumprà* had.'

'And you, Signora?'

She moved her cane a few millimetres to the left. 'I went into the bar.'

'How long were you in there, Signora?'

'Long enough.'

'Long enough for what?' he asked, smiling at her, not at all annoyed by her oblique answer.

'Barbara, the owner, after about eight, she takes all the *tramezzini* that haven't been sold, and she cuts them up into little pieces and puts them on the counter. If you buy a drink, you can eat all you want.'

This surprised Brunetti, unaccustomed as he was to such generosity from the owners of bars; from the owners of anything, for that matter.

'She's a good girl, Barbara,' the old woman said. 'I knew her mother.'

'So how long do you think you were in there, Signora?' he asked.

'Maybe half an hour,' she answered, then explained, 'It's my dinner, you see. I go there every night.'

'Good to know, Signora. I'll remember that if I'm ever over here.'

'You're over here now,' she said, and when he didn't respond, she went on: 'The Americans, they went in there. Well, two of them did,' she added, lifting the cane again and pointing at the bar.

'They're in the back, having hot chocolate. You could probably talk to them if you wanted to,' she said.

'Thank you, Signora,' he said and turned towards the bar.

'The prosciutto and carciofi is the best,' she called after him.

3

Brunetti hadn't been in the bar for years, ever since the brief period when it had been converted into an American ice-cream parlour and had begun to serve an ice-cream so rich it had caused him a serious bout of indigestion the one time he had eaten it. It had been, he recalled, like eating lard, though not the salty lard he remembered from his childhood, tossed in to give taste and substance to a pot of beans or lentil soup, but lard as lard would be if sugar and strawberries were added to it.

His fellow Venetians must have responded in similar fashion, for the place had changed ownership after a few years, but Brunetti had never been back. The tubs of ice-cream were gone now, and it had reverted to looking like an

Italian bar. A number of people stood at the curved counter, talking animatedly and turning often to point out at the now-quiet *campo*; some sat at small tables that led into the back room. Three women stood behind the bar; one of them, seeing Brunetti enter, offered him a friendly smile. He walked towards the back and saw an elderly couple at the last table on the left. They had to be Americans. They might as well have been draped in the flag. White-haired, both of them, they gave the bizarre impression that they were dressed in each other's clothing. The woman wore a checked flannel shirt and a pair of thick woollen slacks, while the man wore a pink V-necked sweater, a pair of dark trousers, and white tennis shoes. Both apparently had their hair cut by the same hand. One could not say, exactly, that hers was longer: it was merely less short.

'Excuse me,' Brunetti said in English as he approached their table. 'Were you out in the *campo* earlier?'

'When the man was killed?' the woman asked.

'Yes,' Brunetti said.

The man pulled out a chair for Brunetti and, with old-fashioned courtesy, got to his feet and waited until Brunetti was seated. 'I'm Guido Brunetti, from the police,' he began. 'I'd like to talk to you about what you saw.'

Both of them had the faces of mariners: eyes narrowed in a perpetual squint, wrinkles seared into place by too much sun, and a sharpness of expression that even heavy seas would not disturb.

The man put out his hand, saying, 'I'm Fred Crowley, officer, and this is my wife, Martha.' When Brunetti released his hand, the woman stretched hers out, surprising him with the strength of her grip.

'We're from Maine,' she said. 'Biddeford Pool,' she specified, and then, as though that were not enough, added, 'It's on the coast.'

'How do you do,' Brunetti said, an old-fashioned phrase he had forgotten he knew. 'Could you tell me what you saw, Mr and Mrs Crowley?' How strange this was, he the impatient Italian and these the Americans who needed to go through the slow ritual of courtesy before getting down to the matter at hand.

'Doctors,' she corrected.

'Excuse me?' said Brunetti, at a loss.

'Doctor Crowley and Doctor Crowley,' she explained. 'Fred's a surgeon, and I'm an internist.' Before he could express his surprise that people their age were still working as doctors, she added, 'Well, we were, that is.'

'I see,' Brunetti said, then paused and waited to see if they had any intention of answering his original question.

They exchanged a look, then the woman spoke. 'We were just coming into what you call the *campo*, and I saw all these purses on the ground and the men selling them. I wanted to have a look and see if there was something we could take back to our granddaughter. I was standing just in front, looking at the purses, when I heard this strange noise, sort of like that fitt, fitt, fitt your coffee machines make when they turn that nozzle thing to make the steam. From my right, three times, and then from the left, the same noise, fitt, fitt, twice that time.' She stopped, as if hearing it all over again, then went on. 'I turned to see what the noise was, but all I could see were the people beside me and behind me, some of the people from the tour, and a man in an overcoat. When I looked back, that poor young man was on the ground, and I knelt down to try to help him. I think I called for Fred then, but it might have been later, when I saw the blood. At first I was afraid he'd fainted; not being used to the cold, or something like that. But then I saw the blood, and maybe that was when I called Fred; I really don't recall. He did a lot of time in the Emergency Room, you see. But by the time Fred got there, I knew he was gone.' She considered this, then added, 'I don't know how I could tell, because all I could see was the back of his neck, but there's a look about them, when they're dead. When Fred knelt down and touched him, he knew, too.'

Brunetti glanced at the husband, who picked up her story. 'Martha's right. I knew even before I touched him. He was still warm, poor boy, but the life had gone out of him. Couldn't have been more than thirty.' He shook his head. 'No matter how many times you see it, it's always new. And terrible.' He shook his head and, as if to emphasize his words, pushed his empty cup and saucer a few centimetres across the table.

His wife put her hand on top of his and said, as if Brunetti weren't there, 'Nothing we could have done, Fred. Those two men knew what they were doing.'

She couldn't have been more offhand about it: 'those two men'.

'What two men?' Brunetti asked, striving to keep his voice as calm as possible. 'Could you tell me more about them?'

'There was the man in the overcoat,' she said. 'He was on my right, just a little bit behind me. I didn't see the other one, but because the noise came from my left, he had to have been on the other side. And I'm not even sure it was a man. I just assume that because the other one was.'

Brunetti turned to the husband, 'Did you see them, Doctor?'

The man shook his head. 'Nope. I was looking at the things on the sheet. I didn't even hear the noise.' As if to prove this, he turned to the side and showed Brunetti the beige snail of the hearing aid in his left ear. 'When I heard Martha call me, I didn't have any idea what was going on. Truth to tell, I thought something might have happened to her, so I pushed right past those people to get to her, and when I saw her down on the ground like that, even though she was kneeling, well, I won't tell you what I thought, but it wasn't good.' He paused as if in pained memory and gave a nervous smile.

Brunetti knew better than to prod him, and

after a few moments, the man spoke again. 'And, as I said, as soon as I touched him, I knew he was gone.'

Brunetti turned his attention back to the woman. 'Could you describe this man for me, Doctor?'

Just at that moment the waitress came by and asked if she could bring them anything. Brunetti looked at the two Americans, but both shook their heads. Though he didn't want it, he ordered a coffee.

A full minute passed in silence. The woman looked at her cup, mirrored her husband's gesture in pushing it away, looked back at Brunetti, and said, 'It's not easy to describe him, sir. He was wearing a hat, one of those hats men wear in movies.' To clarify the description, she added, 'The kind of thing they wore in movies in the Thirties and Forties.'

She paused, as if trying to visualize the scene, then added, 'No, all I remember is a sense that he was very tall and very big. He was wearing an overcoat; it might have been grey or dark brown, I really don't recall. And that hat.'

The waitress set Brunetti's coffee in front of him and moved away. He left it untouched, smiled across at her and said, 'Go on, please, Doctor.'

'There was the overcoat, and he had a scarf; maybe it was grey and maybe it was black. Because there were so many people standing around, all I saw was the side of him.'

'Could you give me an idea of his age?' Brunetti asked.

'Oh, I couldn't be sure of that, no more than to say he was an adult, perhaps your age,' she said. 'I think his hair was dark, but it was hard to tell in that light, and with his hat on. And I wasn't paying much attention to him at that point, not really, because I didn't have any idea of what was going on.'

Brunetti thought of the victim and asked, conscious of how it would sound, 'Was this man white, Doctor?'

'Oh yes, he was European,' she answered, then added, 'but my sense of him was that he looked more Mediterranean than my husband and I do.' She smiled to show she meant no offence, and Brunetti took none.

'What, specifically, makes you say that, Doctor?' he asked.

'His skin was darker than ours, I think, and it looked like he had dark eyes. He was taller than you, officer, and much taller than either one of us.' She considered all of this and then added, 'And thicker. He wasn't a thin man, officer.'

Brunetti turned his attention to the husband. 'Do you have any memory of seeing this man, Doctor? Or of seeing someone who might have been the other one?'

The white-haired man shook his head. 'No. As I told you, my only concern was my wife. When I heard her shout, everything else went out of my head, so I couldn't even tell you which people from our group were there.'

Brunetti turned back to the woman and asked, 'Do *you* remember who was there, Doctor?'

She closed her eyes, as if trying to recall the scene yet again. Finally she said, 'There were the Petersons; they were standing to my left, and the man was behind me on the right. And I think Lydia Watts was on the other side of the Petersons.' She kept her eyes closed. When she opened them she said, 'No, I don't remember anyone else. That is, I know that we were all there in a bunch, but those are the only ones I can remember seeing.'

'How many people are in your group, Doctor?'

The husband answered, 'Sixteen. Plus spouses, that is,' he immediately corrected. 'Most of us are retired or semi-retired doctors, all from the North-east.'

'Where are you staying?' he asked.

'At the Paganelli,' he answered. Brunetti was surprised that a group that large could find room there, and that Americans would have the good sense to choose it.

'And this evening, for dinner? Is the group scheduled to eat somewhere in particular?' Brunetti wondered if he could perhaps locate them all and talk to them now, while whatever memories they had would still be fresh.

The Crowleys exchanged a glance. The man said, 'No, not really. This is our last night in Venice, and some of us decided to eat on our own, so we don't have any plans, not really.' He gave an embarrassed smile and added, 'I guess we're sort of tired of eating with the same people every night.'

'We were just going to walk around until we saw a place we liked and eat there,' his wife added, smiling across at her husband as if proud of their decision. 'But it's awfully late now.'

'And the group?' Brunetti persisted.

'They're booked to eat at some place near San Marco,' the woman said.

Her husband interrupted, 'But we didn't like the sound of it, all that local colour stuff.'

Brunetti had to admit they were probably right. 'Do you remember the name?' he asked.

Both shook their heads regretfully; the man spoke for them. 'I'm sorry, officer, but I don't.'

'You said it was your last night here,' he began, and they nodded. 'What time do you leave tomorrow morning?'

'Not until ten,' she said. 'We take the train to Rome, and then we fly out on Thursday. Home in time for Christmas.'

Brunetti pulled their bill towards him, added the cost of his own coffee to it, and put fifteen Euros on the table. The man started to object, but Brunetti said, 'It's police business,' and that lie seemed to satisfy the doctor.

'I can recommend a restaurant,' he said, and then added, 'I'd like to come and talk to you, and to these other people, in your hotel tomorrow morning.'

'Breakfast's at seven-thirty,' she explained, 'and the Petersons are always right on time. I'll call Lydia Watts, when we get back if you like, and ask her to come down at eight so you can talk to her.'

'Is your train at ten or do you leave the hotel at ten?' Brunetti asked, hoping to be spared the need to be on the other side of San Marco by seven-thirty in the morning.

'The train, so we have to leave the hotel at nine-fifteen. There's a boat coming to take us to the station.'

Brunetti got to his feet and waited while the man helped his wife into her parka and then put on his own. Wearing them, the old people doubled in size. He led the way to the door, and held it open for them. Outside, in the *campo*, he pointed to the right and told them to walk along Calle della Mandorla to the Rosa Rossa and to tell the owner that Commissario Brunetti had sent them.

They both repeated his name, and the man said, 'Sorry, Commissario. I didn't hear your rank when you came in. I hope you didn't mind being called officer.'

'Not at all,' Brunetti said with a smile. They shook hands, and Brunetti stood and watched them until they had disappeared beyond the corner of the church.

When he returned to the place where the man had been killed, he found a uniformed officer standing beside one of the stanchions. He saw Brunetti approach and saluted. 'You alone here?' Brunetti asked. He noticed that all of the sheets and the few bags that had remained had disappeared and wondered if the police had taken them back with them.

'Yes, sir. Santini said to tell you he didn't find anything.' Brunetti assumed this meant not only shell casings, but any traces of whoever might have killed the man.

He looked at the enclosed area and only then noticed an oval mound of sawdust in the centre. Without thinking, he asked, nodding towards it with his chin, 'What's that?'

'It's the, er, blood, sir,' the man answered. 'Because of the cold.'

The image this conjured up was so grotesque that Brunetti refused to consider it; instead, he told the officer to call the Questura at midnight and remind them that he was to be relieved at one. He asked the young man if he wanted to go and have a coffee before the bar closed and then stood and waited for him.

When the uniformed man was back, Brunetti told him that, if he saw any of the other *vu cumprà*, he was to tell them that their colleague was dead and ask them to call the police if they had any information about him. He made a particular point of telling the officer to make it clear to them that they would not have to give their names or come to the Questura and that all the police wanted from them was information.

Brunetti used his *telefonino* to call the Questura. He gave his name, repeated what he had just told the crime scene officer, emphasizing that callers were not to be asked their names, and instructed that all calls relating to the shooting were to be recorded. He called the *Carabinieri* and, unsure of his authority, asked their cooperation in treating any relevant calls they might receive with the same discretion, and when the maresciallo agreed, asked if they would record their calls as well. The maresciallo observed he was very doubtful that any information would be volunteered by the *vu cumprà* but nevertheless agreed to do so.

There seemed little else for Brunetti to do, so he wished the young officer a good evening, hoped it would get no colder, and, having decided it would be faster to walk, turned towards Rialto and home.

4

Paola sat, mouth agape, fearing that everything she had ever tried to do as a parent had failed miserably and she had produced a monster, not a child. She stared at her daughter, her baby, her bright, shining angel, and wondered if demonic possession were possible.

Up until that point, dinner had been a normal enough affair, at least as normal as a meal can be when it has been delayed by murder. Brunetti, who had been called from home only minutes before they sat down, had phoned a little after nine, saying he would still be some time. The children's complaints that they were on the verge of expiring from hunger had by then worn down Paola's resistance, so she fed them, putting her own dinner and Guido's back in the oven to keep warm. She sat with the children, sipping idly from a glass of prosecco that gradually grew warm and flat as the children ate their way through enormous portions of a pasticcio made of layers of polenta, ragù, and parmigiano. To follow there was only roasted radicchio smothered in stracchino, though Paola marvelled that either one of her children could possibly eat anything else.

'Why's he always have to be late?' Chiara complained as she reached for the radicchio.

'He's not always late,' a literal-minded Paola answered.

'It seems that way,' Chiara said, selecting two long stalks and lifting them on to her plate, then carefully spooning melted cheese on top.

'He said he'd be here as soon as he could.'

'It's not like it's so important or anything, is it? That he has to be so late?' Chiara asked.

Paola had explained the reason for their father's absence, and so she found Chiara's remark not a little strange.

'I thought I told you someone was killed,' she said mildly.

'Yes, but it was only a *vu cumprà*,' Chiara said as she picked up her knife.

It was at this remark that Paola's mouth fell open. She picked up her glass of wine, pretended to take a sip, moved the platter of radicchio towards Raffi, who appeared not to have heard his sister, and asked, 'What do you mean by, "only", Chiara?' Her voice, she was glad to note, was entirely conversational.

33

'Just what I said, that it wasn't one of us,' her daughter answered.

Paola tried to identify sarcasm or some attempt to provoke her in Chiara's response, but there was no hint of either. Chiara's tone, in fact, seemed to echo her own in terms of calm dispassion.

'By "us", do you mean Italians or all white people, Chiara?' she asked.

'No,' Chiara said. 'Europeans.'

'Ah, of course,' Paola answered, picking up her glass and toying with the stem for a moment before setting it down, untasted. 'And where are the borders of Europe?' she finally asked.

'What, *Mamma*?' asked Chiara, who had been answering a question put to her by Raffi. 'I didn't hear you.'

'I asked where the borders of Europe were.'

'Oh, you know that, *Mamma*. It's in all the books.' Before Paola could say anything, Chiara asked, 'Is there any dessert?'

As a young mother, Paola, herself an only child and without any previous experience of small children, had read all the books and manuals that gave modern parents advice on how to treat their children. She had, further, read many books of psychology, and knew that there was a general professional consensus that one should never subject a child to severe criticism until the reasons for their behaviour or words had been explored and examined, and even then, the parent was enjoined to take into consideration the possibility of damaging the developing psyche of the child.

'That's the most disgusting, heartless thing I've ever heard said at this table, and I am ashamed to have raised a child capable of saying it,' she said.

Raffi, who had tuned in only when his radar registered his mother's tone, dropped his fork. Chiara's mouth fell open in a mirror of her mother's expression, and for much the same reason: shock and horror that a person so fundamental to her happiness could be capable of such speech. Like her mother, she dismissed even the possibility of diplomacy and demanded, 'What's that supposed to mean?'

'It's supposed to mean that *vu cumpràs* are not *only* anything. You can't dismiss them as if their deaths don't matter.'

Chiara heard her mother's words; more significantly, she felt the force of her mother's tone, and so she said, 'That's not what I meant.'

'I've no idea what you meant, Chiara, but what you *said* was that the dead man was *only* a *vu cumprà*. And you'd have to do a lot of explaining to make me believe that there's any difference between what those words *say* and what they *mean*.'

Chiara set her fork down on her plate and asked, 'May I go to my room?'

Raffi, his own fork motionless in his hand, turned his head back and forth between them, confused that Chiara had said what she did and stunned by the power of his mother's response.

'Yes,' Paola said.

Chiara stood, quietly pushed her chair back under the table, and left the room. Raffi, who was familiar with his mother's sense of humour, turned to her, waiting for the one-line remark he was sure would come. Instead, Paola got to her feet and picked up her daughter's plate. She placed it in the sink, then went into the living room.

Raffi finished his radicchio, resigned himself to the fact that there would be no dessert that night, set his knife and fork neatly parallel on his plate, then took it over to the sink. He went back to his room.

Brunetti returned to this scene half an hour later. Comforted by the scents that filled the entire apartment, he was eager to see his family and talk of things other than violent death. He went into the kitchen and, instead of the family he expected to see eating dessert and eagerly awaiting his return, he found an all-but empty table and dishes stacked in the sink.

He went searching for them in the living room, wondering if there was something interesting on television, impossible as he knew that to be. He found only Paola, lying on the sofa, reading. She looked up when he came in and said, 'Would you like to eat something, Guido?'

'Yes, I think I would. But first I'd like a glass of wine and for you to tell me what's wrong.' He went back into the kitchen and got a bottle of Falconera and two glasses. He opened the wine, dismissed all the nonsense about leaving it unpoured long enough to breathe, and went back into the living room. He sat down near her feet, set the glasses on the table in front of the sofa, and poured out two large glasses. He leaned towards her and handed her one, then used the same hand to take her left foot. 'Your feet are cold,' he said, then pulled a balding old afghan down from the back of the sofa and covered them.

He took a sip large enough to complement the size of the glass and said, 'All right, what is it?'

'Chiara complained that you were late, and when I told her it was because someone had been killed, she said that it was only a *vu cumprà*.' She kept her voice dispassionate, reportorial.

'Only?' he repeated.

'Only.'

Brunetti took another drink of wine, rested his head on the back of the sofa, and swirled the wine around in his mouth. 'Hummm,' he finally said. 'Not nice at all, is it?'

Though he couldn't see Paola, he felt the sofa move as she nodded.

'You think she heard it in school?' he asked.

'Where else? She's too young to be a member of the Lega.'

'So is it something her friends bring in from their parents, or is it something the teachers give them?' he asked.

'It could be either, I'm afraid,' she said. 'Or both.'

'I suppose so,' Brunetti agreed. 'What did you do?'

'I told her what she said was disgusting and that I'm ashamed she's my daughter.'

He turned, smiled, held his glass up and saluted her. 'Always prone to moderation, aren't you?'

'What was I supposed to do, send her to some sort of sensitivity training class or give her a sermon on the brotherhood of man?' Brunetti heard her rage and disgust rekindle as she went on, 'It is disgusting, and I *am* ashamed of her.'

Brunetti was pleased she did not bother to assert that their daughter had never heard such things in their home, that they were in no way responsible for this sort of distortion of mind. Heaven alone knew what was suggested by the conversations he and Paola had in front of the children; no one knew what they could have inferred over all those years. He liked to think he was a moderate person, brought up, like most Italians, without racial prejudice, but he was honest enough to accept that this belief was probably yet another national myth. It is easy to grow up without racial prejudice in a society in which there is only one race.

His father hated Russians, and Brunetti had always thought he did so with good reason, if three years as a prisoner of war is a good reason. For his own part, he had an instinctive distrust of southerners, though it was a feeling that caused him no little discomfort. He was far less troubled by his own distrust of Albanians and of Slavs.

But African blacks? That was an almost entirely unfamiliar category for him, and since he was completely ignorant about them, he doubted that he could have infected his children with his prejudices. More likely it was something, like head lice, that Chiara had picked up in school.

'Do we sit here and castigate ourselves as negligent parents and then punish ourselves for that by not eating dinner?' he finally asked.

'I suppose we could,' she said, her remark entirely devoid of humour.

'I don't like the idea of that,' he said. 'Either one or the other.'

'All right,' she finally said. 'I've been sitting alone in here a long time, which takes care of the castigating, so I suppose we can at least eat dinner in peace.'

'Good,' he said, finishing his wine and leaning forward to take the bottle.

As they ate, some tacit agreement having been made not to discuss Chiara's remark further that evening, Brunetti told her what was said to have happened in Campo Santo Stefano: two men, though no one seemed to have paid much attention to them, appeared out of the darkness and slipped back into it after shooting the African at least five times. It was an execution, not a murder, and certainly there was nothing random about it. 'He didn't have a chance, poor devil,' Brunetti said.

'Who would want to do something like that? And to a *vu cumprà*?' Paola asked. 'And why?'

These were the questions that had accompanied Brunetti on his walk home. 'Seems to me that it's either because of something he did after he got here or something he did before,' Brunetti said, though he knew this was merely to state the obvious.

'That doesn't help much, does it?' Paola asked, but it was an observation, not a criticism.

'No, but it's a place to begin to divide the things we might be looking for.'

Paola, always comfortable when presented with an exercise in logic, said, 'Begin by examining what you know about him. Which is?'

'Absolutely nothing,' Brunetti answered.

'That's not true.'

'What?'

'You know he was a black African, and you know he was working as a *vu cumprà*, or whatever we're supposed to call them now.'

'*Venditore ambulante* or *extracomunitario*,' Brunetti supplied.

'That's about as helpful as "*Operatore ecologico*",' she answered.

'Huh?'

'Garbage man,' Paola translated. She got to her feet and left the room. When she came back, she had a bottle of grappa and two small glasses. As she poured, she said, 'So let's just call him a *vu cumprà* to save time and confusion, all right?'

Brunetti thanked her for the grappa with a

nod, took a sip, and asked, 'What else do you think we know?'

'You know that none of the others stayed to try to help him or to help the police in any way.'

'I'd guess they saw he was dead when he fell.'

'Would it have been that obvious?'

'I think so, yes.'

'And so you know it was an execution,' Paola went on, 'not the result of a fight or an argument that provoked it suddenly. Someone wanted him dead and either sent people to do it or came and did it himself.'

'I'd say he sent people,' Brunetti offered.

'How can you tell?'

'It has that feel about it, the work of professionals. They appeared out of nowhere, executed him, and disappeared.'

'So what does that tell you about them?'

'That they're familiar with the city.'

She gave him a questioning glance, and he elaborated, 'To know which way to leave. Also to know where he was.'

'Does that mean Venetian?'

Brunetti shook his head. 'I've never heard of a Venetian who works as a killer.'

Paola considered this and then said, 'It wouldn't take all that long to learn at least that much about the city. Some of the Africans are pretty much always there, in Santo Stefano, so all they'd have to do is walk around for a day or so to find them. Or ask someone.' She closed her eyes and considered the geography of the area and finally said, 'Afterwards, getting away would be easy. All they'd have to do is go back towards Rialto, or up towards San Marco, or over the Accademia.'

When she stopped, Brunetti continued, 'Or they could go into San Vidal and then cut back towards San Samuele.'

'How many places could they get a vaporetto?' she asked.

'Three. Four. And then they could have gone either way.'

'What would *you* do?' she asked.

'I don't know. But if I wanted to leave the city, I'd probably go up towards San Marco and cut in towards the Fenice and then to Rialto.'

'Did anyone see them?'

'An American tourist. She saw one of them, said he was a man about my age and size, wearing an overcoat, a scarf, and a hat.'

'Half the city,' Paola said. 'Anything else?'

'That there were other people from her group there and they might have seen something. I'm going to talk to them tomorrow morning.'

'How early?'

'Early. I have to leave here before eight.'

She leaned forward and poured him another small glass of grappa. 'American tourists at eight in the morning. Here, take this: it's the least you deserve.'

5

The morning dawned unpleasantly. A thick mist hung suspended in the air, eager to cling to anything that passed through it. By the time Brunetti got to the *imbarcadero* of the Numero Uno, the shoulders of his overcoat were covered by a thin film of droplets, and he pulled in dampness with every breath. The approaching vaporetto slipped silently from fog so thick Brunetti could barely make out the form of the man waiting to moor it and slide back the metal gate. He stepped on board, looked up and saw its radar screen turning, and wondered what it was like out on the *laguna*.

He took a seat in the cabin and opened that morning's *Gazzettino*, but he learned from it considerably less than he had the night before.

43

In possession of few facts, the writer opted for sentiment and spoke of the terrible cost the *extracomunitari* had to pay for their desire for a chance at bare survival and to earn enough money to send back to their families. No name was given for the dead man, nor was his nationality known, though it was assumed he was from Senegal, the country from which most of the *ambulanti* came. An elderly man got on at Sant'Angelo and chose to sit next to Brunetti. He saw the newspaper and mouthed out the headline, then said, 'Nothing but trouble once you start letting them in.'

Brunetti ignored him.

Brunetti's silence spurred the man to add, 'I'd round them up and send them back.'

Brunetti gave a grunt and turned the page, but the old man failed to take the hint. 'My son-in-law has a shop in Calle dei Fabbri. Pays his rent, pays his help, pays his taxes. He gives something to the city, gives work. And these people,' he said, making a gesture that stopped just short of slapping the offending page, 'what do they give us?'

With another grunt, Brunetti folded his newspaper and excused himself to go and stand on deck, though they were only at Santa Maria del Giglio and he had another two stops before he got off.

The Paganelli was a narrow hotel, slipped in, like an architectural dash separating two capital letters, between the Danieli and the Savoia & Jolanda. At the desk he said he was there to meet the Doctors Crowley and was told they were already in the breakfast room. He followed the clerk's gesture down a narrow corridor and entered a small room that held six or seven tables, at one of which the Crowleys sat. With them were another elderly couple and, between them, a woman whose appearance gave evidence of considerable assistance.

When Doctor Crowley saw Brunetti, he got to his feet and waved at him; his wife looked up and smiled a greeting. The other man at the table rose and stayed standing as Brunetti approached. One of the women smiled in Brunetti's direction; the other did not.

The people presented to him as the Petersons were tiny, bird-like people, dressed in colours as inconspicuous as those of sparrows. She had iron grey hair that capped her head in a tight perm; he was entirely bald, his head covered with deep, sun-hardened furrows running from front to back. The woman who had not smiled, introduced as Lydia Watts, had lustrous red hair and lips the same colour. Brunetti saw her push back a vagrant curl with a hand that no surgery and no art could make look the same age as her face and hair.

The table was covered with the aftermath of breakfast: coffee cups and teapots and fragments of buttered rolls. There were two empty bread baskets and an equally empty platter that might have held meat or cheese.

After Brunetti shook hands with all of them, Dr Crowley pulled over a chair from a neighbouring table and offered it to Brunetti. He sat and when the doctor did too, looked around the table at the assembled Americans. 'I'm grateful that you agreed to speak to me this morning,' he said in English.

Dottoressa Crowley answered, 'It's only right, isn't it, to tell you what we saw, if it can help?' There were nods of agreement from the others.

Her husband took over from her and said, 'We've been talking about it already this morning, Commissario.' With a gesture that encompassed all of the people at the table, he added, 'It's probably best that we each tell you what we saw.'

Dr Peterson cleared his throat a few times, then said, speaking with the sort of clarity that comes of the fear that a foreigner might not otherwise understand, 'Well, after we got down into that place you call a *campo*, we were standing sort of in the front, to the left of Fred and Martha, and I was looking down at the purses those fellows were selling. And a man, not the one Martha saw – guy about my height – he moved forward until he was standing just a little bit behind me. He was on my left, but I really didn't pay any attention to him because, as I said, I was looking at the purses. Then I heard the noise, sort of a zip zip – I didn't have any idea what it was – sounded like a staple gun or something, or that thing they use when they take your tyres off – and there was the music from behind us, too – and then this guy stepped back without looking where he was going, and then he was gone. I didn't think anything of it except that I didn't like the way he pushed back like that, right into the people behind him.

'Next thing you know, I looked back and I saw that the guy who was selling the purses, he was down on the ground. And then Martha was kneeling beside him, and then Fred, and then they said he was dead.' He looked at Brunetti, and around at the others.

'I never saw anything like it in my life,' Dr Peterson continued, with what began to sound like indignation, as though he thought Brunetti owed him an explanation. He continued: 'Well, we waited around for a while, I'd say about a half-hour, but nothing happened. No one came. And it was awful cold and we hadn't had our supper yet, so we came back here to the hotel.'

A waiter passed by their table, and Dr Peterson took his attention away from Brunetti long enough to ask for another pot of coffee. The waiter nodded, noticed Brunetti sitting with them, and asked if he would like *un caffè*, a question which seemed to confuse the Americans as much as it relieved Brunetti. He had been in America and knew the difference between coffee and *caffè*.

Peterson turned to his wife and said, speaking to Brunetti, 'My wife was standing on the other side of me, so she didn't see anything, did you, honey?'

She shook her head and said in a very soft voice, 'No, dear.'

'Nothing at all, Signora?' Brunetti asked, ignoring her husband and speaking directly to her. 'Anything at all, no matter how insignificant?' When she still didn't answer, he prompted, 'Did he smoke, say anything, was he wearing anything you noticed?'

The woman smiled and looked at her husband as if to ask him if she had indeed noticed any of these things, but then she shook her head and lowered her eyes.

The woman with the red hair said, 'One of them had very hairy hands.'

Brunetti turned to her and smiled. 'Was this the one who was standing by Dr Crowley or the other one, the one near Dr Peterson?'

'The first one,' she said, 'the one near Martha. I didn't see the other man or, if I did see him, I didn't pay any attention to him. You see, when I was standing there, my shoe was untied.' She saw Brunetti's response to this and explained, 'And someone must have been standing on it, so when I heard that noise, it startled me, and I must have tried to move, but my foot was trapped and I lost my balance for a moment, and by the time I was steady on my feet again, I'd got sort of turned around. So I saw a man backing away, and I was vaguely conscious that he was near Martha. He had his hand up near his face, pulling at his scarf or his hat, and all I could see was that the back of his hand was very hairy, almost like a monkey's. But then I heard Martha calling for Fred, and I turned back around and didn't pay any more attention to him.'

Her appearance had led him to expect her to be flirtatious, but Brunetti found nothing of the coquette in her. She had described the scene simply, and he had no doubt that the man she had seen had hands as hairy as a monkey's.

When it seemed that no one else was going to add anything, Brunetti asked, 'Can any of you recall anything else about either of these men?'

His question was met with silence and a general shaking of heads.

'If I assure you that you will not be kept here to answer further questions and will not be called back to Italy as a result of anything you tell me, will that make it easier for you to answer?' Brunetti had no idea if foreigners feared getting caught up in the machinery of the judicial system as much as Italians did, but he still thought it wise to assure them that they would not be, even if he was not certain this was true.

None of them said a word.

Before he could attempt to rephrase the question, Dottoressa Crowley said, 'It's kind of you to put it that way, Commissario, but you don't have to do that with us. If we'd seen anything, we'd tell you, even if it meant we had to stay here longer.'

Her husband said, 'We asked the others when we got back last night, but no one seems to have noticed these men.'

'Or is willing to say they do,' added Lydia Watts.

The waiter arrived with their coffee and his

caffè. Brunetti added sugar and drank it quickly. He stood and took a number of his business cards from his wallet and handed them around, saying, 'If you should remember anything at all about what happened, please do get in touch with me. Phone or fax or email. Anything at all that comes to you.' He smiled and thanked them for their time and their help, and left the hotel without bothering to get their addresses. The hotel would have them, anyway, should he need to confirm anything, not that they had said anything that he could imagine would need confirmation. A thickset, Mediterranean man with hairy hands and another, shorter, one no one could describe, but no witness who had seen either one of them fire a gun.

The mist had not cleared. In fact, it appeared to have grown thicker, so Brunetti was careful to keep the façades of the buildings on his left in sight as he walked down the *riva*. The mist caused him to pass through the rows of *bacharelle* without seeing them. This added to the uneasiness he always felt when he walked past them and their vendors, so unlike the comfortable familiarity he felt in the rest of the city. He did not bother to analyse this sensation, was aware of it only in some atavistic, danger-sensing part of his mind. Once beyond them and past the façade of the Pietà, the feeling disappeared, just as the mist was beginning to do.

Brunetti arrived at the Questura a little after nine and asked the man on the switchboard if anyone had called with information about the dead man. He was told that no calls had come in. On the first floor he found Signorina Elettra's office empty, which caused him some surprise. The fact that her – and his – immediate superior, Vice-Questore Giuseppe Patta, had not arrived at his place of work, on the contrary, came as no surprise whatsoever. Brunetti stopped in at the officers' room and asked Pucetti, who was alone there, to come upstairs with him.

Once in his office, Brunetti asked the young officer where Ispettore Vianello was, but Pucetti had no idea. Vianello had come in just after eight, made a few phone calls, then left, saying he would be back before lunchtime.

'No idea?' Brunetti asked when they were both seated, unwilling to compromise the young man by asking him outright if he had eavesdropped on Vianello's conversations.

'No, sir. I was taking a call, so I couldn't hear what he said.' Brunetti was relieved to see that Pucetti no longer sat stiffly erect when speaking to him; sometimes he even went so far as to cross his legs. The young officer had begun to look at home in his uniform, less like some fresh-faced schoolboy dressed for Carnevale.

'Was it about this dead man, do you know?'

Pucetti thought a moment, then said, 'I'd guess not, sir. He seemed very relaxed about whatever it was.'

Changing topic, Brunetti said, 'I asked when I came in, but no one's called, which means we have no idea who he is or where he was from.'

'Senegal, probably,' Pucetti suggested.

'I know. That's likely, but we need to be sure if we want to have any hope of identifying him. He had no papers on him, and the fact that no one has called to identify him or to report that one of the *vu cumprà* is missing means we aren't going to get any help from the rest of them.' He was conscious of how dismissive that sounded of an entire class of people, 'the rest of them', but he had no time now to concern himself with niceties of expression. 'So we have to find out who he was, and to do that we need someone who has contact with the others.'

'Someone they trust?' Pucetti asked.

'Or fear,' Brunetti said, not much liking the sound of that, either.

'Who?'

'Whom they fear is probably easier,' Brunetti answered. 'I'd say we start with the people who rent rooms to them. Then we try the wholesalers who sell them the bags. Then the officers here who have arrested them,' he said, holding up a finger as he named each group.

'It might be easier to start with us, sir. That is, those of us who have arrested them,' Pucetti said, adding, 'Because we're right here, if for no other reason.'

'Of course,' Brunetti said. 'That technician get the photos done yet?'

'Not that I know of, sir,' Pucetti answered, starting to get to his feet, 'but I could go down to the lab and see if he's got them.'

'Yes. Do,' Brunetti told him. 'And see if

52

there's any sign of Signorina Elettra while you're down there, would you?'

Pucetti saluted and was gone. Brunetti took the paper out of his briefcase and finished reading the first section, looking in vain for any sort of editorial comment on the death. That was sure to come, he knew.

By the time he started the second section, the first page of which carried a longer, though no more informative, story about the murder, Pucetti was back, carrying in his hand a thick pile of full page photos.

Quickly Brunetti flipped through them, discarding the photos of the whole body in place and selecting those taken from each side and from front on. The man's eyes were closed, and the solemnity of his face was such that no one who saw the photos would expect him ever to open them again.

'Handsome devil, wasn't he?' Pucetti asked, looking down at the photos. 'How old would you say he was?'

'I doubt he was more than thirty,' Brunetti said.

Pucetti nodded in agreement. 'Who'd want to do something like that to one of these guys? They don't cause any real trouble.'

'You ever arrest one?' Brunetti asked.

'A couple,' Pucetti said. 'But that doesn't mean they aren't good people.'

'Does Savarini say that?' Brunetti asked.

Pucetti paused a moment, then finally answered, 'That's different.'

'And Novello?'

'Why wouldn't he?'

'Because they broke his finger the last time he was sent to arrest them.'

'It was an accident, sir,' said an affronted Pucetti. 'He grabbed the big sports bag that held everything the man wanted to sell, and the guy did what anyone would do: he tried to yank it back. Savarini's finger was in the strap, and when the *vu cumprà* pulled at it, he broke his finger. But it wasn't like the guy intended to do it.'

'So it's not broken?' Brunetti asked, curious to see how Pucetti would answer.

'No, of course it's broken. Only he didn't mean to do it, and Savarini doesn't bear him any ill will. I know because he told me so. Besides,' continued an even more heated Pucetti, 'he was one of the cops who jumped into the canal to save the one who fell in.'

'While trying to evade arrest, if memory serves,' Brunetti remarked.

Pucetti started to speak but stopped and gave Brunetti a long look, then asked, 'Are you playing with me, sir?'

Brunetti laughed.

6

An hour later, Pucetti and Brunetti had shown the photos to most of the officers at the Questura. Halfway through the process, Brunetti began to notice an unsettling correlation between their political affiliations and their responses. Most of those he knew to be sympathetic to the current government displayed little sympathy for, indeed, little interest in, the dead man. The further left on the political spectrum, the more likely it was that people would display sympathy for the man in the photo. Only two officers, both of them women, showed real sorrow that a man so young should have been killed.

Gravini, who had been in the squad that had made the last raid on the *ambulanti*, thought he recognized the man in the photo but also said he was sure he had never seen him among the *vu cumprà* he had arrested.

They were down in the officers' squad room, so Brunetti gave an inquiring glance around and asked, 'Do you have photos of those who have been?'

'Rubini has all the papers in his office, sir,' the sergeant answered. 'Arrest reports, copies of their passports, their *permessi di soggiorno*, at least for those who have them, and copies of the letters we send them.'

'Letters?' interrupted Pucetti. 'Why do we bother to send them letters?'

'We don't actually send them,' Gravini answered. 'We give them to them, saying they have forty-eight hours to leave the country.' He snorted at the absurdity of this, then added, 'And then we arrest them a week later and give them another copy of the same letter.'

Brunetti waited for his next comment, which he assumed would be much in line with what the old man on the vaporetto had said that morning. Gravini shrugged and said, 'I don't know why we bother. They aren't hurting anyone, just trying to make a living. And no one forces people to buy the bags from them.'

Pucetti interrupted suddenly, 'Gravini, you're one of the ones who went into the canal, aren't you?'

Gravini lowered his head, as if embarrassed at having been caught at some folly. 'What was I supposed to do? He was new, the one who fell in. It was probably the first time he'd been caught in one of our raids. He panicked, really just a kid, and he ran. What else would he do, with cops all over the place, running at him? It was over by the Misericordia, and he ran up that bridge that doesn't have a parapet. Lost his footing or something and fell in. I could hear him screaming all the way back by the church. When we got there, he was flailing around like a madman, so I did the first thing that came into my head: I went right in after him. Didn't realize until I was in the water that it wasn't very deep, at least not near the sides. I don't know what he was making all the fuss about.' Gravini tried to make himself sound angry but without much success. 'Ruined my jacket, and Bocchese spent a day cleaning the mud out of my pistol.'

Brunetti chose not to comment on this. 'Any idea where you might have seen this one, then?' he asked, tapping his forefinger on the full-face photo.

'No, sir. It doesn't come to me, but I know I've seen him somewhere.' He took the photos and looked through the series. At last he said, 'Can I take these, sir? And maybe show them to some of the men I've arrested?'

Brunetti was not sure how to refer to the other *vu cumprà*. 'Colleagues' of the dead man would sound strange, suggesting as it did an ordered world of work. He finally decided on, 'His friends?'

'Yes. There's one I've arrested at least five times; I can ask him.'

'But what if he sees you coming?' Pucetti asked.

'No, no, it's nothing like that,' Gravini insisted. 'A bunch of them live in an apartment off Via Garibaldi, down near where my mother lives, so I see them when I go to visit her, when . . .' he trailed off, seeking a way to say it. 'Well, when we're both off work. He says he used to be a teacher, Muhammad. I can ask him.'

'You think he'd trust you?' Brunetti asked.

Gravini shrugged. 'No way to know until I ask him.'

Brunetti told Gravini to keep the photos and to show them around, perhaps ask Muhammad if he would do the same among the men with whom he worked. 'Gravini,' he added, 'tell them that all we're asking for is a name and an address. No questions after that, no trouble, nothing else.' He wondered if the Africans would trust the word of the police and suspected that they had no reason to do so. Even though there were men like Gravini, willing to jump into a canal to save them, Brunetti feared that the prevailing attitude of the police would more closely resemble that of the old man on the vaporetto and thus not encourage cooperation.

He thanked both men and went down to Signorina Elettra's office, where he found her at her desk. For some days, Signorina Elettra had been keeping the gloom of winter at bay with a refulgence of colour: she had begun last Wednesday with yellow shoes, Thursday with emerald green slacks and Friday with an orange jacket. Today, to begin the week, she had decided to skip her throat – no doubt because a bright scarf would be too predictable an accessory – and had wrapped her hair in a piece of silk that seemed to be covered with parrots.

'Lovely birds,' Brunetti said as he came in.

She glanced up, smiled, and thanked him. 'I think next week I might suggest to the Vice-Questore that he try the same thing.'

'Which? Yellow shoes or the turban?' Brunetti asked, just to show he had noticed.

'No, his ties. They're always so very sober.'

'Not the tie-pins, though. They have different coloured jewels in them, don't they?' Brunetti asked.

'One would hardly notice, they're so small,' she said. 'I wonder if I should get him some.'

Brunetti had no idea if she meant ties or jewelled pins for them: it hardly mattered. 'And put them down as office expenses?' he asked.

'Of course,' she answered. 'Perhaps I'd list them as "maintenance".' Then, turning to business, she asked, 'What is it I can help you with, Commissario?'

Hearing her, Brunetti wondered when she had last asked anyone what she could do for them, whether himself or the Vice-Questore. 'I'd like you to see what you can find out about the *vu cumprà*,' he said.

'It's all in here,' she answered, pointing at her computer. 'Or in the Interpol files.'

'No,' he said, 'not that sort of information. I want to know what people know, really know,

59

about them: where they live and how they live, what sort of people they are.'

'Most are from Senegal, I believe,' she said.

'Yes, I know. But I want to know if they're from the same place and if they know one another or are related to one another.'

'And,' she continued, 'presumably, you'd also like to know who the murdered man is.'

'Of course,' he answered. 'But I don't think that's going to be an easy thing to find out. No one has called about him. The only people who volunteered anything were some American tourists who were there at the time, and all they saw was a very tall man with hairy hands who they said looked "Mediterranean", by which they mean dark. There was another man, but all they noticed about him was that he was shorter than the other. Aside from that, the shooting might as well have taken place in another city, for all we know. Or on another planet.'

After a thoughtful pause, she asked, 'That's pretty much where they live, isn't it?'

'Excuse me?' he asked, confused.

'They don't have any contact with us, not real contact, that is,' she began. 'They appear like mushrooms, set out their sheets, and do business until they disappear again. It's as if they popped out of their space capsules, then vanished again.'

'That's hardly another planet,' he said.

'But it is, sir. We don't talk to them, or really see them.' She noticed how he responded to this and so insisted, 'No, I'm not trying to attack us for the way we treat them nor trying to defend them, the way my friends do, saying they're all victims of this or that. I simply think it's very strange that they can live among us and yet, for the entire time they aren't on the street, selling things, remain invisible.' She looked to see if he realized how serious she was, then added, 'That's why I say they live on a different planet. The only attention we pay to them on this planet, it seems, is when we arrest them.'

He considered this and had to agree with her. He remembered once, last year, an evening when he and Paola were on their way to dinner and had been caught in a sudden rainstorm, how the streets had instantly blossomed with Tamils, all carrying bouquets of collapsible umbrellas, which they tried to sell for five Euros apiece. Paola had remarked that they seemed – the Tamils – freeze dried: all one had to do was add water, and they sprang to full size. Much the same, he realized, could be said of the *vu cumprà*: they had the same ability to appear as though out of nowhere and then as easily disappear.

He decided to accept her point and said, 'Then that's a way to begin: see if you can find out where it is they go when they disappear.'

'You mean who rents to them and where?'

'Yes. Gravini said there are some who live down in Castello near his mother. Ask him for her address or have a look in the phone book: it can't be a very common name.' He recalled what

Gravini had said about the tenuous nature of his relationship – one could hardly call it friendship, not if it originated in one man arresting the other – with Muhammad. 'All I want is the address. I don't want to do anything until Gravini has had a chance to talk to the one he knows. See what you can find out about any other apartments that might be rented to them.'

'You think there'd be contracts?' she asked. 'There would be copies at the Comune.'

Brunetti doubted the willingness of most landlords to offer the protection of a formal contract to Africans: they were certainly reluctant enough to give them to Venetians. Once a tenant had a contract, the law made eviction difficult, if not virtually impossible. Besides, a formal contract had to state the rent, and thus the income became visible, and taxable: any sane landlord would want to avoid that. So the Africans were probably renting – Brunetti found no way around the obvious pun – *in nero*.

'I think it would be better to ask around,' he answered. 'Try the people at the *Gazzettino* and *La Nuova*. They might know something. They always do a story every time we do a round-up and arrest some of them. They've got to know something.'

His attention wandered and he found himself wondering how Elettra endured wearing the turban. The office was warm, one of those offices on the side of the building where the radiators worked, so surely it must have become uncomfortable to wear it tight to her head all day long.

But he said nothing, thinking that perhaps Paola would be able to explain.

'I'll see what I can find out,' she said. 'Are there fingerprints I could send to Lyon?'

'I haven't got the autopsy report yet,' Brunetti said. 'I'll send the photos to you as soon as I get them.'

'Thank you, sir,' she said. 'I'll see what I can do.'

On his way back to his own office, Brunetti was already running through the list of friends who might be able to help him with information. By the time he reached his desk, he had accepted the fact that there was no one he knew who could supply him with reliable information about the *ambulanti*, which led him to suspect that Signorina Elettra was right and they did indeed live on different planets.

He called down to the office of Rubini, the inspector in charge of the Sisyphean labour of arresting the *ambulanti*, and asked him to come up for a moment.

'About last night?' Rubini asked over the phone.

'Yes. You hear anything?'

'No,' Rubini answered. 'But I didn't expect to.' There was a pause, and then he asked, 'Should I bring my files?'

'Please.'

'I hope you've got a long time, Guido.'

'Why?'

'There must be two metres of them.'

'Then should I come down there?'

'No, I'll just bring the summaries of the ones I've submitted. It will still take you the rest of the morning to read them.' Brunetti thought he heard Rubini laugh quietly but wasn't sure. He replaced the phone.

When Rubini showed up more than ten minutes later, a stack of files in his hands, he explained that the delay was caused by his having searched for the file containing all of the photos that had been taken of the Africans who had been arrested in the last year. 'We're supposed to photograph them every time we arrest them,' he explained.

'Supposed to?' Brunetti asked.

Rubini set a large stack of papers on Brunetti's desk and sat down. From Murano, Rubini had been on the force for more than two decades and, like Vianello, had moved up through the ranks slowly, perhaps blocked by the same refusal to curry favour with the men in power. Tall and so thin as to seem emaciated, Rubini was in fact a passionate rower and every year was among the first ten to cross the finish line of the Vogalonga.

'We did at the beginning, but after a while it seemed a waste of time to take the photo of a man we'd arrested six or seven times and who we say hello to on the street.' He pushed the papers closer to Brunetti and added, 'We call them *tu* by now, and they address us all by name.'

Brunetti pulled the papers towards him. 'Why do you still bother?'

'What, to arrest them?'

Brunetti nodded.

'Dottor Patta wants arrests, so we go and arrest them. It makes the statistics look good.'

Brunetti had suspected this would be the answer, but he asked, 'You think it really does any good?'

'God knows,' Rubini said with a resigned shake of his head. 'It keeps the Vice-Questore off our backs for a week or two, and I suppose if we were to be serious about it, arrest them and take all their bags, they'd simply decide to go somewhere else.'

'But?' Brunetti asked.

Rubini crossed his legs, pulled out a cigarette and lit it without bothering to ask if he could. 'But my men always leave them a couple of bags when they confiscate them, even though they're supposed to take them all. After all, they've got to eat, these guys, whether they're African or Italian. If we take all of their bags, they've got nothing to sell.'

Brunetti shoved the top of a Nutella jar towards the inspector. 'And the bags?' he asked.

Rubini took an enormous pull at his cigarette and let the smoke filter slowly from his nose. 'You mean the ones we leave them or the ones we take?'

'There's the warehouse in Mestre, isn't there?' Brunetti asked.

'Two of them by now.' Rubini leaned forward and flicked ash into the proffered ashtray. 'It's all in there,' he went on, using the hand with the cigarette to point to the files. 'So far this year we've confiscated something like ten thousand bags. No matter how fast we chop them up or burn them, we keep confiscating more. Soon there won't be enough room to store them.'

'What'll you do?'

Rubini crushed the cigarette and said, making no attempt to disguise his exasperation, 'If it were my decision, I'd give them back to the *vu cumprà* so they wouldn't have to pay to buy new ones all over again. But then what happens to all those people who work in the factories in Puglia where they make them?' Abruptly he got to his feet, pointed at the files and said, 'If there's anything else you want to know, give me a call.' At the door, he paused and looked back at Brunetti, and raised a hand in an expression of utter hopelessness. 'It's all crazy, the whole thing,' he said, and left.

7

Brunetti had not read the *Iliad* – his laboured high school translations could hardly be considered a reading of the text – until his third year at university; the experience had been a strange one. Though he had never read the original, it was so much a part of his world and his culture that he knew even before he read it what each book would bring. He experienced no surprise at the perfidy of Paris and the compliance of Helen, knew that bold Priam was doomed and that no bravery on the part of noble Hector could save Troy from ruin.

Rubini's files produced much the same sense of literary *déjà vu*. As he read through the summary of the police's response to the arrival of the *vu cumprà* in Italy, he was conscious of how familiar he was with so many elements of the plot. He knew that the original street pedlars had been Moroccans and Algerians who sold illegally the handicraft articles they brought into Italy with them. Indeed, he could remember seeing their merchandise, years before: hand-carved wooden animals, glass trading beads, ornamental knives and glitzy fake scimitars. Though the report did not explain it, he assumed that their original name had been given to this wave of French-speaking itinerant salesmen in imitation of their attempts to catch the attention of their new customers with some linguistically bastardized invitation to buy.

As the Arabs were supplanted by Africans from further south, the frequency of crimes lessened: though immigration violations and selling without a licence remained, petty theft and crimes of violence virtually disappeared from the arrest records of the men who had inherited the name of *vu cumprà*.

The Arabs, he knew, had passed on to more lucrative employment, many of them migrating north to countries with no choice but to accept the residence permits so easily granted by an accommodating Italian bureaucracy. The *Senegalesi*, with no apparent propensity to crime, had originally been viewed sympathetically by many of the residents of the city, and as Gravini's story suggested, they had earned the regard, however gruffly stated, of at least some of the officers on the street. In the last years, however, the increasing insistence with which they confronted passers-by and their apparently ever expanding numbers had worn away much of the Venetians' original good will.

He searched, but searched in vain, for any arrests during the last few years for crimes other than violations of visa regulations or selling without a licence. There had been one rape, six years ago, but the attacker turned out to be a Moroccan, not a Senegalese. In the only arrest involving violence, a Senegalese had chased an Albanian pickpocket halfway up Lista di Spagna before bringing him to the ground with a running tackle. The African had sat on the pickpocket's back until the police responded to the call one of his friends made on his *telefonino* and arrived to make the arrest. A handwritten note in the margin explained that the Albanian had turned out to be only sixteen, and so, although he had been repeatedly arrested for the same crime, he had been released the same day after being given the usual letter ordering him to leave the country within forty-eight hours.

The last file contained a speculative report on numbers: there had been days during the previous summer when an estimated three to five hundred *ambulanti* had lined the streets; repeated police round-ups had caused a temporary attrition, but the number was now estimated to have crept back to close to two hundred.

When he finished the report, Brunetti glanced at his watch and reached for the phone. From memory, he dialled the number of Marco Erizzo, who answered on the second ring. 'What now, Guido?' he asked with a laugh.

'I hate those phones,' Brunetti said. 'I can't sneak up on anyone any more.'

'Very James Bond, I know,' Erizzo admitted, 'but it lets me do a lot of filtering.'

'But you didn't filter me,' Brunetti said, 'even though you knew I'd be likely to ask a favour.' Brunetti made no attempt at small talk about Marco's family, nor did he expect such questions: long friendship would already have alerted Marco that Brunetti's voice was not the one he used for a social call.

'I'm always interested in knowing what the forces of order are up to,' Erizzo said with mock solemnity. 'In case I can be of service to them in any way, of course.'

'I'm not the Finanza, Marco,' Brunetti said.

'No jokes about them, Guido, please,' Erizzo said in a decidedly cooler tone. 'And try to remember never to use their name when you're talking to me, especially if you call me on the *telefonino*.'

Unwilling to address himself to Marco's unshakeable conviction that all phone calls, to make no mention of emails and faxes, were recorded, especially by the Finance Police, Brunetti instead asked, 'It's not as if you ever use any other telephone, is it?'

'Not one I answer. Tell me what it is, Guido.'

'The *vu cumprà*,' he said.

Marco wasted no time by asking the obvious question of whether this were related to last night's killing and said instead, 'Never been anything like it here in the city, has there, at least not since they shot that *carabiniere* in, when was it, 1978?'

'Something like that,' Brunetti agreed, aware of how long ago those awful years seemed now. 'You know anything about them?'

'That they take nine and a half per cent of my business away from me,' Erizzo said with sudden heat.

'Why so exact?'

'I've calculated what I sold in bags before their arrival and after, and the difference is nine and a half per cent.' He cut off the last syllable with his teeth.

'Why don't you do something about it?'

Erizzo laughed again, a sound utterly lacking in humour. 'What do you suggest, Guido? A letter of complaint to your superiors, asking them to concern themselves with the welfare of their citizens? Next you'll be asking me to send a postcard to the Vatican to ask them to concern themselves with my spiritual welfare.' Bitter resignation had joined anger in Erizzo's voice. 'You people,' Erizzo went on, presumably referring to the police, 'you can't do anything except shake them up for a day or so and let them out again. You don't even bother to slap their wrists any more, do you?' He paused, but Brunetti refused to venture a response into that silence.

'There's nothing I can do about them, Guido. The only thing I can hope is that they don't lay down their sheets in front of one of my shops, the way they do in front of Max Mara, because if they do, the only thing that will happen is that I'll lose more money. The politicians don't want to hear about them, and you guys can't – or won't – do anything.'

Brunetti again thought it expedient not to express an opinion. He persisted, 'But what do you know about them?'

'Probably not much more than anyone else in the city,' Erizzo said. 'That they're from Senegal, they're Muslims, they mostly live in Padova, some of them here, they don't cause much trouble, and the bags are of good quality and the prices are right.'

'How do you know about the quality of the bags?' Brunetti asked, hoping to divert his friend from his anger.

'Because I've stopped on the street and looked at them,' he said. 'Believe me, Guido, even Louis Vuitton himself, if there is such a person, couldn't tell the difference between the real ones and the ones these guys are selling. Same leather, same stitching, same logo all over the place.'

'Do they sell imitations of your bags?' Brunetti asked.

'Of course,' Erizzo snapped.

Brunetti chose to ignore the warning in his friend's tone and went on, 'Someone told me that the factories are in Puglia. Do you know anything about that?'

Voice no warmer, Erizzo said, 'That's what

I've been told. The factories are the same. They work for the legitimate companies during the day, then they turn the fake ones out at night.'

'"Fake" doesn't have much meaning any more, not if it's the same factories, I'd say,' Brunetti observed, trying to lighten the mood that had come over their conversation.

There was to be no jollying Marco. 'I suppose so,' was his only comment.

'Do you have any idea of who's behind it?' Brunetti persisted.

'Only an idiot wouldn't be able to figure that out, it's so big and so well organized.' Then, in a voice grown minimally less cool, Erizzo added, 'They've got only one problem.'

'What?' Brunetti asked.

'Distribution,' Erizzo surprised him by answering.

'Huh?'

'Think about it, Guido. Anyone can produce. That's the easy part: all you need is raw materials, a place to assemble them, and enough people who are willing to work for what you pay them. The real problem is finding a place to sell whatever it is you've made.' Brunetti remained silent, so he proceeded, 'If you sell it in a shop, you've got all sorts of expenses: rent, heat, light, a bookkeeper, salespeople. Worst of all, you've got to pay taxes.' Brunetti wondered when he had ever had a conversation with Marco in which the subject of taxes had not been mentioned.

'That's what I do, Guido,' his friend went on,

73

voice veering back towards anger. 'I pay taxes. I pay them on my shops, and for my employees, and on what I sell, and on what I manage to keep. And my employees pay taxes on what they earn. And some of it stays here, in Venice, Guido, and what they earn they spend here.' The warmth in Marco's voice was not that of friendship or returning intimacy.

'You tell me how the city profits from what the *vu cumprà* earn,' Marco demanded. 'You think any of that money stays here?' Even though it was a rhetorical question, Erizzo paused, as if daring Brunetti to answer. When he did not, Erizzo said, 'It all goes south, Guido.' There was no need for him to say more about the destination of this money.

'How do you know that?' Brunetti demanded.

Brunetti heard him take a deep breath. 'Because no one bothers them, that's why. Not the Guardia di Finanza, and not the *Carabinieri*, and not you people, and because they seem to come into this country pretty much as they please, and no one bothers to stop them at the borders. That means that no one wants to be bothered or that someone doesn't want them to be bothered.' The pause after this last sentence was so long that Brunetti thought Marco had finished, but his voice came back, 'And if I thought you had the stomach to listen to any more of this, I'd add that they also enjoy the protection of everyone who refuses to see them as illegal immigrants who spend their days

74

breaking the law while the police stroll back and forth in front of them.'

Brunetti was at a loss about how to deal with his friend's rage, so he let a long time pass before he said, voice calm, 'Longest definition I've ever heard of "distribution".' Before Marco could react, he added, 'Also the most illuminating.'

Marco paused for an equally long time, and Brunetti could almost hear the wheels of friendship spinning about in search of the road they had left. 'Good,' Marco finally said, and Brunetti thought he heard in that monosyllable the same relief that they had come back to firm ground. 'I'm not sure all of this is true, but at least it makes sense.'

Was this the historian's plight, Brunetti wondered, never to know what was true but only what made sense? Or the policeman's? He drew himself away from these reflections and started to thank Marco, but before he could say more than the other man's name, Marco said, 'I've got another call. I've got to go.' And then silence.

The call had gained Brunetti no new information, but it had strengthened his belief that the *ambulanti* enjoyed the protection of – for a moment, he was at a loss how best to express this, even to himself – the protection of 'forces that function at variance with those of the state' was the euphemism he finally summoned.

He took a notebook and opened it to the centre page, where he found the phone number he wanted. Adding one to each of the digits in it and embarrassed at this simple code, he dialled. When a man answered on the fifth ring, Brunetti said only, 'Good morning, I'd like to speak to Signor Ducatti.' When the man told him he must have dialled a wrong number, Brunetti apologized for disturbing him and hung up.

Immediately Brunetti regretted that he had not gone down to the bar at the bridge for a coffee before phoning: now he was trapped in his office until Sandrini called him back. To pass the time, he took some papers from his in tray and began to read through them.

It was more than half an hour before his phone rang. He answered with his name, and the same voice that had told him he had dialled a wrong number said, 'What is it?'

'I'm very well, Renato,' Brunetti answered. 'Thanks for asking.'

'Tell me what you want, Brunetti, and let me get back to the office.'

'Just stepped out to make a phone call, did you?' Brunetti asked.

'Tell me what you want,' the man said with badly suppressed anger.

'I want to know if your father-in-law's – what shall I call them – if his business associates had anything to do with last night?'

'You mean the dead nigger?'

'I mean the dead African,' Brunetti corrected him.

'That all?'

'Yes.'

'I'll call you,' he said and hung up.

If Renato Sandrini were better behaved, perhaps Brunetti's conscience would have troubled him about blackmailing and intimidating him. As it was, the man's consistent rudeness, as well as the arrogance that characterized his public behaviour, made it almost pleasant for Brunetti to exercise his power over him. Twenty years ago, Sandrini, a criminal lawyer in Padova, had married the only daughter of a local Mafia boss. Children followed, as did an enormous amount of very well-paid defence work. The repeated success of Sandrini's defences had turned him into something of a local legend. As the size of his legal practice increased, so too did that of his wife, Julia, until, at forty, she had come to resemble a barrel, though a barrel with very expensive taste in jewellery and an alarmingly possessive love for her husband.

None of this would have worked to Sandrini's disadvantage, nor to Brunetti's advantage, were it not for a fire in a hotel on the Lido that had filled some of the rooms with smoke and caused four people to be taken to the hospital, unconscious. There, it was discovered that the man in room 307, who had given his name as Franco Rossi, carried the *carta d'identità*, as well as the credit cards, of Renato Sandrini. Luckily, he had regained consciousness in time to prevent the hospital from calling his wife to alert her to his condition, but not before the police had been called to report the disparity in names that appeared on the documents. All of this would have passed as an easily overlooked clerical error were it not for two things: the other person in the room with Sandrini was a fifteen-year-old Albanian prostitute, and the police report containing this information landed the following morning on the desk of Guido Brunetti.

Caution prevented him from approaching Sandrini until he had spoken at some length with the prostitute and her pimp and had obtained both videotaped and written statements from them. They were willing to talk only because they believed the man in question to be Franco Rossi, a wholesaler of fitted carpets from Padova. Had they had the least idea of who Sandrini was – more importantly, had they had any idea of the identity of his father-in-law – both would surely have preferred prison to having had the long conversations with the pleasant commissario from Venice.

It had taken only one meeting with Sandrini for Brunetti to persuade the lawyer that it might be wiser, given the rather Victorian ideas of some members of the Mafia as to the sanctity of the marriage vows, to give the occasional piece of information to the pleasant commissario from Venice. To date, Brunetti had maintained his promise never to ask Sandrini to compromise his professional relationship with his clients, but he knew the promise was a false one and that he would grind information out of Sandrini mercilessly should it serve his own purposes.

Brunetti placed the files into his out tray and, strangely cheered by the consideration of his own perfidy, went home for lunch.

8

If he had thought to leave uncertainty and unease behind him at the Questura, he was much mistaken, for he found both within the walls of his home. Here they manifested themselves in the aura of moral outrage which both Paola and Chiara carried about with them, much in the fashion of Dante's usurers, passing through eternity with their money bags hung round their necks. He assumed that both his wife and his daughter believed themselves in the right. When, after all, had a person involved in an argument believed themselves to be in the wrong?

He found his family at table. He kissed Paola's cheek and ruffled Chiara's hair, but she pulled her head quickly aside, as if unwilling to be touched by a hand that had rested on her opponent's shoulder. Pretending not to have noticed, he took his place and asked Raffi how school was. His son, in a manifestation of male solidarity in the face of female moodiness, said things were fine, then began a long explanation of the arcana of a computer program he was using in his chemistry class. Brunetti, far more interested in his linguine with scampi than in anything to do with computers, smiled and asked what he did his best to make sound like relevant questions.

Conversation chugged along through a plate of sole fried with artichoke bottoms and a rucola salad. Chiara pushed her food around on her plate, leaving much of it uneaten, an unmistakable sign that this situation was affecting her deeply.

Upon learning that there was no dessert, she and Raffi evaporated; Brunetti set his empty glass down and said, 'I have the feeling I ought to have one of those blue helmets the UN peacekeepers wear when there's danger they might be caught in crossfire.'

Paola poured them both a bit more wine, the Loredan Gasparini his father-in-law had sent him as a birthday present, one he would like to be able to drink in happier circumstances. 'She'll get over it,' Paola said and set the bottle on the table with an authoritative clunk.

'I have no doubt of that,' Brunetti answered calmly. 'I just don't want to have to eat my lunch in this atmosphere until that happens.'

'Oh, come on, Guido. It's not that bad,' Paola said in a voice that suggested she would be quite happy, if given sufficient provocation, to divert her irritation towards him. 'She'll realize what she's done in a few days.'

'And then?' he asked. 'Apologize?'

'For starters,' Paola said.

'And then what?'

'Think about what she said and what that says about her as a person.'

'It's been a day,' he said. 'And she's not over it.'

Paola allowed a long time to pass before she asked, 'What does that mean?'

He tried to find a way of saying what he wanted to say without angering her. 'That I think you've offended her,' he finally offered.

'Her?' Paola said with false incredulity. 'How?'

He poured some more wine into his glass but left it on the table. 'By assaulting her without giving her a chance to explain.'

Her look was long and level. '"Assaulting?"' she repeated. 'Does that mean there's some explanation or justification for ideas like hers, that the death of a man can be dismissed with a cavalier "only", and that her listener is somehow obliged to let the remark pass unobserved? Or that to object to it is to "assault" the person who made it?'

'Of course not,' he said, trained by Paola herself to recognize and dismiss the *argumentun ad absurdum*. 'I'm not saying that.'

82

'Then what are you saying?'

'That you might have been better advised to see where she got these ideas and try to reason with her.'

'Rather than assaulting her, as you put it?' she asked, beginning to show her anger.

'Yes,' he answered calmly.

'I'm not in the habit of attempting to reason with racial prejudice,' she said.

'Then what do you want to do with it, beat it with a stick?'

He saw her start to answer, then bite it back. She took a sip of her wine, then another, then set the glass down. 'All right,' she finally said. 'Perhaps I was a little too severe with her. But it was so embarrassing, to hear her say those things and to think I might have been responsible, in some way, for her having said them.'

'Are we talking about Chiara here, or about you?' he surprised her by asking.

She pursed her lips, glanced across at the window that looked off to the north, nodded in acknowledgement of the accuracy of his question, and said, 'You're right.'

'I'm not interested in being right,' Brunetti said.

'What are you interested in, then?'

'Living in peace in my own home.'

'I suppose that's pretty much all anyone wants,' she said.

'If only it were that simple, huh?' he asked, got to his feet and leaned over to kiss her on the head, then went back to the Questura and to the investigation of the death of the man who was only a *vu cumprà*.

The African's death, or at least the cause of it, was catalogued in the print-out of the autopsy report that lay on Brunetti's desk. The speed with which it had arrived surprised Brunetti, and he flipped to the back to see if Rizzardi had given a reason. His surprise grew when, instead of the pathologist's name, he found a blank where the name of the responsible pathologist should have appeared. Deciding to waste no time in attempting to figure out why Rizzardi might have failed to fill this in, he began to read.

The victim was estimated to have been in his late twenties, and although there was evidence he had been a heavy smoker, he was in excellent health, as were his organs. He was 1.82 metres tall and weighed 68 kilos. A set of his finger-prints had been forwarded to Lyon for possible identification.

In total, five bullets had struck him, a number which corresponded to the number of sounds the Americans had heard. Either of two of them would have sufficed to kill him: one had severed his spine, and one had perforated the left ventricle of the heart. The remaining three had pounded into his torso; one had lodged in the liver, while two had simply buried themselves in his flesh without damaging any organs. The fact that all five shots had struck him spoke to Brunetti of proximity as much as marks-manship, for from what the Americans had described, the killers had been little more than a metre from their victim. The angles of the paths of the bullets suggested that one man was taller than the other; the fact that the bullets had lacked the force to emerge from the body suggested that the guns were of low calibre. The bullets had been extracted and sent to the lab for analysis, though a layman's guess was that the gun that fired them would turn out to be a .22, a weapon Brunetti knew was not unknown to paid killers.

'Layman,' Brunetti said aloud, setting the report to one side. Rizzardi, who had worked in Naples a decade ago, had probably seen more signs of violent death than anyone else in the city, so he would hardly have used such a term when writing an autopsy report.

The report had arrived by email, which meant that the photos would be on view in Signorina Elettra's computer. Brunetti, however, had no desire to see them: the sight of wounds had always caused him pain and disgust. It was only the idea of the motivation that had caused them that interested him. He admitted to himself that he had little real knowledge of Africa, thought of the continent as a vague, amorphous mass where things went wrong and people suffered and starved while they lived amidst a wealth of natural resources that had been strewed about them with nature's most prodigal hand.

He had read of the colonial past of the continent, but the closer history moved towards the present, the less interest he took in it. But this, he realized, was true of his interest in history in general.

Brunetti gazed out of the window of his office at the crane that still, after years, towered over the *casa di riposo* of San Lorenzo. A man who made his living selling counterfeit bags. A man who had been executed by a pair of professional killers. The first could be said of all of the *vu cumprà*: that was what they did, sell bags. The second, however, most decidedly could not: in the cases he could recall of violent death involving *extracomunitari*, none had been Africans, neither the victims nor the killers.

Brunetti tried to consider the factors that might bear on the murder and could come up with nothing more helpful than the man's origins and past behaviour or something he might be involved in now. As for his past, Brunetti admitted he knew nothing, not even the man's country of origin, though Senegal was a safe guess. And for the present, he imagined possibilities only to exclude them immediately: jealous husbands did not in general send killers to vindicate their honour; and the wholesalers of the bags, so far as Brunetti knew, hardly needed the example of murder to keep their employees in line. The Africans were surely only too grateful for any chance of work to risk losing their jobs through attempting to cheat their employers. Beyond these thoughts, the possibilities stretched out, both unknown and unlimited.

He took a copy of that week's staff assignments and flipped it over. On the back he began a list of the things they needed to know about the dead man: 'Name, nationality, profession, criminal record, how long in Italy, address, family, friends.' He thought about how to begin to penetrate the mystery of the man's existence, remembered someone who might be able to help him, picked up the phone and called down to the officers' room.

As he had hoped, Vianello answered.

'You free?' Brunetti asked.

'Yes.'

'Two minutes,' Brunetti said and added, 'We'll need a boat.'

It took him more than that time to put on his overcoat and find a spare pair of gloves, which were stuffed into the pockets of a down vest that had been forgotten in his closet. He went down to the entrance hall.

Vianello was waiting at the front door, wearing so many layers of sweaters and vests under his coat as to seem almost twice his normal size. 'We're not going to Vladivostok, you know,' Brunetti said in greeting.

'Nadia's got flu, the kids have colds, and I don't want to get sick and have to stay at home.'

'Who's with them?' Brunetti asked.

'Nadia's mother. You know how close she lives, so she's in and out all day.' Vianello waved the officer on duty aside and pulled open the front door, allowing a gust of frigid air to sweep around them and into the hall. He stuffed his gloved hands into the pockets of his parka and stepped outside.

The pilot stood on deck, no more of his face visible than a small triangle of eyes and nose swaddled in the fur-lined hood of his jacket. Stepping on board, Brunetti said, 'Could you take us over to San Zan Degolà?' before hurrying down the steps and into the cabin.

Vianello followed him inside, allowing the double doors to slap closed behind him. The cabin was cold, but at least they were out of the wind that buffeted the doors. When he was seated opposite Brunetti, Vianello asked, 'What's over there?'

'Don Alvise.'

At the mention of the former priest's name, Vianello nodded in immediate understanding. Alvise Perale had for years been a parish priest in Oderzo, a small, torpid town north of Venice. In his time as *parroco* of the local church, he had dedicated his considerable energies not only to the spiritual well-being of his parishioners but also to the material well-being of the many people whom the currents of war, revolution, and poverty had washed up on the banks of the Livenza river. Among these people were Albanian prostitutes, Bosnian mechanics, Romanian gypsies, Kurdish shepherds, and African shopkeepers. To Don Alvise, regardless of their nationality or religion, they were all children of the god he worshipped and thus worthy of his care.

His parishioners responded to his activities with mixed feelings: some believed he was right to divide the wealth of the Church with these poorest of the poor, but others preferred to worship a less open-handed god and eventually protested to their bishop when Don Alvise invited a family from Sierra Leone to move into the rectory with him. In his letter to Don Alvise, ordering him to tell the family to leave, the bishop explained his motives by stating that 'some of these people worship stones'.

Upon receipt of this letter, Don Alvise went to the local bank and withdrew the bulk of the money from the parish account. Two days later and before responding to the bishop's letter, he used the money to buy a small apartment in the nearby town of Portogruaro, title to which was given to the father of the family from Sierra Leone. That same evening, Don Alvise wrote to his bishop, explaining that he saw no other course open to him than to renounce his vocation, for to continue to live it as he thought it should be lived was clearly to create perpetual strife with his superiors. In closing, he added, in the most respectful terms, that he would prefer the company of people who worshipped stones to that of people who had them in place of hearts.

The many friends he had accumulated over the years rose to his aid, and within weeks he had a position as a social assistant in Venice, the city of his birth, where he was given charge of a hostel that provided lodging and food for people claiming political asylum in Italy. Though he was a civil servant and no longer a member of the clergy, the people with whom he worked persisted in using his honorific in addressing him, and so he was never referred to as 'Signor Perale' but always as 'Don Alvise'. He could wear jeans, he could grow a moustache that any macho would envy, he could even be seen in the company of women: nothing could take the title from him. Don Alvise he had been and Don Alvise he would remain.

Brunetti had met him some years before, when he was investigating the disappearance of a woman from Kosovo who was believed to be involved in the drug trade. The woman had never been found, but he and Don Alvise had remained in friendly contact since then, each occasionally able to do the other a favour or provide information that could be of use in the pursuit of their different goals.

Brunetti knew that there was an official, governmental structure that would provide him with information about the *extracomunitari*; the Questura certainly had ample documentation on them. But he knew that Don Alvise's information, though it could not be considered in any way official, would be far more accurate. Perhaps the difference lay in the fact that, to the public administration, these people were problems, while to Don Alvise they were people *with* problems.

As the boat made its way slowly up the Grand Canal, Brunetti explained to Vianello why he wanted to see the former priest. 'They trust him,' he said, 'and I know he helps find houses for a lot of *clandestini*.'

'The Senegalesi?' Vianello asked. 'I always thought they were a sort of closed community. And I think they're Muslim, most of them.'

Brunetti had heard the same, but Don Alvise was the only person he could think of at the moment who might be able to help, and he knew that the former priest cared little what god a person chose to worship. 'Maybe,' he temporized. 'That is, maybe he knows them or some of them.' When Vianello did not offer agreement, Brunetti asked, 'Can you think of anyone else?'

Vianello didn't answer.

The launch turned left into Rio di San Zan Degolà. Brunetti got to his feet and, lowering his head as he left the cabin, went up on deck. 'Up there, before the bridge,' he told the pilot, who pulled the boat to the side of the canal, flipped the motor into reverse, and drew silently up to the moss-covered steps. Brunetti studied them for a moment, but before he could decide whether to risk stepping from the bobbing boat, the pilot walked around behind him and, towrope in hand, jumped up on to the *riva* and pulled the front of the boat tight to the wall. He tied the end of the rope to a metal ring in the pavement and leaned across to offer Brunetti, and then Vianello, a hand.

Brunetti suggested the officer go and get himself a coffee and said they shouldn't be more than half an hour. As the officer headed for a bar that stood to the right, Brunetti led Vianello around to the left of the façade of the church and down a narrow *calle*.

'Calle dei Preti,' the ever-observant Vianello read. 'Seems the right place for him to live.'

Brunetti, turning left at the end of the street and heading back towards the Grand Canal, said, 'Well, almost, except that we're on the Fontego dei Turchi.'

'He probably helps them, too,' Vianello began, 'so it's probably just as good a name.'

Brunetti remembered the door, a heavy green *portone* with twin brass handles in the shape of lions' heads. He rang the bell and waited. When a voice from the answerphone asked who it was, he gave his name, and the door snapped open, allowing them to enter a long narrow courtyard with a capped well at one end, wooden doors lining both sides. Without hesitating, Brunetti went to the second door on the left, which was open. At the top of the first flight of steps was another open door, where a short, stooped figure stood waiting for them as they climbed to the top.

'*Ciao*, Guido,' Perale said, taking Brunetti by the elbows and rising up on his toes to kiss him on both cheeks.

Moved by real affection for the man, Brunetti embraced him and took his right hand in both of his. Turning away from the priest, he said, 'This is Lorenzo Vianello, my friend.'

No stranger to the forces of order, Don Alvise recognized a policeman when he saw one but extended his hand and shook Vianello's warmly. 'Welcome, welcome. Come inside,' he said, pulling on Vianello's hand to bring him into the apartment.

He turned just inside the door and closed it after them, then asked for their coats, which he hung on two hooks on the back of the door. He was at least a head shorter than Brunetti, though his stoop made him appear shorter still. His mop of grey hair looked a stranger to both comb and barber, lopped off unevenly on the sides and growing well below his collar at the back. He wore glasses with black plastic frames and lenses so thick they distorted his eyes. His nose resembled nothing so much as a lump of clay that had been pressed on to his face, and his mouth, lurking under the macho moustache, was small and round as a baby's.

His appearance would have made him faintly ridiculous, even grotesque, were it not for the aura of sweetness that radiated from his every word and glance. He seemed a man who gazed on all he saw with approval and affection, who began every interchange with deep and abiding regard for the person in front of him.

He led them into a room which, because of the desk that stood at an angle in a corner, might have been an office, were it not for the bed set against one wall and the long board above it that served as a shelf and on which lay a few pairs of faded jeans, a pile of sweaters, and neatly folded underwear. Don Alvise pulled the chair behind the desk around in front and set it beside the single chair that stood there. He gestured to them and went to the desk and sat on it, though he had to give a little hop to get up, and his feet hung in the air as he sat.

'How may I help you, Guido?' he asked when his guests were seated.

'It's about the man who was murdered last night,' Brunetti answered.

Don Alvise nodded, 'I thought it would be,' he said.

'I thought you might know him or know about him.' Brunetti kept his eyes on the priest's as he spoke, looking for some flicker of recognition, but he saw none. He stopped there, waiting for the priest to answer his unspoken question.

'You didn't bring a photo,' Perale said.

Brunetti gave him a long look before he answered. 'I didn't think it would be necessary. If people know that you knew him, they would have told you about it.' Some impulse of charity, as well, had kept him from bringing the photo.

Don Alvise said, 'That's true.'

Brunetti allowed a pause to elapse before he said, 'And?'

Like a small child under examination or observation, Perale looked down at the floor and began to bang his heels, one after the other, softly against the front of the desk. One two, one two, one two, his feet counted out, while his face remained hidden from the other men. Finally he looked at Brunetti and said, 'I have to think about this and ask some questions before I say anything to you.'

'Before you say anything or before you can say anything?' Brunetti asked.

'Isn't it the same thing?' the priest asked innocently.

Brunetti was uncertain how to greet the priest's prevarication. 'Come on, Don Alvise,' he finally said then, laughing, added, 'you weren't a Jesuit when I first met you. Don't start acting like one now.'

Tension and reticence vanished; ease slipped back into the room to take up its place among the three men. 'All right, Guido, I understand. But I still need to speak to some people before I can talk to you.'

'And if they tell you not to talk to me?'

Again, the small feet began to tap out their rhythm, as if their certainty could help Don Alvise resolve his own lack of it. 'Then I'll have to think about it,' he said.

'For whatever it's worth,' Brunetti said, 'the Immigration Police aren't involved in this, and, no matter what you tell me, they won't be.'

The drumming stopped and the priest looked over at him. 'Doesn't that depend on what I tell you?' he asked.

Brunetti decided to risk it. 'If I give you my word that, no matter what you tell me, I won't tell them, will you believe me?'

The tiny mouth broadened into a smile and Don Alvise said, 'Guido, if you gave me your word that politicians are honest men, I'd believe you.' Then, seeing Brunetti and Vianello's astonishment, he added, 'Though I'd still keep my hand on my wallet in their company.'

Brunetti decided to leave it at that. He knew that Don Alvise would tell him what he decided was wisest for him to know, and there would be no changing that. He could do nothing more than trust in the former priest's wisdom. Having decided that, Brunetti got to his feet, and the three men exchanged polite farewells before Brunetti and Vianello left.

9

'He always that sly?' Vianello asked as they stepped outside.

'Sly?' Brunetti asked.

'Clever. Whatever you want to call it.' To explain his tone, which was something approaching anger, Vianello said, 'He knows who the man is. Anyone could see that, and yet he gives you this runaround that he has to ask people before he can tell you.' He let out an angry puff of breath which both men could see in the cold air. 'If he knows him, or knew him, he has to tell you,' he insisted. 'That's the law.'

Surprised to find Vianello, of all people, thinking in such legalistic terms, Brunetti temporized. 'Well, he does and he doesn't.'

'Why doesn't he?' Vianello asked.

Instead of answering directly, Brunetti swerved across the *calle* towards a bar. 'I need a coffee,' he said as he pushed open the door. The overheated air wrapped around them and, as if on cue, the espresso machine let out a jet of steam that imitated Vianello's angry huffing of a few moments ago.

At the bar, Brunetti glanced at Vianello and, at his nod, ordered two coffees.

While they waited, he said, 'He doesn't have to tell me if he believes what he says will put someone else in danger.' Before Vianello could cite the law at him, Brunetti added, 'That is, he knows he has to, legally, but that wouldn't mean anything to him, not if he thought the information could cause someone harm.'

'But you promised him not to go to the Immigration Police,' Vianello insisted. 'Doesn't he believe you?'

'The danger might come from somewhere else,' Brunetti said.

'Where?' asked Vianello.

The coffees came, and they busied themselves with ripping open envelopes of sugar and spilling the contents into the tiny cups. After his first sip, Brunetti set his cup back in the saucer and said, 'I've no idea. But for the moment, all I can do is wait to see what he tells me, or what he doesn't tell me. And if he doesn't tell me, then I've got to find the reason he won't.'

Vianello did no more than wave his coffee cup in Brunetti's direction by way of interrogation.

Brunetti went on. 'Whatever he does – whether he gives me an answer or not – he's still giving me information. And now that I have that, I can start thinking about what to do.'

Vianello shrugged and together they left the bar to go back to the launch.

The pilot had kept the motor running all the time they were gone, so they found the cabin comfortably warm. Brunetti had no idea whether it was the warmth or the boost given by the coffee and the sugar, but something lifted his spirits and allowed him to take joy in the beauty of the trip back to the Questura. *Palazzi* swept by on both sides, the drunken promiscuity of their styles competing for his attention: here a severe Gothic window, there a façade of parti-coloured mosaic, on the left the water-flooded atrium of Ca' d'Oro, and opposite it the yawning space, deserted now, where Paola had that morning bought fish.

That thought turned his mind to his family and to the tension that had seeped into him during lunch. What to do about Chiara? For a moment, he thought of taking her to the morgue at the hospital and showing her the black man's corpse, evidence of what could happen when you thought of them as 'only' *vu cumprà*. But this would be nothing more than cheap melodrama, and there was surely no guarantee that Chiara would agree with him that one thing led to the other. And did he know – know for certain – that the one thing had led to the other? This in turn took his thoughts back to Don Alvise.

Palazzo Ducale approached from the left, and its beauty pulled him to his feet. 'Come on,' he said to Vianello and went back up on deck. The cold hit him like a blow and the wind pushed tears from his eyes, distorting his vision and transforming the *palazzo* into a shimmering, shivering form suspended in the light reflected from the dancing waves.

Vianello came up the stairway and stood beside Brunetti. The flags on the tall poles in front of the *basilica* flapped wildly in the wind; boats and gondolas tied to the moorings bounced up and down and side to side, creating a series of booms so loud they could be heard above the wind. The Piazza seemed filled with huddled, bent shapes; the tourists kept their heads down, as protected from glory as they were from the wind.

Had it been better once, he wondered, when all of this was new and La Serenissima controlled the seas? Or had it been just as easy then to arrange the murder of some nameless Moor, certain that his insignificance and anonymity would serve to protect his killers? He closed his eyes for a moment, and when he opened them again, the *palazzo* had given way to the Bridge of Sighs and then to the façades of the hotels that lined the *riva*. The cold ate at him, worse here on the open water, but he stayed on deck until they docked at the Questura, when he thanked the pilot and asked Vianello to come up to his office with him.

The last part of the ride had chilled both of

them to the bone, and it was more than five minutes before they felt sufficiently warm to remove their overcoats. As he was putting his own in the *armadio*, Brunetti said, 'Wicked. It's colder than I can remember its ever being at this time of year.'

'Global warming,' Vianello said, tossing his own coat over the back of one of the chairs in front of Brunetti's desk and sitting down in the other.

Completely at a loss, Brunetti waited until he too was seated before he asked, 'What do you mean, "global warming"? Isn't that supposed to make it hotter?'

Vianello, still rubbing his hands together for warmth, said, 'It is, or it will. That's little, but it's certain. But it will also make a mess of all the seasons. Remember how much it rained in the autumn and last spring?' At Brunetti's nod, Vianello said, 'It's all tied together. It has to do with ocean and air currents.'

Because Vianello sounded so certain, Brunetti asked, 'Where did you get all this?'

'I read the UN Report on Global Warming. Well, some of it. It's all in there. The cherry on the cake is that the last place that will feel the influence – well, at least if all these scientists know what they're talking about – you know which country, well, which continent will suffer the least and suffer last?'

Brunetti was still entirely lost and shook his head to admit it.

'North America. That means the Americans.

They're protected on both sides by enormous bodies of water, and the currents are favourable to them, so while the rest of us are choking on their gases or dying from the heat, they'll be able to go on the same as ever.'

Brunetti was alarmed by Vianello's tone, which he found uncharacteristically heated. 'Aren't you being a bit severe, Lorenzo?'

'Severe? Severe because they'll shorten my life and kill my children?'

Too late Brunetti registered that he had once again stepped up and taken a seat on Vianello's hobby horse: the ecology of the planet. Keeping his voice moderate, he said, 'None of this is proven, you know, Lorenzo.'

'I know. But it's also not proven that, if I started smoking again and smoked three packs a day, I'd die of lung cancer. But the likelihood is pretty high.'

'You think so? In this case?'

The sincerity of Brunetti's question was so patent that Vianello answered in a much calmer tone. 'I don't know. I'm not an expert on these things. I just know what I read, and I know this report was commissioned by the UN, and the people who wrote it are climatologists from all over the world. So it's good enough for me, at least until I read something more persuasive.'

'You think there's anything to do?' Brunetti asked. Vianello's knitted brows caused him to clarify by adding, 'About this, I mean.'

'There doesn't seem to be. It's probably too late.'

'Too late for what?' Brunetti asked, suddenly very interested in what his inspector had to say.

'To avoid the consequences of what we've done in the last half-century.'

'That's a gloomy prospect,' Brunetti said, surprised to hear Vianello speak so seriously about this. For years, people at the Questura had kidded Vianello about his interest in the environment, but Brunetti had always put it on the same level as his own children's insistence that they not drink mineral water that came in plastic bottles or that they carefully collect all of their waste paper and take it to the ecological bins at Rialto. This, however, was a far more sombre vision than he had ever heard from Vianello.

'Is there really nothing we can do?' Brunetti asked.

Vianello shrugged.

For a moment, it looked as though Vianello were going to get up and leave; Brunetti feared that he would. He was very curious to hear Vianello's answer and so prodded. 'Well?'

'Live life and try to do our jobs, I think,' Vianello said after some time. Then, as if the subject had never been raised, he asked, 'What about this black guy? How do we find out who he is if your Don Alvise decides not to tell us?'

Accepting that the subject of global warming was closed, Brunetti answered Vianello's question. 'Gravini says he knows one of the Africans; he lives down by his mother in Castello. He's going to see if he can get anything from him.

And I've asked Signorina Elettra to ask around to see if she can find the people who rent to them.'

'Good idea. He's got to have lived somewhere.' Then, realizing just how silly that sounded, Vianello added, 'That is, here in the city, if he didn't have anything on him except a pair of keys.'

'Did you read the autopsy report?' Brunetti asked, surprised at himself for having forgotten to ask Vianello about it on the way to Don Alvise's.

'No.'

'It says he was in his late twenties and in good health, and that either of two of the shots would have killed him.'

'God, what a world,' Vianello answered. He looked across at Brunetti, pulled his lips together in a gesture of confusion, and added, 'It's strange, that we don't know anything at all about them, or about Africa, isn't it?'

Brunetti nodded but said nothing.

'Enough that they're black, huh?' Vianello asked with an ironic raising of his eyebrows.

Brunetti ignored Vianello's tone and added, 'We don't look like Germans, and Finns don't look like Greeks, but we all look like Europeans.'

'And?' Vianello asked, obviously not much impressed by Brunetti's observation.

'There must be someone who knows more about them,' Brunetti said.

It was at this point that Signorina Elettra came into the office, carrying a sheet of paper Brunetti hoped would shed light on the identity of the *vu cumprà*. Even as he heard this term reverberating in his mind, he told himself to substitute it with *ambulante*.

'I found two of them,' she said, nodding a greeting to Vianello. He stood and offered her his chair, pulled the other one over and moved his parka to the back, then sat down again.

'Two what?' asked an impatient Brunetti.

'Landlords,' she said, then explained, 'I called a friend of mine at *La Nuova*.' She saw their response to the name of the newspaper and said, 'I know, I know. But we've been friends ever since elementary school, and Leonardo needed the job.' Having excused her friend's choice of employer, she added, 'Besides, it allows him to meet some of the famous people who live here.' That was too much for Vianello, who let out a deep guffaw. She waited a moment and joined him. 'Pathetic, isn't it? Famous for living here? As if the city were contagious.'

Brunetti had often reflected on this, finding it especially strange in foreigners, this belief that some cachet adhered to their address, as if living in Dorsoduro or having a *palazzo* on the Grand Canal could elevate the tone of their discourse or the quality of their minds, render the tedium of their lives interesting or transmute the dross of their amusements into purest gold.

If he thought about it, he felt happiness in being Venetian, not pride. He had not chosen where to be born or what dialect his parents spoke: what pride to be taken in those things?

Not for the first time, he felt saddened by the vanity of human wishes.

'. . . over near Santa Maria Materdomini,' he heard Signorina Elettra saying when he tuned back into her conversation with Vianello.

'Bertolli?' Vianello asked. 'The one who used to be on the city council?'

'Yes, Renato. He's a lawyer,' Signorina Elettra said.

'And the other one?' Vianello asked.

'Cuzzoni. Alessandro,' she said, then waited to see if the name meant anything to either of them. 'He's originally from Mira, but he lives here now and has a shop.'

'What sort of shop?'

'He's a jeweller, but most of the stuff he sells is factory made,' she said with the easy dismissal of a woman who would never wear a piece of machine-made jewellery.

'Where's the shop?' Brunetti asked, not because he was particularly interested but to show them that he really was listening.

'Off Ventidue Marzo. On that *calle* that goes up towards the Fenice, down from the bridge.'

Brunetti sent his memory walking towards Campo San Fantin, down the narrow *calle* towards the bridge, past the antique shop. 'Opposite the bar?' he asked.

'I think so,' she answered. 'I haven't checked the address, but it's the only one there, I think.'

'And these two rent to *extracomunitari*?' Brunetti asked.

'That's what Leonardo tells me. No long-term

contracts, no questions about how many people will eventually live in the apartment, and everything paid in cash.'

'Furnished or unfurnished?' Vianello asked.

'Either, I think,' Signorina Elettra replied. 'If you can call it furnished. Leonardo said they did a story once, about two years ago, about one of the apartments they were living in. He said you wouldn't believe the place: seven of them sleeping in the same room, roaches all over the place. He said the kitchen and bathroom were unlike anything he'd ever seen, and when I asked him what it was like, he made it clear that I didn't want to know.'

'And was one of these two the landlord?' Brunetti asked.

'I don't know, and he didn't say. But Leonardo told me they probably rent to *extra-comunitari*.'

'Did he know where the apartments are?' Brunetti asked.

'No. As I say, he's not even absolutely sure that they do rent to them, but he says he's heard their names when people talk about who's willing to rent to *extracomunitari*.'

'Is this his office?' Brunetti asked, looking at the address listed for Renato Bertolli and trying to calculate where it might be.

'Yes. I checked it in *Calli, Campielli e Canali*, and I think he's got to be just before the *fabbro*, the one who makes keys.' This was enough for Brunetti. He had been over there a few times, about five years ago, to have a metal banister made for the final flight of stairs leading to their apartment. He knew the area, though it seemed a strangely out of the way location for a lawyer's office.

'I'm not sure how to approach them,' Brunetti said, taking the paper and waving it gently in the air. 'If we ask about the apartments, they'll worry that we'll report them to the Finanza. Anyone would.' It did not for an instant occur to him that either man would be declaring the rent on the apartments and thus paying taxes on the money. 'Can you think of anyone who might be able to get them to talk to us?'

'I've some friends who are lawyers,' Signorina Elettra said cautiously, as if admitting to some secret vice. 'I could ask if anyone knows them.'

'You, Vianello?' Brunetti asked.

The inspector shook his head.

'What about the other one, Cuzzoni?' Brunetti asked.

This time both Signorina Elettra and Vianello shook their heads. Seeing Brunetti's disappointment, she said, 'I can check at the Ufficio del Catasto and see what apartments they own. Once we know where they live, then we just have to check if there are rental contracts for their other apartments.'

Brunetti's uncle, who lived near Feltre, used to go hunting, and with him went Diana, an English setter whose greatest joy, aside from gazing adoringly at his uncle as he stroked her ears, was to chase birds. In the autumn, when the air changed and the hunting season began, a wild restiveness came over Diana, who knew no peace until the day his uncle could finally take down his shotgun and open the door that led to the woods behind his home.

Looking at Signorina Elettra poised on the edge of her chair, Brunetti was struck by how much she resembled Diana: there were the same liquid dark eyes, the flared nostrils, and the badly restrained nervousness at the thought of prey that was to be seized and brought back. 'Can you find everything with that thing?' he asked, not needing to name her computer.

She turned towards him and she sat up straighter. 'Perhaps not everything, sir. But many things.'

'Don Alvise Perale?' he asked. He sensed, rather than saw, Vianello's start of astonishment, but when he turned to look at him, Brunetti saw that the inspector had managed not to display his surprise. Brunetti permitted himself a half-smile, and after a moment Vianello was forced to shake his head in rueful appreciation of Brunetti's inability to trust anyone fully.

He remembered that Diana needed no encouragement or explanation: a flutter of motion and she was off, like the wind. Signorina Elettra wasted no time with questions or clarifications. 'The ex-priest, sir?'

'Yes.'

She rose to her feet in a single graceful motion. 'I'll go and see what I can find.'

'It's almost eight, Signorina,' he reminded her.

'Just a quick look,' she said and was gone.

When the door closed behind her, Vianello said, 'Don't worry, sir. She doesn't have a bed here. So she'll go home eventually.'

10

Brunetti found a seat at the back of the cabin, on the left-hand side of the vaporetto, so his view was of San Giorgio and the façades on the Dorsoduro side of the canal. He studied them as he headed up towards San Silvestro, but his attention was far removed from Venice, even from Europe. He considered the mess that was Africa, and he considered the endless historical argument of whether it was caused by what had been done to the Africans or by what they had done to themselves. It was not a subject upon which he believed himself sufficiently expert to comment, nor one where he thought there was much hope that people would arrive at the kind of consensus that passes for historical truth.

His memory filled with images: Joseph

Conrad's battleship, firing round after futile round into the jungle in an attempt to force it to submit to peace; shoals of bodies washed up on the shores of Lake Victoria; the shimmering surface of a Benin bronze; the yawning pits where so many of the earth's riches were mined. No one of these things was Africa, he knew, any more than the bridge under which the boat was passing was Europe. Each was a piece in a puzzle no one could understand. He remembered the Latin words he had once seen on a sixteenth-century map to mark the limit of Western exploration of Africa: *Hic scientia finit*: Knowledge Stops Here. How arrogant we were, he thought, and how arrogant we remain.

At home he found peace, or perhaps it is more accurate to say that he found a truce that seemed to be holding. Chiara and Paola talked as usual at dinner, and if the way Chiara packed away two helpings of pasta with broccoli and capers and then two baked pears was any indication, her appetite had returned to normal. Taking this as a good sign, he allowed himself to stretch out on the sofa in the living room after dinner, the smallest of small glasses of grappa on the table beside him, his current book propped on his stomach. For the last week, he had been rereading Ammianus Marcellinus' history of the later Roman Empire, a book which Brunetti enjoyed chiefly for its portrait of one of his greatest heroes, the Emperor Julian. But even here he found himself drawn into Africa, with the account of the siege of the town of Leptis in

Tripolis and of the perfidy and duplicity of both attackers and defenders. Hostages were killed, men were condemned to have their tongues cut out for speaking the inconvenient truth, the land was laid waste by pillage and slaughter. He read to the end of the twenty-eighth book but then closed it and decided that an early night would be better than this reminder of how little mankind had changed in almost two millennia.

In the morning, after the children had left for early classes, he and Paola spoke about Chiara, but neither of them was sure what her apparent return to normal behaviour implied. He also repeated his concern about the source of the opinion she had expressed.

'You know,' Paola said, after listening to him, 'all these years the kids have been in school, I've listened to their friends' parents respond to their kids' bad grades. It's always the fault of the teacher. No matter what the subject, no matter who the student: it is always the fault of the teacher.'

She dipped a corner of a biscuit in her caffè latte, ate it, and continued. 'Never once have I heard anyone say, "Yes, Gemma's really not very bright, so I understand why she didn't do well in mathematics" or, "Nanni is a bit of a dope, you know, especially at languages." Not a bit of it. Their children are always the best and the brightest, are perceived as spending every waking moment bent over their books, and into the lambent clarity of their minds no teacher has ever been capable of adding even the dimmest light or glimmer of improvement. Yet these are the same kids who come home with Chiara or Raffi and talk of nothing but pop music and films, seem to know nothing about anything except pop music and films and, when they can tear their attention away from pop music and films, do nothing except call one another on their *telefonini* or send SMS's to each other, the grammar and syntax of which I most sincerely hope to be spared.'

Brunetti ate a biscuit, took another, looked across at her and asked, 'Do you prepare these speeches when you're washing the dishes, or do such rhetorical flourishes come to you un-rehearsed?'

She considered his question in the spirit in which it had been asked and answered, 'I'd say they come to me quite naturally, though I imagine I'm aided by the fact that I see myself as the Language Police, ever on the prowl for infelicities or stupidities.'

'Lots of work?' he asked.

'Endless.' She smiled, but the smile disappeared and she said, 'All of that means I have no idea where she got it from.'

During all of this, his thoughts had never been far from the dead man, and so when she paused, he asked, 'If you have any time left over after patrolling the language, could you think of someone at the university who might be able to identify an African by looking at a photo? I mean his tribe or where he might come from.'

'The one who was shot,' she said.

Brunetti nodded. 'All we know is that he's an African – presumably from Senegal – and not even that for sure. Is there anyone there who might help?'

She dipped another biscuit, ate it, took a sip of coffee, and said, 'I know a man in the archaeology department who spends six months a year in Africa. I could ask him.'

'Thanks,' Brunetti said. 'I'll ask Signorina Elettra to send the photos to you at the university.'

'Couldn't you just bring them home and give them to me?'

'They're in the computer file,' Brunetti said, speaking calmly so that it would sound as if he understood how this was possible.

She glanced at him, surprised. Then, reading his expression, she asked, 'Who's my little computer genius, then?' She smiled.

Chagrined, he returned the smile, and asked, 'How did you know?'

'It's part of being on the Language Police. We detect all forms of mendacity.'

He finished his coffee and set the cup down. 'I should be home for lunch,' he said as he got to his feet, then bent and kissed her on the head. 'From policeman to policeman,' he said, and left for the Questura.

When he reached his office, he found papers on his desk. The first page was a list of the addresses of the apartments owned by Renato Bertolli and Alessandro Cuzzoni, with a note stating that Cuzzoni was not married, and

Bertolli's wife owned nothing more than a half-interest in the apartment in which they lived.

Bertolli, whose home address in Santa Croce was given, owned six apartments, for two of which formal rental contracts were on record in the Ufficio delle Entrate. The fact that those two contracts dated back thirty-two and twenty-seven years, when Bertolli would have been a boy, suggested that they were in the hands of Venetian families whose right to remain in them, by now, was virtually beyond challenge. Bertolli and his wife were listed as resident in the third, but no contracts existed for the other apartments, suggesting they were empty, a suggestion which the information from Signorina Elettra's friend called into question.

Attached was a note in Signorina Elettra's hand, which read, 'I called your friend Stefania at the rental agency and asked her to call around for me. She called back to say Bertolli rents all three of the apartments to foreigners by the week or month. She also asked me to tell you she's still trying to sell the place near Fondamenta Nuove.'

Cuzzoni, then. He lived in San Polo, at an address only a few numbers distant from Brunetti's, owned the apartment where he lived and a house in Castello, though no contract was on file at the Ufficio delle Entrate to indicate that the house was being rented.

How convenient, that the city offices never bothered with even the most simple cross-check. If no rental contract was on file, then there was no reason to believe that the owner was being paid rent, and who could be expected to pay tax if an apartment was empty? A person of a certain turn of mind might so argue, but Brunetti had spent decades looking into the myriad ways citizens cheated one another and everyone cheated the state, and so he assumed that there was some other game afoot here, some way that money was being made on the house and taxes avoided. Renting to illegal immigrants seemed as good a way as any.

He pulled down his copy of *Calli, Campielli, e Canali* and looked for Cuzzoni's address: he found it on the other side of Rio dei Meloni, literally the building next but one to his own, though getting to it from his home would require walking up to Campo Sant'Aponal, then turning back towards the water. Using the same book, he checked the address of the house Cuzzoni owned. It was a high number in Castello, a location that was, for many Venetians, as far away as Milano.

He could easily speak to Cuzzoni, either at home or in his shop, but first Brunetti decided he would go and have a look down in Castello to determine if there was any sign that people were living in his house and who those people might be. He remembered his promise to Gravini, not to act until the officer had had a chance to speak to the African he knew, but looking did not count as acting.

The weather had not changed, and cold assaulted him the instant he stepped from the door of the Questura. One end of his scarf whipped out like an eel on a fishing line and tried to fly away from him. He grabbed it and wrapped it around his neck, hunkered down, and went over the bridge in the direction of Castello.

His memory of the map was clear: also, he knew the building because a former classmate of his in middle school had lived in the house next door. To spare his face from the wind, he kept his eyes on the pavement and navigated by radar more than vision. He walked past the Arsenale, the lions looking far more pleased than they should have been at finding themselves out in this cold.

He turned left into Via Garibaldi and walked past the monument to the hero who, gazing down at the frozen surface of the water in the pool at his feet, looked more concerned about the cold than had the lions. He took the second turn on the right, made a quick left, and then as quickly another right. The number he sought was the second building on the left, but he walked quickly past it and went into a bar in the small *campiello* just ahead.

Three old men wearing overcoats and hats sat playing cards at a table in the corner, small glasses of red wine at their right hands. One of them tossed a card face-up on the table, followed by the second man, and then the third, who swept up all three with arthritic difficulty, tapped them into order on the table in front of him, closed his cards and then quickly fanned them open and laid a new card on the table. Brunetti went to the bar and ordered *un caffè corretto*, not because he wanted the grappa, but because it looked like the kind of bar where real men drank *caffè corretto* at eleven in the morning.

He walked to the end of the bar and opened the copy of *La Nuova* that lay there. When his coffee came, he accepted it with muttered thanks, stirred in two sugars, and turned a page of the newspaper. The old men continued to play cards, none of them talking, even when the hand came to an end and the winner shuffled the cards and dealt them out again.

On page twelve there was an article about the murder. 'God, next thing you know, they'll be shooting us, too,' Brunetti said to no one in particular, careful to speak in Veneziano. He finished his coffee and placed the cup back in the saucer. He continued reading to the end of the story, looked at the bartender, and asked, 'Filippo Lanzerotti still live up at the corner?'

'Filippo?'

Brunetti gave the explanation that had obviously been asked for, 'We went to school together, but I haven't seen him in years. I just wondered if he still lived down here.'

'Yes. His mother died about six years ago, so he and his wife moved into the house.'

Brunetti interrupted him here. 'I remember, with those windows looking back over the garden. We didn't appreciate it then, that view.' He put the paper on the counter and pushed it aside, reached into his pocket and pulled out some change. He gave an inquiring glance and paid what was asked.

He nodded towards the paper he had left open to the story of the murder and asked, 'You have any of them around here, the *vu cumprà*?' Even as he spoke, he regretted it: the words sounded leaden and forced, filled with inappropriate curiosity.

It was some time before the barman answered, 'Not so anyone would notice.'

'They come in here?'

'Why do you ask?'

'No reason,' Brunetti said. 'Just that I know a lot of people don't like them, but I've always found them very polite.' Then, as if remembering, 'One of them even lent me his *telefonino* one day when I forgot mine and had to make a call.' He was talking too much and knew it, but still he could not stop.

His example must have fallen short as proof of human solidarity, for the barman said only, 'I've got no complaint against them.'

'Not like the Albanians,' came a sepulchral voice from the card table. By the time Brunetti turned to look at them, the three men's attention had returned to their cards, and there was no way to know which one of them had spoken. From the placidity of their faces, the voice might well have belonged to any member of the chorus.

'If you see Filippo,' Brunetti said, 'tell him Guido said hello.'

'Guido?'

'Yes, Guido from maths class. He'll remember.'

'Good, I'll do that,' the barman said just as one of the men at the table called for more wine, and he turned away to take down a clean glass.

Outside, Brunetti retraced his steps until he was back on Via Garibaldi. He went into the fruit and vegetable shop on the left, saw that the endive was described as coming from Latina, and asked for a kilo. While the woman was selecting the stalks, he asked, still in dialect, 'Is Alessandro still renting to the *vu cumprà*?' He jerked his head back in the direction of the Cuzzoni address.

She looked up, surprised by his leap from endive to real estate. 'Alessandro. Cuzzoni,' Brunetti clarified. 'A couple of years ago, he tried to sell me that house of his back there, around the corner, but I bought a place in San Polo. Now my nephew's getting married, and they're looking for a place, and so I thought of Alessandro. But someone told me he was renting to the *vu cumprà*, and I wondered if he still was. Before I say anything to my nephew, that is.' Then, before she could grow suspicious of his question and of him, he said, 'My wife told me to get some *melanzane*, but the long ones.'

'All I've got are the round ones,' she said, clearly more comfortable talking about vegetables than about the business of her customers.

'All right. I'll tell her it was all I could find. Give me a kilo of the round ones, then, as well.'

She pulled out a second paper bag and selected three plump *melanzane*. As if comforted by their solidity, she said, 'I don't think it's for sale any more, that house.'

'Ah, all right. Thank you,' Brunetti said, understanding that she had answered his question without seeming to. She handed him the plastic bag of vegetables and he paid, hoping that Paola could find some use for them.

He decided to go home, where Paola was pleased at the quality of the endive and said they'd have it that evening. She made no comment on the aubergines, and he forbore to explain that they were, in a certain sense, part of his investigative technique.

Because the children were not home for lunch, the meal was, at least by Brunetti's standards, spartan, nothing more than risotto with *radicchio di Treviso* and a plate of cheese. Seeing his badly concealed disappointment at the sight of the selection of cheeses, Paola came and stood close beside him. 'All right, Guido. I'll make the pork tonight.'

Brunetti cut a piece of taleggio and set it on his plate. Interested, he looked up at her and asked, 'Which one?'

'The one with olives and tomato sauce.'

'And the endive?'

She looked away from him and addressed, it appeared, the light fixture, 'How did this happen to me? I married a man, and I find myself living with an appetite.'

'With butter and parmigiano?' he asked,

spreading a thick layer of the cheese on a slice of bread.

Deciding to ignore his promise to Gravini, he left the apartment at three-fifteen and walked up to Sant'Aponal, then back towards Fondamenta Businello, where the apartment had to be. He found the number, where the only doorbell bore the name Cuzzoni. He rang, waited a moment, then rang again.

'Sì?' a man's voice finally asked.

'Signor Cuzzoni?'

'Yes. What do you want?'

'To talk to you. It's the police.'

'Talk to me about what?' the voice went on calmly.

'Some property of yours,' Brunetti said with equal calm.

'Come up, then,' the man said, and the door snapped open.

Brunetti pushed it back and stepped into a large garden that gave evidence, even in its winter sleep, of being the pampered recipient of considerable care. Two Norfolk pines stood on either side of a brick path flanked by waist-high hedges still bearing their tiny leaves. Other bricks had been set into the grass to create two diamond-shaped gardens, where Brunetti saw flowers that looked like pansies huddled under large sheets of milky plastic sheeting. At the far end of the garden was a single door, flanked by enormous windows protected by a thick metal grating.

The door was open, and he went in and then

up the broad flight of low marble steps that led to the *piano nobile*. As he reached the top of the steps, the door opened inward and he found himself looking at a face that had been familiar to him for years.

The man was a few years younger than he, though his hair, Brunetti was satisfied to notice, was far thinner than his own, something he had suspected in the past but could now confirm. As tall as Brunetti, though thinner, Cuzzoni had an elegant nose and large brown eyes, perhaps too large for his face. He was as surprised as Brunetti to find himself confronted by a face he recognized.

Recovering sooner than Brunetti, he extended his hand and said, 'Alessandro Cuzzoni.' Brunetti took the offered hand, but before he could say his name, Cuzzoni went on, 'It's very strange to meet you, after seeing you pass on the street all these years. It's as though we know one another already.'

'Brunetti, Guido,' he said and followed Cuzzoni into the apartment. The first thing he noticed was a tremendous water stain on the back wall of the entrance hall and an equally dark circle on the ceiling above it. His eyes followed it down to the floor, where he saw strips of parquet lying about in concave ruin.

'My God. What happened?' he couldn't stop himself from asking.

Cuzzoni looked at the wreckage of ceiling, wall, and floor and quickly away, as if to spare himself a painful experience. He raised a finger to the centre of the ravished ceiling. 'It happened four days ago. The woman upstairs put a wash in her washing machine and went out to Rialto. The tube that's supposed to drain the water came loose, so the entire cycle ended up coming down my wall. I had already gone to work, and she was out all morning.'

'Oh, I'm sorry,' Brunetti said. 'Water. Nothing's worse.'

Cuzzoni shrugged and tried to smile, but it was obvious that his heart was not in it. 'Luckily – for her, at least – the building's all lopsided, so the water ran towards the wall and came down here. She didn't have much damage at all.'

As the other man spoke, Brunetti studied the far wall, where he thought he saw rectangles of darker paint. The other walls held paintings and, ominously, prints and drawings, one of which might have been a Marieschi. 'What was on the wall?' he finally asked.

Cuzzoni took a deep sigh. 'The title page of the *Carceri*. The first impression, and with a signature added that was probably his. And a small Holbein drawing.'

As when someone spoke of serious illness in their family, Brunetti didn't know how to ask or what to say. 'And?' was the best he could think of.

'Better not to ask.'

'I'm sorry,' Brunetti said. He knew better than to mention insurance. Even if Cuzzoni had it or the woman above had it, some things could not be repaired, nor could they be replaced. Besides, insurance companies never paid.

'Come into my study. We can talk there,' Cuzzoni said, turning to the right and opening a door. It was only then that Brunetti realized how hot the apartment was. Cuzzoni saw him start to unbutton his overcoat and said, 'Here, let me take that. I have to keep the heat as high as possible until it's dried out. The painters can't do anything until the walls are dry.'

'And the parquet?' Brunetti asked, handing over his coat.

Cuzzoni hung it on a coat rack and waved Brunetti towards a long sofa against one wall. Cuzzoni seated himself in a comfortable looking old armchair that faced him and said, 'The parquet is what I mind most, in a way. It's cherry, eighteenth century, and I'll never be able to replace it.'

'Can it be saved?'

Cuzzoni shrugged. 'Maybe. I've talked to someone who's worked for me in the past, a retired carpenter, who said he'd come and have a look. If he thinks there's anything he can do, he'll pull it up and take it to his workshop. His son's running the business now, but he still works. He may be able to soak it and put it under a press until it comes straight again. But he said it would be discoloured and he'd probably have trouble getting the same patina back.'

He shrugged again. 'I keep telling myself it's just a thing. They're all just things. But they've survived hundreds of years, it seems a shame for anything to happen to them now.'

Though Signorina Elettra had told him that Cuzzoni came from Mira, Brunetti thought it better to seem to know nothing about him and so asked, making a gesture that encompassed the room, 'Is it your family home?'

'No, nothing like that. I've only been in here for about eight years. But it's become precious to me, and I hate to see something like this happen to it.' He smiled and shook his head as if apologizing for his sentimentality, then said, 'But surely the police aren't here to ask about my neighbour's washing machine.'

Brunetti smiled in return and said, 'No. Hardly. I'm here to ask about a house you have down at the end of Via Garibaldi.'

'Yes?' Cuzzoni asked, curious but nothing more.

'I'd like to know if you've rented it to *extracomunitari*.'

Cuzzoni sat back in the chair, rested his elbows on the arms, and brought his fingers together in a triangle beneath his chin. 'May I ask why you want to know this?'

'It has nothing to do with rent or taxes,' Brunetti assured him.

'Signor Brunetti,' Cuzzoni said, 'I have little fear that an officer of the police would busy himself with whether or not I pay taxes on the rent for my apartments. But I am curious to know why it is you're interested.'

'Because of the man who was killed,' Brunetti

said, deciding that he would trust Cuzzoni at least this far.

Cuzzoni lowered his head and rested his mouth on the top of his laced fingers. After some time, he looked back at Brunetti and said, 'I thought so.' He allowed more time to pass and then went on, 'Yes, there are *extracomunitari* in the building. In all three apartments. But I don't know if one of them was the man who was killed.' Brunetti knew that the newspaper account of the killing had not given a name, nor had it supplied a photo of the dead man.

'Do you know who they are, the men who live there?' Brunetti asked.

'I've seen their papers, their passports and, in one case, a work permit. But I have no way of knowing if the passports are legitimate or, for that matter, if the work permit is.'

'And yet you rent to them?'

'I let them stay in my apartments, yes.'

'Even though it might be illegal?' Brunetti asked, his voice curious but entirely without censure.

'That is not for me to determine,' Cuzzoni answered.

'May I ask why you do this?' Brunetti asked.

Cuzzoni let the question hang in the air for a long time before he answered it with another question, 'May I ask why you want to know this?'

'Because I'm curious,' Brunetti said.

Cuzzoni smiled and unlatched his fingers. He put his hands on the arms of the chair and said,

'Because we are too rich and they are too poor. And because a friend of mine who works with them told me that the men asking to live in those apartments were decent men in need of help.' When Brunetti didn't respond to this, Cuzzoni asked, 'Does that make sense to you, Signor Brunetti?'

'Yes,' Brunetti said without hesitation, and then he asked, 'Would it be possible for me to go and see these apartments?'

'To see if the dead man was one of the men living there?'

'Yes,' Brunetti said and then added, because he thought it would make a difference, 'No harm will come to the men living there because of me.'

Cuzzoni considered this and finally asked, 'How do I know you're telling me the truth?'

'You can ask Don Alvise,' Brunetti said.

'Ah,' Cuzzoni answered and sat looking at Brunetti for what seemed a long time. Finally he pushed himself to his feet and said, 'I'll get you the keys.'

11

Brunetti left Cuzzoni's apartment, uncertain as to whether he should go back down to Castello immediately and take a look at the apartments to which the other man had given him the keys. The three separate sets each had two keys, presumably one to the front door of the building and one to each apartment. All the way to the Rialto bridge, he wavered between going and not going. When he reached the top of the bridge, a sudden gust of wind, sent, he was sure, from Siberia and directed specifically and with malice towards him, swept by with such force that he temporarily lost his footing. This could have served as an excuse not to go, had it not occurred to him that this time of day, when the shops were open, was precisely the time when the men who lived in the apartments were likely to be at home and thus able to answer his questions.

He took out his *telefonino* and dialled the direct line to the officers' room. Alvise answered and passed the phone to Vianello. 'Can you meet me at the end of Via Garibaldi in about twenty minutes?' he asked.

'Where are you now?'

'At Rialto, just going to the 82.'

'Right. I'll be there,' the inspector said and hung up.

Better than that, Vianello got on the boat at the San Zaccaria stop, again padded and muffled to twice his normal girth. Briefly, Brunetti told him about his conversation with Cuzzoni and added that he preferred having someone with him when he went to talk to the Africans.

'You afraid of them?' Vianello asked.

'I don't think so. But they're likely to be afraid of me.'

'And you think reinforcements will help?' Vianello asked.

'No, not necessarily. But it will limit the ways they can show their fear.'

'Meaning they won't get away?' Vianello asked, indicating with his mittened hands the front of his body, as if to demonstrate the unlikelihood of his being able to give successful chase to far younger and far slimmer men.

Brunetti smiled at the gesture and said, 'No. Hardly.' He didn't know how to tell Vianello that he thought his presence would have a calming influence on the Africans, as it so often did on witnesses. Nor did he know how to tell Vianello that he would himself find his company comforting when going into the presence of an unknown number of young men, most of them illegal immigrants working at illegal jobs and now somehow caught up in a murder investigation.

They got off at Giardini and started down Via Garibaldi; as they walked, Brunetti recounted his conversation with Cuzzoni, though he said nothing more about the man than that he seemed undisturbed to learn that the police were interested in his tenants and indeed seemed almost proud to have them living in his apartments.

'A do-gooder?' Vianello asked.

Hearing the term used that way, Brunetti was struck by the paradox that it had become a pejorative. However had that come about, that it was now wrong to want to do good? 'Not at all,' he answered, 'but I think he might be a good man.'

Vianello, as prone as Brunetti to making snap judgements about people's characters, said nothing.

Brunetti followed the same path he had that morning but this time stopped in front of one of the buildings on the left of the narrow *calle*. 'Do we ring and tell them we're coming or just go in?' Vianello asked.

'It's their home,' Brunetti said. 'Seems to me

we have to ask them to let us in.' There were three doorbells; Brunetti rang the lowest one.

After a few moments, a man's voice inquired, '*Sì?*'

'We've come from Signor Cuzzoni,' Brunetti answered, deciding it was true enough. After all, he had the keys to prove it.

There was a long pause, and then the voice asked, 'What do you want?'

'I want to talk to you.'

'Who?'

'All of you.'

There followed a long pause. The man at the other end of the speaker phone didn't bother to cover the mouthpiece, so Brunetti and Vianello heard questions and answers being fired about in some language neither of them recognized. One voice was raised angrily, but then it seemed as if someone talked it into silence. After some time, the first voice returned and said, 'Come in.'

The door opened for them and they stepped inside. There was a single flight of steps in front of them; at the top, three black men stood abreast, barring the way. Brunetti went first, Vianello behind him. When he was two steps from the top, Brunetti stopped and looked up at the men. The one in the centre was both taller and older than the others, with a broad nose that looked as if it had been made even broader by having been broken. The one on the left was short and stocky and wore a heavy jacket, as though he had just come in or was just going out. The third was painfully thin; his narrow-cut jeans billowed out around his legs. Though his skin was darker than that of the others, his features were finer, with an almost European nose and a thin mouth, tight with disapproval.

'Thank you for agreeing to talk to me. My name is Commissario Guido Brunetti, from the police,' Brunetti said.

The man on the right, the thin one, wheeled away from the other two. As he turned, his right arm swung out from his body and around to his back, where his hand banged against his buttock. The one in the centre stepped back, making room on the landing. Brunetti paused at the top of the steps, waited until Vianello was standing beside him, and then put out his hand. '*Piacere*,' he said, first to one man and then to the other.

Surprised, both of them extended their hands, though they remained silent. Then Vianello stepped forward, gave his name, and also shook hands with both men. That seemed to leave them with no choice but to respond with the habit of politeness. The tall one stepped towards the door and made a graceful gesture, inviting them to enter.

Brunetti went inside but not before muttering a courteous request to do so; Vianello did the same. The first thing Brunetti noticed was the smell: the strong odours of meat and spices – mutton, perhaps, though he could not identify the spices. The other smell was that of men, men who lived close together and who did not or could not wash their clothing often enough.

134

The man with the limp arm had moved to the back of the room. Four others stood inside, waiting for them. Two of them smiled in Brunetti's direction while the others nodded; their greeting was cordial and entirely without menace. Brunetti and Vianello nodded towards them and waited to see who would speak.

The tall man, who had followed them inside, seemed to be their leader, or at least the others kept glancing back and forth between him and the white men. Brunetti was conscious of the spareness of the room, which seemed to serve as both kitchen and dining room. A linoleum-topped counter ran along the back wall. On it stood a double gas ring, a rubber tube running down to a squat gas canister. He remembered this sort of stove from the apartment they had lived in when he was a child and wondered where on earth you could still buy those canisters today.

Large cooking pots stood on top of the burners, and the sink, which appeared to have only one tap, was filled with dishes. The counters, however, were clean, as was the table.

'What is it you want?' the tall man asked. His Italian was accented in a way Brunetti could not identify, his voice deep but not at all loud.

'I want to know whatever you can tell me about the man who was killed last night,' Brunetti said.

Before the tall one, to whom Brunetti had addressed the question, could answer, the one who had turned away on the stairs said, 'And we must know about him because we're black, too?' Though he was knife-thin, his voice was even deeper than the other man's, a resonant bass, a voice that could fill a concert hall or hold an audience.

How quickly people learn resentment, Brunetti thought. Who did they expect him to ask about the death of an African, the Chinese? He bit back this question, and turned his attention once again to the older man. 'I came to you because I thought you might work with him or know him.'

Before he answered, the older man pulled a plastic chair away from the linoleum-topped table, another relic from Brunetti's youth, and turned it towards Brunetti. He indicated another chair, and the man in the jacket pulled it out for Vianello.

When both men were seated, the older man said something in a language Brunetti did not understand, and one of the others opened a wall cabinet and took down two glasses. He opened a drawer and pulled out a dish towel and wiped the glasses, then set them on the table. From another cabinet he took out a plastic bottle of mineral water, unscrewed the cap, and filled both glasses.

Brunetti thanked him, nodded to the man he now thought of as the leader, and drank half of the water. Vianello did the same. He put the glass down, rested his hands on the edge of the table, and looked at the leader, saying nothing.

At least two minutes passed during which

none of the men in the room spoke. Finally the leader said, 'You say you are a policeman?'

'Yes,' answered Brunetti.

'And you want to know about him?'

'Yes.'

'What do you want to know?'

'I would like to know his full name and where he came from. I would like to know where he lived and what he did for work before he came here. And I would like to know if any of you can think of a person who would want to do him harm or some reason why this could have happened to him.'

The leader considered the series of questions and finally said, 'It seems like you want to know everything.'

'No,' Brunetti said in a normal voice. 'It's not everything. I have no interest in how he got here or what sort of papers he had, not unless you think it might have something to do with his death. And I have no official interest in any of you or how you got here or what you do to make a living, so long as it has nothing to do with this man's death.'

'No official interest?' the man asked.

'As a policeman, I have no interest in those things.'

'And as a man?'

'As a man, I know nothing about any of you. I don't know for certain where you come from or why you chose to come here, and I have no idea how long you intend to stay. I do know, however, that you are said not to be men who have come here to steal or rob or to cause trouble, but that you are here to work, if you can find work.'

'That is a lot of information to have,' the man said, 'for someone who takes no interest.'

'Yes, it is,' Brunetti admitted. 'But you have been here, you or colleagues of yours, for years, and so I know, or I think I know, some things.' Quickly Brunetti added, 'I don't know about your culture, but ours is one where most information passes from mouth to mouth, and each time it passes, something is added to it or taken away from it, so each time it is passed on, the information is changed. So there is no way to know if what you are told, or what you think you know, is true.' He watched to see that this long speech had been understood. 'So I have no idea, really, if what I think I know about you, or your friends, is true or not,' Brunetti said and finished his glass of water. When the man who had poured him the first glass of water stepped forward to refill it, he thanked him and said he had had enough.

The leader turned to the other men in the room and asked them something. While he waited to see what response they would make, Brunetti allowed himself to settle into the room and pay attention to it. He noticed, first, that it was cold, so cold that he was glad he had kept his coat on, and that, for all the disorder, it was clean. The linoleum of the floor was grey, but it appeared to have been recently swept. And from what he had been able to tell, his glass had been wiped as an act of respect, not of necessity. For a long time, none of them spoke, and then the young man in the too-big jeans said something. No one else said a word, and so he went on, his voice growing more heated as he spoke. At one point, he raised his left hand and pointed at Brunetti and Vianello while he said something that could have been 'police', but the word was buried in a long sentence that went on for some time and then ended abruptly on an angry note. During all of this, his right arm remained immobile at his side.

The leader spoke to him in a calmer tone, then placed his hand on his shoulder in a gesture that echoed the soothing tone of his voice. The young man, however, remained unpersuaded and let off another stream of fiery words; this time the word 'police' was audible twice.

The leader listened with no sign of impatience until the young man was finished, then turned to Brunetti. 'He says that we cannot trust the police.'

It seemed to Brunetti that the young man had had time to say considerably more than that, though Brunetti had to admit that what he said was probably true. They were in Italy illegally and stood on the street during the day, selling counterfeit bags. They lacked the funds to buy or rent shops, restaurants, or bars, so the resulting protection of wealth would not be offered them: no helpful functionary would intervene in obtaining work or residence permits, no assistance would be offered in getting the Finance

Police to ignore those pesky rules about the origins of large amounts of cash; no convenient phone call made the night before planned police raids. Without these civic fairy godmothers, the Africans were liable to suffer the abuse and arrogance of the police, and so their lack of trust seemed an intelligent option.

Brunetti remained silent as he considered all of this, hoping that these men might interpret his silence as a sign of respect for their leader. One of the others, a young man who could not have been much older than Raffi, spoke, but briefly, barely a few words. The leader said something to the next man, the one in the jacket, who answered with a monosyllable, and then to the others, who answered only with quick shakes of their heads.

After a long silence, the leader turned his attention to Brunetti and said, 'My friends have told me that they would prefer not to speak about this matter.'

Brunetti waited a moment and then asked, 'Even though they know that I could have all of you arrested?'

The leader smiled, and wrinkles spread across his face in genuine amusement. 'It is not very clever of you to say that to us, knowing that we could disappear before the other police you call could get here to arrest us.'

Brunetti returned his smile and asked, 'And don't you think I could rise up and arrest you all?'

'And carry us all to prison?' the African asked

amiably. Then, puckishly, he added, 'All by yourself?'

As they spoke, it had become evident to Brunetti that this man and the young, thin one were the only ones whose Italian was good enough to follow what was said. The others perhaps followed the major words and phrases, but he doubted they could understand much more than that.

'Where, I am sure,' Brunetti said with such false menace that it was evident he believed not a word of what he was about to say, 'we could easily persuade you to tell us everything we want to know.'

At this, the younger man gasped and took a step towards Brunetti, his left hand rising in the air, his right still lifeless at his side. A glance from the older man stopped him, and he stood there, hand still raised, eyes wide with rage, breathing heavily. Vianello had got to his feet with surprising speed and taken a step towards him, but when he saw that the young man had stopped, he retreated to his chair, but he did not sit down again.

The older man turned to Brunetti and said, with real regret, 'Perhaps it would be best for you not to talk of persuading us to tell you things, Signore.'

Moving very carefully, Brunetti got to his feet and walked over to the young man. Very slowly, he reached up and took his raised hand in his own, bringing it down to waist level. He took his left and covered the back of the young man's hand with it, holding it prisoner between both of his own. The young man closed his eyes and tried to pull his hand away, but Brunetti held it close.

Finally, when the young man opened his eyes and looked at him, Brunetti said, 'I ask your pardon for what I said. I ask it of you and of all of the men in this room, and of your dead friend. I was not thinking when I said it, and I was foolish.' The man tried to pull his hand away again, but the gesture was weaker.

Brunetti went on, still trapping his hands and his eyes. 'Because of what happened to your friend and because no man should die like that, I want to find the men who killed him.'

He released the young man's hand and stepped back from him, his own arms at his sides, completely undefended. The young man stared at him but said nothing. At last Brunetti turned to the older man and said, 'Signor Cuzzoni has given me the keys to the other apartments, and I am going to go and have a look at them.'

'Why do you tell me this?'

'Because you are living in these apartments with the permission of the owner, who has given me the keys and told me I can go into them. It would not be correct of me not to tell you what I am going to do.'

'To ask us?' the older man said.

'No,' Brunetti said, shaking the idea away. 'Tell you.'

Brunetti glanced in Vianello's direction and

walked towards the door. He turned when he got to it and said, speaking to all of them, 'My name is Brunetti. If you want to speak to me, you can call me or find me at the Questura.'

The men looked at him, silent as obsidian statues, and then he and Vianello left the apartment.

12

'Well, I handled that brilliantly,' Brunetti said as they stepped out into the hall.

'I didn't realize what you'd said, that is, how threatening it would sound to them, until I saw him raise his hand,' Vianello said by way of consolation. 'It sounded pretty much in line with the conversation you were having with the *capo*.'

'But if I had thought about what it would mean to them, to be threatened . . .' Brunetti began.

'If my grandfather had wheels, he'd be a bicycle,' Vianello answered, then, turning back to the business at hand, asked, 'Upstairs?'

As Brunetti started up the stairs he felt relieved that Vianello had cut him off. He knew what the police in various countries were capable of doing to the people they arrested and had heard even more from a friend who worked for Amnesty International. He simply had not been thinking when he spoke. Regretting the effect on the men's willingness to trust him was a waste of time, though he did regret offending them by his seeming callousness. He left these thoughts behind him as they climbed to the next floor.

Brunetti had brought the keys from the dead man's pocket, some instinctive caution having told him not to fill out a request for them in the evidence room but simply to open the envelope and take them. At the door to the apartment on the second floor, he tried them and then the first set of keys Cuzzoni had given him, but none of the keys fitted. Then one of the keys on Cuzzoni's second set did turn. He pushed open the door and was greeted by the same heavy male smell that had been so strong in the other apartment, though because this apartment was not heated at all, the smell was slightly less powerful. The kitchen had only cups and glasses in the sink, suggesting that they ate communally in the apartment downstairs. The sitting room had two camp-beds placed against one wall, and the bedroom held five single beds lined up against the walls. The small wardrobe was stuffed with jackets and jeans folded over hangers; its bottom was crowded with countless pairs of running shoes. The smell that seeped out when he opened the door was so strong that

Brunetti quickly closed it and moved towards the bathroom.

It was, not to put too fine a point on it, disgusting. The small bathtub was grey and crusted, and a long green-blue streak ran down one side under the dripping tap. Towels, none of them clean, were bunched over the side of the tub, and more of them hung from nails in the back of the door. The toilet had lost its seat, which leaned against a wall. The sink was filthy with hair and dried shaving cream and other substances Brunetti did not want to think about. White spots and countless fingerprints blurred the surface of the mirror. A tin pot sprouted toothbrushes.

'You want to go back and look through the closet?' Brunetti asked Vianello, who had been looking under the beds.

'I'd rather not, if that's all right,' he said. 'After all, we don't even know what we're looking for.'

Brunetti was forced to agree. 'All right,' he said, 'let's try the next floor.'

They went back into the hall, locked the door behind them, and went up to the third floor. The steps were wooden and very narrow, while the ones below had been stone and considerably wider. From the outside of the building, Brunetti had seen no sign of a third floor, but perhaps this one had been added, like his own apartment, as an afterthought and without permissions.

At the top, there was no landing. The last step

simply stopped at a wooden door. Brunetti took the set of keys from the evidence room and tried the lock. The first one turned. When he opened the door, light filtered in from behind him. He leaned inside and patted the wall on the left, found a switch, and flicked on the light.

A forty-watt bulb hung naked from the ceiling of what must once have been a storage room. There were no windows, and above them they saw the terracotta tiles of the roof set on a lattice-work of beams. No insulation shielded the room from the outside: both Brunetti and Vianello saw their breath turn to vapour as they stepped inside.

A single bed piled with shabby woollen blankets stood against the far wall. There was room only for a small table on which was a single electric hot plate, its wire running to the light switch beside the door, where someone had attached it with a great deal of tape and very little skill. Next to the hotplate were a metal cup and a box of tea bags; under the table stood a metal bucket, covered with a towel. A single step took Brunetti to the table. He lifted the towel and saw that the top of the water was covered with a thin sheet of ice.

He had only to lean towards the door to be near enough to shove it closed. On the back, a pair of jeans and a red sweater hung from two nails. Almost without thinking, Brunetti slipped his hand into the pockets of the jeans. He felt something hard at the bottom of the right pocket and pulled it out. The object, about the size of an egg, was wrapped in a clean white cloth. He set it on the table and unwrapped it.

He exposed a wooden carving of a human head, an object that Brunetti could easily have cradled in his hand were it not for the jagged pieces of wood sticking out from the bottom, suggesting that it had been broken off from the rest of the statue.

'What's that?' Vianello asked, coming over and standing beside him.

'I don't know. A woman, I think.' Brunetti picked it up to bring it closer to both of them. The woman's nose was a pinched triangle, her eyes narrow slits carved within perfect ovals. The workmanship of the hair was particularly fine and suggested tight braiding arranged in elaborate, symmetrical patterns. In the centre of her forehead was carved an odd geometric pattern, four triangles arranged around and pointing towards a central diamond, all of it carved in one continuous line.

'It's beautiful, isn't it?' Vianello asked.

'Yes, wonderful,' Brunetti agreed. He turned it upside down, exposing the rough edges of wood on the bottom.

'Snapped off at the neck, I'd say,' Brunetti said. He rewrapped the head and slipped it into his own pocket.

Vianello went over to the bed and knelt down to push aside the edges of the blankets. He pulled out a cardboard box, got to his feet, and set it on the bed.

There was nothing else in the room: no toilet,

no source of water, no cabinet or wardrobe of any sort. Brunetti pointed to the metal cup. Turning to Vianello, he said, 'He must have heated water in this.'

Vianello gave no sign that he thought this worthy of comment. He looked down at the box, pushed the contents around with his forefinger, and said, 'Nothing here.' He knelt beside the bed again and reached for the box.

'What's in it, Vianello?'

'Just some food.'

'Wait a minute,' Brunetti said. Vianello sat back on his heels.

Brunetti bent over the box and saw a packet of plain biscuits, a bag of shelled peanuts, an open box of rough cooking salt, four tea bags, a piece of cheese he thought might be Asiago, two oranges, and a transparent bag filled with the paper envelopes of sugar that bars served with coffee.

'Why salt?' he asked.

'Excuse me?'

Brunetti used the same hand to gesture around the room. 'Why would he have a box of salt? There are no pans. He doesn't cook. So why does he have salt?'

Vianello said, 'Maybe he uses it to brush his teeth,' then stuck his forefinger in his mouth and made a scrubbing motion to show how it could be done.

Brunetti leaned forward and picked up the box of salt. 'No, look at it. It's *sale grosso*, for cooking. You can't brush your teeth with this:

the pieces are too big.' The top of the box had been sliced open on three sides and the top partly pulled back to allow easy pouring. Brunetti saw the clumsy grains, the size of lentils, on the top. He licked his finger and stuck it into the salt, pulled it out and tasted it. Saltiness filled his mouth.

Brunetti set the box on the bed, pulled out his handkerchief and spread it smooth on top of the blanket. Then he poured the salt slowly out on to his handkerchief. Towards the middle of the box, the size and colour of the grains began to change: they lost the dull opacity of salt and, as if the subject of some beneficent transformation, grew in clarity and size until they fell from the box absolutely clear, some of them almost the size of peas.

'*Dio mio,*' Vianello said involuntarily.

Brunetti looked at the pile on the handkerchief, silenced by possibility. In the dull light from the single bulb, the stones lay there, inert and clear. Perhaps sunlight would bring them to life: he had no idea. He was not even certain what they were: no facets had been cut or ground into them to give them recognizable shape or lustre as gemstones. For all he knew, they could have been the castoffs of some Murano glass-blower, little chunks of clarity meant to form, say, the ears of glass bears or the noses of transparent bunnies.

But if that was all these glassy things were, they were unlikely to be hidden in the room of a murdered man.

Vianello got to his feet. 'What do we do with them?' he asked. Brunetti thought of some of his colleagues at the Questura and how, were one of them to ask the question, he would interpret it as an inquiry into the best way of pocketing the stones. From Vianello, however, the question was no more than an echo of his own concern about how to keep them from falling into those other hands. How many villas had sprung from police evidence rooms? How many vacations had been paid for by sequestered drugs and money?

'Give me your mittens,' Brunetti said.

'What?' asked a startled Vianello.

'Your mittens. We can put them in there to carry them out of here.'

'We're going to take them?'

'Would you leave them here?' Brunetti asked. 'When the men downstairs know we're interested in him, and when Cuzzoni knows?'

'You said you trusted him.'

Brunetti pointed at the squat pyramid on the bed. 'Until I know if these are real, I don't trust anyone.'

'And when you do know? Who will you trust then?' Vianello asked, pulling his mittens from the pockets of his jacket.

Ignoring the question, Brunetti picked up the handkerchief by the four corners and jiggled it until he created a chute that would allow it to pour easily. The salt and stones hung heavily, a fat lump at the bottom of a not entirely clean white handkerchief. Vianello held the first mitten under it, and Brunetti poured until they came within a few centimetres of the top. Vianello shook the stones until the thumb stood out rigid from the side. He set it on the bed while he slipped his watch off and tried to wrap the expandable band around the stuffed mitten, but it did not work, so he replaced the watch and contented himself with giving the mitten a few more shakes. He slipped it into the right pocket of his jacket and zipped the pocket closed.

They did the same with the second mitten, which went into Vianello's left hand pocket. That left Brunetti with a pile the size of an orange at the bottom of his handkerchief. He tied the corners together, then slipped it into the inside pocket of his jacket and buttoned the pocket.

Careful of the box now that it might carry fingerprints, he used the keys to slit open the bottom flap, then pressed the box flat and slid it into the outside pocket of his jacket. When that was done, he took out his *telefonino* and called the number of the technical squad at the Questura. He told them where the apartment was, said it might be the home of the man who was murdered, and asked them to send someone over to fingerprint the room. He was not to be in uniform and was to ring the top bell in front of the house. Yes, he and Vianello would wait.

When he hung up, Vianello said, 'You didn't answer my question.'

'Which one?' asked a distracted Brunetti.

'Who you'll trust, once you find out if they're real?'

For the first time since they had entered the building, Brunetti smiled. 'No one.'

The technician took almost an hour to get there, which left Brunetti and Vianello to sit side by side on the bed in the freezing room and discuss possibilities. When the cold became too intense, they went down one floor to the other apartment and let themselves in again. There, at least, it was minimally warmer, and one of them could stand at the partially open door to see that no one went past it and up to the next floor.

Brunetti went into the kitchen and came out with two plastic bags. At his request, Vianello unzipped his pockets and put both mittens in one of the bags. Brunetti tied the neck of the bag closed and slipped it into the other. While they did all this, they talked about what they had found, but neither of them could come up with a satisfactory explanation, though Brunetti did think of someone whom he could ask about the stones. While Vianello stood at the door, he called Claudio Stein and asked if he could come and talk to him the following morning.

Claudio, like most people Brunetti knew, believed that a telephone was an open conduit to various offices of the government, and so he asked no questions and said that he would be in his office after nine and would, of course, be delighted to see Brunetti. When Brunetti hung up, Vianello asked, 'Who is he?'

'A friend of my father's. They were in the war together.'

'How old is he, then?'

'Past eighty, I'd say,' Brunetti answered, then, 'I don't really know.' He had no idea if Claudio was older or younger than his father, only that he had been one of the few men his father trusted and one of the even fewer who had remained a friend all during the long twilight of his father's last years.

The sound of the doorbell announced the arrival of the man from the technical squad. When he got to the second floor, Brunetti explained that he wanted prints from the room on the floor above. He pulled the salt box from his pocket and, holding it by a corner, waited for the technician to take an evidence bag out of his briefcase. 'The prints on this should match the dead man's; the others should be mine,' Brunetti said. 'I'd like to know if there are any others.' He told the man that the door upstairs was open and added that he'd like Bocchese to get on to this as quickly as he could. As the man turned towards the stairs, Brunetti said, as an after-thought, 'When you're finished, wipe off any sign that you've been up there, all right? And then do this place here.'

The man waved a hand over his head in acknowledgement and started up the steps. There was no reason for them to remain, and so they went downstairs. Brunetti stopped at the doorway to the first floor apartment and knocked, but no one answered the door.

'You think they're gone?' Vianello asked.

Brunetti looked down at his watch, surprised to see that it was after seven, which meant they had spent more than two hours inside the building. 'If nothing else, they've gone to work.' Both of them knew that, to avoid direct competition with shop owners, the *vu cumprà* worked primarily when the shops were closed for lunchtime or after they closed in the evening. 'There's no way they'll be back here before midnight,' Brunetti said.

'And so?'

'So we go home for dinner, and then tomorrow I'll go and see Claudio.'

'Would you like me to come with you?' Vianello asked.

'To protect me again?' Brunetti joked, pointing to the door behind which the black men lived.

'If he's in the business I think he's in, perhaps it's Signor Claudio who could use a bit of protecting,' Vianello answered, but he smiled when he said it.

'Claudio and my father walked back from Berlin in 1946. I don't think danger has any real meaning for a person who did that,' Brunetti said, thanked Vianello nonetheless for his offer, and went home to his pork with olives and tomato sauce.

13

Claudio Stein ran his business from a small apartment over near Piazzale Roma, at the end of a blind *calle* near the prison. Brunetti had been there many times. In his youth, he had gone with his father and had listened while the two men spoke of their shared past, both as young men in Venice before the war and then as young soldiers in Greece and in Russia. Over the course of the years spanned by the friendship of the two men, Brunetti had come to know all their stories: the priest in Castello who told them it was a sin not to join the Fascist party, the woman in Thessaloniki who gave them a bottle of ouzo, the wild artillery captain who had tried to kidnap them into his unit and had been turned away only by the sight of a pistol. In all of their stories, the two men emerged victorious: but then the fact that they had survived the war at all was, all things considered, sufficient sign of victory.

After years of listening to their stories, Brunetti eventually realized that the hero of all of the adventures that took place before the war was his father: extroverted, generous, clever, a natural leader of the neighbourhood boys. After the war, however, command passed to the far less volatile Claudio: cautious, honest, reliable and, in his relationship with his friend, protective and loyal. Claudio had learned how to deflect the retelling of stories when they veered towards subjects that might bring on one of the elder Brunetti's cataclysmic rages: he always turned the conversation away from politicians, officers, or equipment and back to their repeated triumphs in the search for food and amusement. How many of these stories were true? Brunetti had no idea, nor did he care. He loved them and had always loved hearing them because of the pictures they gave him, however out of sequence or distorted by the lens of the teller, of the man his father had been before the war had had its way with him.

Claudio opened the door soon after his first ring, and the first thing Brunetti thought was that the old man had forgotten to put his shoes on. They embraced, and Brunetti took the opportunity to look down the back of the old man's legs, but there indeed were the heels of his shoes. He stepped back and took another look and saw that it was nothing more than the inevitable betrayal of age that had slipped in and stolen five or more centimetres from Claudio since the last time they met.

'How good to see you, Guido,' the old man said in the same deep voice that had been a beacon of calm to Brunetti during most of his youth. He led Brunetti into the apartment, saying, 'Here, give me your coat.' Brunetti set his briefcase on the floor and removed his coat, waiting as Claudio hung it up. It had been Claudio, he remembered, who had given him a thousand lire for his sixteenth birthday, a fortune then, money he had taken to the neighbourhood bar and spent in a single night on buying drinks for his friends. Such were the times that most of the money had been spent on Coca-Cola and limonata: after all, wine was available at home, so why celebrate with that?

Claudio led them down the corridor and into the room he always referred to as his office, though it was simply a room in an apartment with a large desk, three chairs, and an enormous safe as tall as a man. In all the years Brunetti had come here, the surface of the desk had always been empty. Only once, and that was six years ago when he had come to interview Claudio in his official capacity as a policeman, had anything appeared on the desk. Then it had been nothing more than the soft suede jeweller's case that had been left by a pair of swindlers who had somehow substituted it for the one Claudio had himself filled with the stones they claimed they were going to buy.

The case was a classic, a well-prepared sting that had probably taken the pair more than a year to set up. They had studied Claudio's behaviour, befriended members of his family, and in the process had learned enough about his private life and his business to persuade him that they were old clients of his father, who had run the business before leaving it to Claudio.

On the day of sale, they had come to this same office, and Claudio had given them the pride of his collections, gems to a value so large that he had begun to sob after confessing everything to Brunetti. Carefully they had selected the stones, letting Claudio place them, one by one, in the suede case. At the very last, the one who subsequently turned out to be the leader had selected an enormous diamond solitaire ring and had placed it in the centre of the case, then watched as Claudio folded it closed and secured it with its bands of black elastic. 'That way,' the man had said, pointing at the little leather bump that indicated the ring, 'you'll be sure which case is ours.'

And it had happened then, in the half-second between the time Claudio finished securing the package and the moment when he inserted it on the top shelf of the safe. Had one of them asked him a question, pulled out a cigarette case? Later, when he discovered the substitution, Claudio could not remember anything about that crucial moment when the two cases had been switched. He realized what had happened only two days later, when the men did not come back to pay him and collect their stones. Later, he said he knew already when he opened the safe and took the case, knew it though he could never believe that it was possible, that they could have managed to switch the cases, not with him there, not with him paying attention. But they had.

He had made Brunetti, after telling him how much the stones were worth, promise to tell no one: he knew he would not be able to endure the shame, were his wife to learn how great had been his carelessness, nor could he bear hers if she learned that the men she had so proudly spoken to about her husband one day on the train were the very men who had come back to cheat him.

That the men were subsequently arrested and jailed made no difference to Claudio, for the money had long since been lost in the casinos of Europe, and his insurance company had declared the claim unpayable because he had not submitted to them, when he applied for his policy, a complete list of the stones in his possession, their origin, price, weight, and cut. That Claudio was a wholesaler and thus had thousands of stones and would have had to spend months preparing the inventory was judged irrelevant in their decision to disallow the claim.

This stew of memories filled Brunetti's mind as Claudio led him down the corridor towards his office. 'Can't I offer you something to drink, Guido?' the old man asked as they entered the office.

'No, nothing, Claudio. I just had a coffee. Perhaps when we're finished.' From long experience, he knew that Claudio would not take his place behind the desk until his guest was seated, so Brunetti pulled out a chair and sat, placing his briefcase between his feet.

Claudio walked behind the desk and sat. He folded his hands and leaned forward in a familiar gesture. 'Paola and the kids?' he asked.

'Fine. Everyone,' Brunetti said, part of the familiar ritual. 'They're all doing well at school. Even Paola,' he added with a laugh. Then he asked, 'And Elsa?'

Claudio tilted his head to one side and grimaced. 'The arthritis is getting worse. It's in her hands now. But she never complains. Someone told us about a doctor in Padova, and she's been going to him for a month. He's giving her some medicine from America, and it seems to help.'

'Let's hope it does,' Brunetti said. 'And Riccardo?'

'Happy, working, and going to make me a grandfather for the third time in June.'

'He or Evvie?' Brunetti asked.

'Together, I think,' Claudio said.

Formalities disposed of, Claudio asked, 'What is it you wanted to see me about?' From force of habit, he wasted no time, even though life had slowed for him in the last few years, and he found himself with so much time that he would like to be able to waste some.

'I've found some stones,' Brunetti said. 'And I'd like you to tell me whatever you can about them.'

'What kind of stones?' Claudio asked.

'Let me show you,' Brunetti said and reached for his briefcase. He opened it, pulled out the plastic bag that contained Vianello's two mittens, and set it on the desk. Then he removed his handkerchief and placed it next to the bag. He glanced across at Claudio and saw both confusion and interest.

He started with the handkerchief, pulling at the first knot with his fingernails and then, when that was untied, the second. He let the corners fall to the surface of the desk and pushed the handkerchief closer to Claudio. Then he opened the plastic bag, removed the mittens and poured their contents on to the pile at the centre of the handkerchief. A few wayward stones rolled free across the surface of the desk; Brunetti picked them up and placed them on the pile, saying, 'I'd like you to tell me about these.'

Claudio, who had probably seen more precious stones in his life than anyone else in the city, looked at them soberly, making no motion towards them. After more than a minute had passed, he licked the tip of his forefinger and placed it on one of the small pieces, picked it up and licked it. 'Why are they mixed with salt?' he asked.

162

'They were hidden in a box of it,' Brunetti explained.

Claudio nodded, approving of the idea.

'Do you need them?' he asked Brunetti.

'Need them how? As evidence?'

'No. Need them now, to keep with you, to take back with you.'

'No,' Brunetti, who had not thought of this, answered. 'I don't think so. Why? What do you want to do with them?'

'First, I have to put them in hot water for half an hour or so and get rid of the salt,' Claudio said. 'That will make it easier to see how many there are and how much they weigh.'

'Weigh?' Brunetti asked, 'as in grams and kilos?'

Returning his attention to the stones, Claudio said, 'They're not measured in kilos: you should know at least that much, Guido.' There was no reproach in his voice, nor disappointment.

'When you do that,' Brunetti said, 'will you be able to tell me what they're worth? Or where they come from?'

Claudio pulled his own handkerchief from the breast pocket of his jacket and wiped his forefinger clean with it. Then, using the same finger, he poked and prodded at the pile, smoothing out the hill Brunetti had created and moving the stones around until there was one level surface. He switched on a segmented desk lamp and angled the head until the light fell on the area directly in front of him. He opened the centre drawer in his desk and took out a pair of

163

jeweller's tweezers. With them, he selected three of the bigger stones, each slightly smaller than a pea, and set them on the desk in front of him. Idly, not bothering to look at Brunetti, he said, 'The first thing I can tell you is that someone has selected these stones carefully.' To Brunetti, they still looked like pebbles, but he said nothing.

From the same drawer Claudio took a jeweller's loupe and a set of balance scales, then pulled out a small box. When he opened it, Brunetti saw a series of tiny cylindrical brass weights. Claudio looked down at the things on his desk, shook his head, and smiled at Brunetti, saying, 'Force of habit, these scales.' He opened a side drawer and pulled out a small electronic scale and switched it on. As the light flashed, revealing a window in which a large zero could be seen, he said, 'This is faster and more accurate.'

Using the tweezers, he picked up one of the stones he had set aside. He placed the stone on the scale, turned it so that he could read the weight, added the second stone, and then the third. He reached into the drawer again and pulled out a black velvet pad about half the size of a magazine, which he placed to the left of the scale. With the tweezers, he set the three stones on the pad. He picked up the loupe and, as Brunetti watched the crown of his head move from left to right, examined the three stones in turn.

He set the loupe on the desk and looked across at Brunetti. 'Are they African?' Claudio asked.

'I think so.'

The older man nodded in evident satisfaction. He picked up the tweezers and gently poked at the pile, pushing stones to one side or another until three more, each larger than the first three, lay in the middle of the small circles he had created. Claudio picked them up with the tweezers and set them on the velvet cloth, to the left of the others; with the loupe, he examined each of them thoroughly.

When he was finished, he removed the loupe and set it beside the handkerchief, then lined up the long tweezers parallel to the border of the smoothed-out cloth. 'I won't know for sure until tomorrow, when I can count them and weigh them, but I'd say you've somehow managed to acquire a fortune, Guido.'

Ignoring the verb and the question implicit in it, Brunetti asked, 'How much of a fortune?'

'It will depend on how much salt there is and whether the smaller ones are as good as I think those ones are,' the jeweller said, pointing at the six stones he had examined.

'If they aren't cut, how can you tell what they're worth?' Brunetti asked. 'They don't have any – what do you call them? – facets.'

'The facets come later, Guido. You can't add them to a stone that isn't perfect. Or, that is, you can add them, but only a perfect stone is going to give you the right lustre when you add the facets.' He waved his hand at the pile of stones. 'I've looked at only six of them. You saw that. But those look to me as though they might be perfect; well, at the very least of excellent quality. I can't be sure, of course, that they're perfect in nature or that they'll be perfect when they're cut and polished, but I think they might be.' He glanced at the wall behind Brunetti for a second, then looked back at him and pointed at the stones. 'It will be in the hands of the cutter. To bring out what's there.'

As if suddenly eager to examine them again, Claudio picked up the loupe and screwed it back in place. He leaned over and again studied all six stones, working from left to right. At one point he took the tweezers and turned one of the stones over, then looked at it from this new angle. When he was done, he removed the loupe and placed it back exactly where it had been. He nodded, as if assenting to a question from Brunetti. 'I don't know when I've last seen such things.' With the tweezers he touched a few of the stones lying in the pile, though there was nothing at all special about them, so far as Brunetti could see.

'Could you give me some idea of what they'd be worth, no matter how vague?' Brunetti asked.

'Just look at them,' Claudio said, his eyes aglow with what Brunetti recognized as passion. Then, sensing the urgency in his friend's voice, the old man brought himself back to the world where diamonds had value, not just beauty. 'When the big ones are cut and polished, each one could be worth thirty, perhaps forty, thousand Euros, but the price will depend on how much is lost when they're cut.' Claudio picked up one of the raw stones and held it towards Brunetti. 'If there are perfect stones to be had from these, they're worth a fortune.'

Then what had they been doing, Brunetti wondered, in a room with no heat, no water, and no insulation? And what were they doing in the possession of a man who earned his living by selling counterfeit bags and wallets on the street?

'How can you tell they're African?' Brunetti asked.

'I can't,' Claudio admitted. 'That is, not for sure. But they look as though they might be.'

'What tells you that?' Brunetti wanted to know.

Claudio considered the question, no doubt one he had heard before. 'Something about the colour and light in them or off them. And the absence of the flecks and imperfections that you find in diamonds from other places.' Claudio looked at Brunetti, then back at the stones. 'To tell the truth,' he finally said, 'I probably can't tell you why, at least not fully. After you've looked at thousands of stones, hundreds of thousands of stones, you just know – or at least you think you know – where they're from.'

'Is that how many you've looked at, Claudio?'

The old man sat up straighter, though the action made him no taller in his chair. He folded his hands in that professorial gesture and said, 'I've never thought about that, Guido – it was just a phrase – but I suppose I have. Tiny six-teenth of a carat stones filled with imperfections, and some glorious ones that weighed more than thirty, forty carats, so perfect it was like looking at new suns.' He paused, as though listening to what he had just said. Then he smiled and added, 'I suppose it's like women. It doesn't matter what they look like, not really: there's always something beautiful about them.'

Brunetti, in full agreement, grinned at the simile. 'Is there any way you could be sure where they're from?' he asked.

Claudio considered this and finally said, 'The best I can do is show a few of them to friends of mine and see what they think. If we all agree . . . well, then either they're from Africa or else we're all wrong.'

'Can you tell where, specifically? That is, what country?'

'Diamonds don't acknowledge countries, Guido. They come from pipes, and pipes don't have passports.'

'Pipes?'

'In the ground. Deep craters that are more like thin, deep wells than anything else. The diamonds were formed down there – kilometres down – millions of years ago, and over the years, they gradually work their way up to the sur-face.' Claudio relaxed into the graceful authority of the expert, and Brunetti listened, interested. 'They come in clusters, some pipes, or they can be single ones. But it's possible that the clusters can cross what are now national borders and fall into the territories of two countries.'

'What happens then?' Brunetti asked.

'Then the stronger side tries to take them from the weaker.'

As he had learned from his reading of history, Brunetti knew this was the normal operating procedure for most international disputes. 'Is this the case in Africa?'

'Unfortunately, yes,' Claudio said. 'It gives those poor people another reason for violence.'

'Hardly necessary, is it?' Brunetti asked.

The sombre topic halted the flood of Claudio's garrulity, and he said, 'You can come and get them tomorrow.' Then, as a joke, he added, 'If you think I can be trusted with them, that is.'

Brunetti leaned forward and placed his hand on Claudio's arm. 'I'd like you to keep them, if you will,' he said.

'For how long?'

Brunetti shrugged. 'I've no idea. Until I've decided what to do with them.'

'Is this police evidence?' Claudio asked, but he seemed interested in clarity, not security.

'In a way,' Brunetti said evasively.

'Does someone else know you have them?' Claudio asked.

'Yes.'

'Thank God,' the old man said.

'What difference would that make?' Brunetti asked.

'Then I'm less likely to steal them,' Claudio said and got to his feet.

14

On his way back to the Questura, Brunetti pondered what Claudio had told him. Because it was all new to him, the older man's talk of diamonds had seemed important, but the part that applied or might apply to the African, upon closer examination, was precious little: some vast amount of Euros and a probable African origin for the stones. It was certainly interesting to know these things, but Brunetti could not see how the knowledge brought him any closer to understanding the connection between the stones and the dead man or between the stones and the man's death. Greed was one of the most reliable motives for crime, but if the man's killers had known about the stones, why had they not gone and taken them after he was dead? And if what they wanted was the stones, then why kill the man at all? It was hardly as though the police were likely to believe a *vu cumprà* who came into the Questura to report that he had been robbed of a fortune in diamonds.

As he walked back, Brunetti decided that the best strategy was to speak immediately to his superior, Vice-Questore Giuseppe Patta, and seek his permission to continue to lead the investigation, though in order to achieve this, he would somehow have to persuade Patta that he did not particularly want the job. He went directly to Patta's office, outside which he found the man he sought in conversation with Signorina Elettra.

As if someone had whispered the word 'diamonds' into the ears of the staff of the Questura as they were dressing for work that morning, Patta wore a new and unusually garish tie-pin, a tiny gold panda with diamond eyes. Signorina Elettra, as though alerted by a sartorial advance warning system, wore a pair of tasteful diamond chip earrings which diminished, though they could not overcome, the impact of Patta's panda.

With an air of studied casualness, Brunetti greeted them both and asked Signorina Elettra if she had succeeded in locating that *Gazzettino* article about the former director of the Casinò. Though this was a question Brunetti had invented on the spot to justify his arrival in the office, Signorina Elettra said she had and reached across her desk to hand him a folder.

'What are you working on at the moment, Brunetti?' Patta inquired.

Holding up the file, Brunetti said, 'The Casinò investigation, sir,' in much the same tone Hercules might have used had he been asked why he was spending so much time in the stables.

Patta turned towards his office. 'Come with me,' he said. The remark could have been addressed to either one of them, but the absence of 'please' indicated that it was directed at Brunetti.

An Iranian friend had once told Brunetti that underlings there acknowledged the commands of their superiors with a word that sounded like *'chasham'*, a Farsi word meaning 'I shall put it on my eyes', which conveyed that the person of lesser importance placed the command of his superior upon his eyes and would do – indeed, see – nothing until the command had been executed. Brunetti often regretted the absence of a similarly servile expression in Italian.

Inside, Patta went to stand at the window, thus preventing Brunetti from taking a seat. He stood just inside the door and waited for Patta to speak. The Vice-Questore stared out of the window for a long time, so long that Brunetti began to wonder if Patta had forgotten about him. He cleared his throat, but the noise evoked no response in Patta.

Just when Brunetti was on the point of speaking, Patta turned from the window and asked, 'They called you the other night, didn't they?'

'About the African, do you mean, sir?' Brunetti asked.

'Yes.'

Brunetti nodded.

'At home?'

'Yes.'

'Why?'

'Excuse me, sir?'

'Why did they call you?'

'I'm not sure I understand, sir. I suppose they called me because I live closest, or perhaps someone here suggested they call me. I really don't know why.'

'They didn't call me,' Patta said, not without a note of petulance.

After considering what might be the safest answer, Brunetti said, 'I imagine they simply called whatever name came to mind. Or, for all I know, there's a list, and they call us at home in turn when it's necessary for someone to attend the scene of a crime.' Patta turned back to the window and Brunetti added, 'Besides, sir, they probably didn't want to burden someone so senior with the opening stages of an investigation.' He did not mention that it was precisely those stages which often proved most important in solving a case.

When Patta still did not speak, he added, 'After all, sir, your skills surely lie in deciding who is best suited to investigate a particular case.' Brunetti realized how close to the wind he was sailing and decided to say nothing more.

After another long pause, Patta asked, 'And do you think you're particularly well suited to this case?'

Brunetti counted to five, very slowly, before he said, 'No, not particularly.'

As soon as he spoke, Patta was upon him. 'Does that mean you don't want it?'

This time Brunetti made it to seven before he answered, 'I don't want it and I don't *not* want it equally, sir,' he lied. 'I am of the opinion that it will turn out to be some story of rivalry between different gangs of blacks and we'll end up questioning dozens of them, who will all say they have no idea who the man was or who he could have been. And in the end, we'll learn nothing and just close the case and send it to the archives.' He tried to sound both disapproving and bored at the same time. When Patta remained silent, Brunetti asked, 'Is that what you wanted to see me about, sir?'

Patta turned back to him and said, 'I think you'd better take a seat, Brunetti.'

Suppressing any sign of surprise, Brunetti did as he was told. His superior chose not to move away from the window. Clouds were gathering, and the light was rapidly dimming. Patta's face had grown less visible since they entered the room, and Brunetti found himself wishing he dared go over and turn the light on, the better to illuminate his superior's expression.

Finally Patta said, 'I find your lack of interest unusual, Brunetti.'

174

Brunetti began to speak, decided to show reluctance, and so waited a few seconds before he said, 'I suppose it is, sir. But I'm busy at the moment, and I have a feeling that any investigation here will prove futile.' He glanced at Patta, saw from his stillness how attentive he was, and went on. 'From the little I've heard about the *vu cumprà*, I'd say they live in a closed world, and there's no way we can get into it.' He tried to think of an appropriate comparison, and the best he could come up with was, 'Like the Chinese.'

'What?' Patta demanded sharply. 'What did you say?'

Startled by his tone, Brunetti said, 'That they're like the Chinese here, sir, in that they're a closed world, a private universe, and we have no understanding of the relationships and rules that operate there, in either case.'

'But why did you mention the Chinese?' Patta asked in a calmer voice.

Brunetti shrugged. 'Because they're the only other large group I can think of here. Ethnic group, that is.'

'The Filipinos? The people from Eastern Europe?' Patta asked. 'Aren't they ethnic groups?'

Brunetti thought about this before he answered, 'I suppose so.' Then he added, 'But if I have to tell the truth, it's because they're so racially different from us, the Africans and the Chinese, that I lump them together. Maybe that makes them seem more alien, somehow.' When

Patta made no response, he asked, 'Why do you ask, sir?'

At that, Patta moved away from the window. He did not, however, sit down behind his desk but chose to take a chair opposite Brunetti, a decision that filled Brunetti with a strange disquiet.

'We don't trust one another, do we, Brunetti?' Patta finally asked.

Ordinarily, Brunetti would lie about this and insist that they were both policemen and so it was obvious that they had to trust one another if they were to work together in the best interests of the force, but something warned him that Patta was in no mood for such nonsense, and so he said, 'No, we don't.'

Patta considered his answer, glanced at the floor, then back again at Brunetti. At last he said, 'I want to tell you something that I will not explain, but I want you to trust me when I tell you it's true.'

Instantly Brunetti thought of a conundrum proposed by his professor of logic: if a person who always lies tells you he is lying, is he telling you the truth or is he lying? Years had passed and he could no longer remember the correct answer, but Patta's remarks sounded suspiciously similar. He remained silent.

'We have to leave this alone,' Patta finally said.

When it was obvious that he was going to say no more, Brunetti asked, 'I assume this means the murder of the black man?'

Patta nodded.

'Leave it alone how? Not investigate it or only look like we are, and find nothing?'

'We can look like we are. That is, we can question people and make reports. But we are not to find anything.'

'Anything like what?' Brunetti asked.

Patta shook his head. 'That's all I have to say on this matter, Brunetti.'

'You mean we're not to find the men who killed him?' Brunetti asked in a hard voice.

'I mean only what I said, Brunetti, that we are to leave this alone.'

Brunetti's impulse was to shout at Patta, but he suppressed it and, instead, asked in a voice he managed to keep calm, 'Why are you telling me this?'

Patta's was just as calm as he answered, 'To spare you trouble, if I can.' Then, as if provoked to the truth by Brunetti's silence, he added, 'To spare us all trouble.'

Brunetti got to his feet. 'I appreciate the warning, sir,' he said and walked to the door. He waited there for a moment, curious to see if Patta would ask if he understood and would obey, but the Vice-Questore said nothing more. Brunetti left, careful to shut the door quietly.

Signorina Elettra looked up eagerly as he emerged and started to speak, but Brunetti did nothing more than slide the empty folder back on to her desk. He put his forefinger to his lips and then gestured that he was going back upstairs.

As a kind of insurance that he would not give in to Patta, Brunetti called Paola and described the wooden head, asking her to add it to the information to give to her friend at the university and encouraging her to make the call. Then he opened his mind to possibility. The fact that the Vice-Questore should warn him off an investigation meant that he had himself been warned off, and that raised the question of who would deliver such a warning. And from whom would a warning carry sufficient force to persuade him within less than a day? Patta respected wealth and power, though Brunetti was never sure which meant more to him. Patta would always defer to money, but it was power that could compel his obedience, so the admonition must come from some source powerful enough to force Patta into submission.

Patta had hinted that his warning arose from concern for Brunetti's safety, a possibility which Brunetti dismissed out of hand. Its origin was more likely to be found in Patta's fear that Brunetti could not or would not be prevented from continuing the investigation once he began it, even if commanded to do so. The cunning of the snake became evident in Patta's seeming concern, as if his main priority were Brunetti's safety and not his own.

The source of a power so great as to force compliance from a Vice-Questore of police? Brunetti closed his eyes and began to run over the rosary beads of possibility. The obvious candidates fell into the general categories of governmental, ecclesiastical, and criminal; the great tragedy of his country, Brunetti mused, was how equal they were as contenders.

15

Signorina Elettra's arrival interrupted these reflections. She knocked and came in without waiting to be told to do so, approached his desk, and all but demanded, 'What did he want?' Then, as if aware of the effrontery of her question, she stepped back and added, 'He seemed so eager to talk to you, I mean.'

An impulse Brunetti recognized as protective led him to answer, as calmly as though hers had been a normal question, 'To ask about the murder of the black man.'

'He was in a very strange mood,' she volunteered, prodding for a more satisfactory answer.

Brunetti shrugged. 'He's always upset when there's trouble. It reflects badly on the city.'

'And that reflects badly on him,' she completed.

'Even if the victim isn't one of us,' Brunetti said, conscious as he spoke of how much he sounded like Chiara. Before Signorina Elettra's universalist sympathies were offended, he explained, 'A Venetian, I mean.'

She appeared to accept this and asked, 'But why one of those poor devils? They never cause any trouble. All they want to do is stand there and sell their bags and try to have a chance at a decent life.' She drew herself from these sentiments and asked, 'Did he assign it to you?'

'No, not specifically. But he didn't say he wanted anyone else to handle it, so I assume I'm to continue.' As he said these bland things, his mind kept attempting to follow the trail that led from Patta's warning back to its source: if Patta had been threatened to warn Brunetti away, then those who continued the investigation would be in danger.

How had Patta phrased it? 'We have to leave this alone'? How typical that was of him, to make the statement as though it were the result of long consideration and general assent. And 'have to', as if it were a truth universally acknowledged that the case was to be abandoned, the man's murder forgotten or quietly assigned to the realm of forgetting, that overcrowded land.

A Patta who had never existed might have said, 'I'm being threatened into silencing you, and the thought of losing my job or being hurt fills me with such fear that I will do whatever I can to corrupt the system of justice and stop you from doing your job, just to keep myself safe.' This phantom Patta's voice was so real that it all but blocked out Signorina Elettra's speaking one. Brunetti blinked a few times and drew his attention back in time to hear her ask, '. . . still report to you?'

'Yes, of course,' he answered, as if he had heard the first half of her question. 'I'll go on as though I were in charge until I'm told otherwise.'

'And then?' she asked.

'And then I'll see who he puts in charge and either help that person or else continue to do things on my own.' It was not necessary to name the person whose appointment would lead to the latter possibility: even in an organization that did not often hunger and thirst for justice's sake, Lieutenant Scarpa's contempt for it was noteworthy. Some of the other commissari were unlikely to achieve success in a case that presented difficulties or complexities, but under the direction of a competent magistrate, they would at least make an attempt to apprehend the guilty and would be handicapped only by inexperience or lack of imagination. Scarpa, however, knew no motivation save self-advancement, and even a whisper from his superior – or from forces Brunetti was reluctant to name – that the case not be pursued would suffice to guarantee its doom.

182

Luckily, the case could not be given to Scarpa, still only a lieutenant, in spite of all of Patta's efforts to have him promoted. A commissario would still be the chief police officer in charge of the investigation, though nothing could prevent Patta, should he choose to do so, from assigning Scarpa to the case, as well.

'If only we didn't have to worry about him,' Brunetti said, knowing it was unnecessary to pronounce Scarpa's name and bemused to hear himself sounding so much like an English king trying to resolve a personnel problem.

Her smile began in her eyes, then progressed across the rest of her face. Finally she said, 'Don't tempt me, sir.'

'Only in the sense of transferring him, Signorina,' he said with exaggerated emphasis, never quite sure where his suggestions might take her.

She gazed out of the window in contemplation of the façade of the church of San Lorenzo. 'Ah,' she breathed in a sigh that seemed to go on for ever, and then silence. She tilted her head to one side, as if adjusting her vision to the contemplation of some object only she could see, and then at last she smiled.

'The Interpol class on technological surveillance,' she said.

Amazed, Brunetti asked, 'The one in Lyon?'

'Yes.'

'But isn't that open only to officers who have been selected by them, before they're transferred to Interpol?'

'Yes,' she answered. 'He's been applying to Interpol for years.'

'But always unsuccessfully, I thought.'

With her most minimal smile, Signorina Elettra remarked, 'So long as Georges runs the personnel office there, Lieutenant Scarpa's application will remain unsuccessful.'

'Georges?' Brunetti inquired, as if they had discovered they had the same accountant.

'I was much younger then,' she offered by way of explanation.

Brunetti, as if he understood exactly what this meant, said only, 'Of course,' and then, trying to reel her back, 'Scarpa?'

She returned to the present and explained the future. 'He could be invited to Lyon and do the course, but then when it's finished, someone could discover that the invitation was meant to go to some other Lieutenant Scarpa.'

'What other Lieutenant Scarpa?' Brunetti asked.

'I've no idea,' she said impatiently. 'Surely there must be a score of them in the police.'

'And if there aren't?'

'Then surely there has to be a Lieutenant Scarpa in the Army, or the *Carabinieri*, or the Finanza or the Polizia di Frontiera.'

'Don't forget the Railway Police,' Brunetti reminded her.

'Thank you.'

'How long does this course last?' he asked.

'Three weeks, I think.'

'And Interpol will pay for it?'

'Of course.'

'Are you sure Georges will do it?'

If she had been an antinomian questioned about the importance of faith, she could have looked no more surprised, but still she did not deign to answer. When Brunetti said no more, she moved towards the door. Pausing there, she said, '*J'appellerai Georges*,' and left.

Brunetti took the thought of who might be behind the warning given to Patta to a lunch of fellow police officials from the Veneto, and it kept him silent company as he talked amiably with his colleagues and listened to the usual speeches about the need to protect the social order from the forces which menaced it from all sides. Idly, Brunetti flipped over his menu and took a pen from his pocket. As the minutes – and then the quarter-hours – passed, he made a list of the concrete nouns that were most frequently invoked as well as any proposal for a specific course of action. As the second hour began, he had three nouns on his paper, 'home', 'family', and 'security', but no note of a specific project or plan beyond 'decisive action' and 'swift intervention'. Why can we never talk in the concrete? he asked himself. Why must we always speak in generalities as glowing as they are meaningless?

Back in his office, Brunetti remembered that this was one of the days when Paola did not have to go back to the university after lunch, leaving her free to spend the afternoon at home, reading or commenting on student papers or, for all he knew, lying on the sofa and watching soap operas. How wonderful it would be, he thought, to have such a job. Five hours a week in the classroom, seven months a year, and the rest of the time free to read. Paola was expected to attend various faculty meetings and sit on two separate committees, though she had never succeeded in communicating to him just what it was these committees were meant to do, nor did she seem ever to attend the meetings.

He had once asked her, years ago, why she bothered to keep the job, and she had explained that, if nothing else, her active participation in classes exposed the students to at least one professor who did something more than stand in front of them and read from a textbook she had herself written some years before. At this accurate description of his own years at university, Brunetti realized how long he had harboured the hope that, at least in the humanities, these days things would somehow be different.

He looked over the papers on his desk, filled to the point of pain with the awareness that all he would do, if he were to remain in the office, would be to add to their quantity. He longed to be away from there: in the mountains, the tropics, some island where he could walk on the beach, ankle deep in warm water. He put out a hand to draw some papers towards him, a phantom hand rejecting the temptation to get up and leave. But after a while he realized how meaningless the words beneath his eyes were and gave in to his desire for freedom. Telling no one what he was doing, he left the Questura and took the first vaporetto to San Silvestro and home.

Biancat was open, so he went in and asked for a dozen irises. While the salesman was selecting them, Brunetti decided to take flowers to Chiara, as well, and asked for a dozen yellow tulips. When he got home, he went into the kitchen and set the tulips on the counter, then went down to Paola's office, carrying the irises.

She smiled when he came in, refrained from asking why he was home so early, and said, 'Guido, how sweet.'

Warmed by her smile and hoping for another, he said, 'I brought some tulips for Chiara, too.'

Her smile disappeared. 'Bad move,' she said, getting to her feet. She kissed his cheek, and took the flowers from him.

'What?' he asked of her retreating back, following her towards the kitchen.

She started to remove the paper from the bouquet and said, 'She read an article about the way they're shipped all over the world.'

'And?' he asked, utterly at a loss.

'And the article talked about how much fuel is consumed just in shipping them, then how much is consumed keeping the greenhouses warm in the winter, and how much fertilizer is used to nourish them and how it leaches into the soil.' This said, she turned her attention to Chiara's tulips, removed the paper wrapping, then bent to take out a dark brown vase. She filled it with water.

187

'More eco-criminals?' he asked ironically. 'It sounds like she believes we're surrounded by them.'

Paola slipped the tulips one by one into the vase, pausing after every few to see how they looked. She took a step back, the better to examine them, then drew close to the counter and finished arranging them. 'It's a valid position, I'd say,' she answered calmly.

'Does she seriously mean this?' Brunetti demanded. 'Now she's declared war on flowers?'

Paola turned and placed a calming hand on his arm. 'Don't get so excited, Guido. And try to remember that she's right.' She pointed to the tulips. 'These were probably grown in the Netherlands, shipped here by truck. They'll last four or five days, then they'll go into a plastic bag and into the garbage, and we'll use more petroleum to burn them.'

'That's a terrible way to look at flowers,' he insisted.

'What would make it less terrible?' she asked. 'If the product were ugly? Plastic gondolas made in Hong Kong and flown here by air freight? Those dreadful masks?'

'But they're flowers, for heaven's sake,' he insisted, pointing at the vase as if demanding that the beauty of the flowers confirm his judgement or that they stand up straighter and defend themselves.

'And we like flowers, and they're beautiful, but the point I'm trying to make, Guido, is that

188

they are no more necessary than are the plastic gondolas or the masks. We could just as easily live without them, but we choose to live with them, and because we do, we are forced to pay the ecological cost to get them here from wherever it is they come from.' He thought she had stopped, then she added, 'But we don't mind, or we mind less, because they're beautiful. So we persuade ourselves that it's somehow different. Only it isn't.' Another moment's pause and then she concluded, 'Or so Chiara believes.'

Brunetti felt suddenly at sea, as though he had stepped into the shallow waters at the Alberoni and been swept off his feet by an invisible current. 'She worries about the flowers, but she can still dismiss the death of a *vu cumprà*?' he asked, fully conscious of how illogical a question it was but unwilling to stop himself from asking it.

Paola smiled as if to suggest she had already asked herself the same question. 'I think she's still too young for us to expect much consistency in her ideas, or in her ideals,' she said.

'What does that mean?'

'Exactly what I said: she's still a child in many ways, so she's discovering all the fine and noble causes for the first time, and she still sees each one as a discrete unit: she hasn't seen the connections or contradictions among them; not yet.'

She looked across at him, but he said nothing, merely stood there looking unconvinced, so she went on. 'I remember when I was her age, Guido, and the causes I thought were good ones. I'm embarrassed by some of them now and positively ashamed of one or two.'

'For instance?' he asked, making no attempt to disguise his scepticism.

'For instance the Red Brigades,' she answered instantly, suddenly far more serious than she had been. 'I'm ashamed now to remember what I thought of them, that they were idealists who wanted to bring about a revolution that would lead to social and political justice.' She closed her eyes at the memory of the person she had been then.

Not without a certain discomfort, Brunetti recalled his own enthusiasm for the slogans and the professed ideals that had been in fashion then. 'And now?' he finally asked.

She tilted her head and shrugged, then said, 'Now I think they were just a bunch of spoiled young people who wanted to attract the world's attention and didn't much care who they hurt or killed in the attempt. All suffering from *protagonismo*, all infected with the same disease of needing to be the centre of the world's attention. And we gave them all the attention they wanted, and some of us gave them our praise and approval.' She picked up the vase of tulips and walked towards the living room. 'So if there's a certain inconsistency in Chiara's enthusiasms or beliefs, and if she repeats slogans or ideas she's heard from other people, I think we have to be patient with her and hope she'll come to her senses.'

'The way we did?' he asked, following her down the hall.

'I think so.'

'Have you said anything to her?' Brunetti asked.

'About what she said?'

'Yes.'

'No,' Paola answered, stopping beside the narrow table that held a majolica bowl and a small marble bust of Hermes. 'That's not necessary.' She set the flowers down to the left of the statue, moved the vase a few centimetres forward, then stepped back to admire it.

'What do you mean, it's not necessary?' he asked, making no attempt to disguise his disapproval.

Paola looked at him. 'She knows what she said was wrong, and she's been thinking about it since she said it. Or, rather, since I jumped on her for saying it. But she hasn't finished thinking about it yet, and when she does, she'll say something.'

Brunetti folded his arms and asked, 'And you're not only the earth mother? In your spare time you double as a mind-reader?'

Paola smiled and waved him out of her way. Heading back to the kitchen, she said over her shoulder, 'Something like that.'

He followed, reluctant to acknowledge his conviction that she was right. He compromised by asking, 'And what about the flowers?' nodding with his chin at the irises, which she had begun to slip into the tall blue vase she always used for them.

'When I'm finished putting them into the vase, I'll put them in my study, and then anyone who sees them will enjoy looking at them.'

'And if she says something?' he asked.

'I'll tell her I agree entirely with her principles, but that you brought them to me, so she will have to address her comments or criticisms to you.'

He laughed, opened the door to the cabinet under the sink, and stuffed the wrappers into the garbage. 'You really are a snake, Paola,' he said, not without admiration.

'Yes, I know,' she agreed. 'It's a form of adaptive behaviour forced upon me by the nature of my work.'

'Me too,' he said, then asked, 'Shall we go and have a coffee?'

She slid the vase of irises to one side of the counter and stepped back to admire them. 'Yes, if we can go to Tonolo and have *un cigno*. And while we're over there, we could go to San Barnaba and see if they have any of that good bread.'

It would take, he calculated, more than an hour. First a cream-filled swan and a coffee at Tonolo, then the walk to Campo San Barnaba and the store that sold the good cheese and the bread from Puglia. He had fled his office in search of peace and quiet, seeking some evidence that sanity still existed in a world of violence and crime, and his wife suggested they spend an hour eating pastry and buying a loaf of bread. He leaped at the chance.

As they walked, occasionally stopping to say hello to people they met or to look into shop windows, he told her about Patta's warning and what he thought it might mean. She listened, saying nothing, until they had had their cream-filled swans and coffee and were on the way to Campo San Barnaba.

'You think he's afraid for his job or for his life?' she asked, then added, 'or his family?'

Brunetti stopped at the first of the two produce-filled boats moored to the *riva*, then moved on to the second. Ignoring Patta for the moment, they discussed dinner and bought a dozen artichokes and a kilo of Fuji apples. As they moved away, Brunetti returned to Paola's question and said, 'I'm not sure, only that he's frightened.'

'Could be any one of them, then,' she said, turning into the store. Ten minutes later, they emerged with an entire loaf of the Pugliese bread, a wedge of pecorino, and a jar of the pesto sauce the owner swore was the best in the city.

'What do you think?' she asked in a voice so level he had no idea if she was talking about the pesto or the reason for Patta's fear. He waited, knowing his silence would prod her to explain. 'You know him better than I do,' she finally said, 'so I thought you'd be able to sense which it is, his job or his safety.'

Brunetti thought about this for some time and

finally admitted, 'No, nothing more than that he's very frightened.'

'If you keep going, you'll find out,' she volunteered.

'Investigating, you mean?'

She stopped and looked at him, surprised. 'I assumed you'd continue to investigate, no matter what he said. What I meant was if you continue to let him know that you're doing it.'

'I'll try to see that he doesn't find out,' Brunetti said.

'To spare his feelings?'

Brunetti laughed. 'No, to spare my job.'

'He can't fire you, can he?' she asked, and he could already see her marshalling the forces of her family and their network of connections.

Brunetti considered this, then answered, 'No, I don't think he could do that on his own. But he could suggest that I be transferred. That's the usual way of getting rid of people.'

'What sort of people?' she asked.

Walking at her side, he occasionally fell back a step to allow others to pass them on the narrow *calli*. 'Inconvenient people,' he answered finally.

'Which means?'

'People who ask questions and who try to prevent the entire system from becoming hopelessly corrupt,' he said, surprising himself with his own seriousness.

She reached and took his arm and tucked

it under her own. He had no idea if the gesture was a request for help or an offer to provide it. It didn't much matter to him which it was.

16

Brunetti woke the next morning to bright sun-light. For the last week, the fog had been trying to transform itself into rain but had managed to do nothing more than drape a slick film on the pavements. During the night the rain had finally come – Brunetti had a vague memory of hearing it slash against the windows while he slept – but some time before dawn it had given up and left the day to the sun.

He lay in bed, made happy by the strip of light that spread across the bottom of the covers. He turned on to his back and stretched to his full length and, yes, his feet found that, at the very bottom of the bed, where the sun had been shining for some time, it was warm.

A half-hour later he woke again, this time

suddenly, remembering that Christmas was only four days away, and he had, once again, done nothing about getting gifts for anyone. His first impulse was to blame Paola for not having reminded him, but the instant he caught himself thinking that, he cringed away, embarrassed, from the idea. A few minutes later, she came into the room, carrying a large cup of caffè latte. She wore a green woollen dress he did not remember having seen before. She set the cup and saucer on the table beside him, sat on the edge of the bed, and said, 'I wanted to be sure you were up before I left.'

'Where are you going?'

'To meet my mother and take her shopping.'

He picked up the cup and pulled it close to his mouth before asking, 'Christmas shopping?'

'Yes. I don't know what to get my father.'

He took three small sips, drawing in life with each one. 'I don't know what to get anyone.'

'You never do,' she said mildly and with great affection. 'If you meet me at four at San Bortolo, we can go and get some things together.'

'You're not home for lunch?' he asked, trying not to sound aggrieved.

'I told you last night, Guido. My mother and I are invited to Aunt Federica's for lunch today.'

That explained the dress, then. He drank more coffee and stifled the impulse to ask her how she could stand the thought of two hours in the company of her aunt. But if she was willing to go shopping with him, something she loathed even more than he did, then he would forgo comment on her family.

'We go every year; you know that,' she said. She saw the face he made when she spoke of certain members of her family, and it prompted her to say, 'Remember that she's the one who brought a successful case against the diocese of Messina for fraud.'

He covered his eyes with his left hand and asked, 'Must you always brag about your family?' When Paola made no reply, he looked out at her from between his fingers. She did not smile.

He set the cup on the saucer, chose the noble path and said, as if he approved of her destination, 'Sorry. I'd forgotten you told me you were going. Four o'clock is fine. I'll try to think of what I'd like to get everyone.'

She leaned forward and kissed his cheek. 'I love it when you lie to me.' She pushed herself away from him and was about to get up from the bed when he lunged and seized her in both arms.

He pulled her towards him, watching her astonishment, delighted by it. He squeezed. She laughed. He squeezed again. She giggled. Suddenly he let her go and she jumped to her feet.

'Will you do that to Patta the next time he accuses you of lying to him?' she asked.

He looked her up and down. 'Only if he wears a dress as short as that one.' He pushed the covers aside and got out of bed.

Strangely enough, the sun appeared to have had no effect on the temperature: when Brunetti left the house, it felt even colder than it had the day before. By the time he got to Rialto, he felt the cold in his ears and nose, and he regretted the light-hearted optimism that had encouraged him to leave his gloves and scarf at home. As if the fog of the previous week had also dropped from his eyes, he registered for the first time that the city was ready for Christmas: tinsel and bulbs hung in almost every shop window.

He looked up and saw that strings of lights crossed above his head: how could he have walked home in the dark for weeks and not have noticed this? His thoughts turned to Paola's Aunt Federica. Brunetti knew that she had taken Paola aside, years ago, and warned her that her marriage to a man 'of his class' would be her ruination, not only personally but also, and far more importantly, socially. It was not until the birth of their second child that Paola had told him about her aunt's remark, and he had been so drunk with joy at the sight of Chiara's toes that he had said only, 'Socially?' and laughed: a Falier could marry the dustman and suffer no social consequences.

He was glad to enter the Questura if only for the warmth to be found in some parts of the building. In his office he shed his overcoat and headed back down towards Signorina Elettra's office. Unfortunately, he ran into Patta on the stairs. 'Good morning, Commissario,' he said. 'I'd like a word with you.'

'Of course, sir,' Brunetti answered, falling into step with him and giving every indication that he was a man who had been in the office for hours, was already well entrenched in his work for the day. He resisted the temptation to ask what it was that Patta wanted or to display his surprise at finding Patta at work so early and followed him into the small anteroom where Signorina Elettra and her computer held court.

She smiled at them but said good morning only to her superior before returning her attention to her computer screen. Patta went into his office; Brunetti turned at the door and looked back, but Signorina Elettra had time only to give a small shrug before he closed the door and followed Patta over to his desk. His superior removed his overcoat and laid it over the back of the second visitor's chair, careful to fold it so that Brunetti could see the Ermenegildo Zegna label. Brunetti made an attempt to look suitably impressed and waited for Patta to take his seat before sitting down himself.

'I want to talk to you about this *vu cumprà* thing,' Patta announced.

Brunetti nodded but made sure to look inattentive, as if to suggest that he had heard about the *vu cumprà* some time in the past and would not mind being reminded just what they were.

'Don't pretend you don't know what I'm talking about, Brunetti,' Patta said irritably.

Brunetti nudged his expression a little closer to intelligence and asked, 'Yes, sir?'

'As you might recall, I told you I thought it would be too complex a case for us to handle,' Patta began; Brunetti resisted the impulse to tell him that, no, he had not said that but had ordered him – without explanation – to stay away from the case. He contented himself with nodding, waiting to see what manoeuvre Patta had devised. 'I was right,' Patta said with every indication of modesty at what must to him have seemed embarrassing redundancy. 'It has ramifications far beyond Venice, and so it's been assigned to special investigators from the Ministry of the Interior, who will take over from you.' He looked at Brunetti to assess his response.

When his subordinate said nothing, Patta went on, 'They're already here and have begun their investigation. I've had all the records and documents handed over to them.' Again he stopped, but in the face of Brunetti's continuing silence was forced to resume. 'They believe the killing is related to another case they're dealing with at the moment.'

'And what case would that be, sir?' asked a respectful Brunetti.

'They are not at liberty to tell me that,' Patta answered.

'I see,' Brunetti said, his imagination spawning possibilities as quickly as a cell divides.

'I think this is a case of what the Americans call "need-to-know",' Patta said, unable to disguise his pride in having thought to use – and managed to pronounce – the foreign term. Then, as if concerned that Brunetti might not have understood, he added, 'That is, only people who are directly involved in the case will have access to the information obtained.'

Brunetti nodded, silent.

Patta paused for so long that he began to give evidence of finding the silence embarrassing. He pushed himself back in his chair and crossed his legs, trying to wait Brunetti out and force him to speak. The silence grew. Finally Patta could stand it no longer and asked, 'Do you understand?'

In a completely neutral voice, Brunetti said, 'I think I do,' and then asked, 'Will that be all, sir?'

'Yes.'

Brunetti got to his feet and left the room. As he closed the door, he glanced in Signorina Elettra's direction but left her office without speaking to her.

He went to the officers' room and walked over to Vianello, who was at his desk. 'Do you have copies of the files?' Brunetti asked.

'You mean about the African?'

'Yes.'

Vianello got up and went over to the battered filing cabinet that stood between the windows of the far wall. He pulled open the top drawer and flicked through some folders until he reached the back of the drawer, then went back to the front and looked through them again. He pushed the drawer closed and returned to his desk. He looked into the two files that lay to the right of the telephone, then opened all of the desk drawers, one by one. He looked up at Brunetti and shook his head.

Together, without bothering to speak, they went upstairs to Brunetti's office, but his own search for the files proved just as fruitless as Vianello's. 'Scarpa?' Brunetti asked.

'Probably,' Vianello agreed. 'But it's so stupid to take them. She's got them on her computer, so she can simply make more copies.'

Both of them considered this, then it occurred to Brunetti to wonder if this were indeed the case. He was reluctant to appear anywhere near Signorina Elettra so soon after having left Patta's office, and he did not want to use the internal phone to ask her about them. 'I'd like you to go down and ask her if she's still got copies,' he told Vianello.

The inspector left the office. During the time Vianello was gone, Brunetti considered the situation. He knew how easy it would be to remove a file, any file, multiple files, from the various cabinets or offices in the Questura, but he failed to understand how, or if, information could be removed from Signorina Elettra's computer. Instinct and past experience suggested that Lieutenant Scarpa was the person most likely to have been involved in the removal of the actual documents, but Patta's reference to the Ministry of the Interior meant that there was now a different level of competence to be reckoned with. To pass the case over to them would effectively end it in Venice and would enable Patta to reach safety; Scarpa, had he been the one to remove the files, would earn the gratitude of his superior. But, beyond the two of them, who gained – and what was to be gained – by suppressing the investigation of the death?

A week ago he had used false identification to buy a second *telefonino* in the name of Roberto Rossi: he had given the number to no one, not even Paola. He took it out now and dialled the number of Rizzardi's office. When the doctor answered with his name, Brunetti said only, 'It's me, Bruno. Carlo.' He paused, giving the doctor time to register the name and the warning of caution it contained. 'I wondered if by any chance you saw that report your office sent me?'

'Ah, yes, Carlo,' Rizzardi answered after the shortest of pauses, 'how nice to hear your voice. I didn't see it until this morning and I've already called once, but you weren't there. I've got a few photos of that, ah, new line in sweaters. I'm not sure you're going to like them, but I think they're something you might want to have a look at. I think we do have a few patterns you'll really want to see.' Rizzardi paused, then added, 'I thought it might be more convenient if you could stop by to pick them up yourself.'

'Ah, thanks,' Brunetti answered. 'I don't think I can do it myself today. You know how busy we always are at the beginning of a season, but I'll send one of my salesmen over to pick them up. In about half an hour, say?'

'Fine,' Rizzardi answered. 'I'll just get them ready and put them in an envelope. Tell your salesman I'll have them with me, and he can come to my office and get them.'

'I'll do that, and thanks. I look forward to seeing them.'

'Yes, I thought you would. They're very interesting. I'll put a price list in with them, shall I?'

'Yes. Thanks, Bruno.'

He thought he heard a muffled laugh, or perhaps it was nothing more than a snort of disgust from Rizzardi that they had to resort to this sort of cloak and dagger caution, but whatever it was, it was over as soon as heard, and Rizzardi put the phone down.

Knowing Vianello would wait when he came back from Elettra's office and found Brunetti's office empty, Brunetti went down to the officers' room and asked Pucetti to go over to the Ospedale Civile to pick up an envelope from Dottor Rizzardi. 'But you better go home first,' Brunetti cautioned him, 'and change out of your uniform.'

'I've got clothes in my locker, sir,' Pucetti said, getting to his feet. 'So I can go over now, soon as I've changed.'

Brunetti went back to his office, burdened by the weight of what he was forced to do. Secret phone calls, coded messages, policemen shedding their uniforms in order to do their jobs. 'We're all mad, we're all mad,' he caught himself muttering as he climbed the steps. Next thing he knew, he'd be wearing a disguise to come to work and setting up bank accounts in the Channel Islands. It helped, he realized, to expand it all to the *reductio ad absurdum*, for to consider their behaviour objectively would be to summon despair.

Vianello came in, saying as he entered, 'She said someone managed to get into her computer and destroy things.' Before Brunetti could ask, he said, 'No, not her physical computer, but into her files. She said whoever did it was very sophisticated.'

'What was destroyed?' Brunetti asked.

'The autopsy report that was attached to the email. And the original report of the crime.'

'And the other things? The addresses of Bertolli and Cuzzoni?' Brunetti asked, alarmed that whoever had destroyed the other files would have found these and known where their investigation was heading. Which, he reflected with sudden cynicism, was considerably more than he knew.

Vianello shook his head in what Brunetti interpreted as a gesture of relief. 'She said she had it all hidden, not only the addresses, but copies of the original report and the one from the pathologist – God knows where: in a folder of recipes, for all I know. She said the autopsy report and the original crime report were the only things on her computer that anyone could find.'

Brunetti had no option but to believe her and hope that she was right.

'Can she find out who did it?' he asked.

'I think that's what she's trying to do now.'

Brunetti went around his desk and sat down. 'I think the only thing to do now is to make it look like we've stopped,' he said.

'Patta will never believe it,' Vianello objected.

'If there's no sign that we're doing anything, then he'll have to believe it.'

Vianello's glance displayed his scepticism, but he said nothing.

'I called Rizzardi,' Brunetti said. 'He said he found something.'

'What?'

'He didn't say. Only that it was interesting and I ought to see it. So I sent Pucetti over.' Brunetti translated the rather childish code of his conversation with the pathologist.

'You called him from here?' Vianello asked, unable to disguise his astonishment.

Brunetti explained about Signor Rossi's *telefonino* and gave the number to Vianello.

'So this is what we're reduced to?' Vianello asked, just as Pucetti came in, wearing Doc Marten boots and a long leather coat.

Neither man commented on Pucetti's attire. The young officer placed an envelope on Brunetti's desk then stood there, looking uncertain what to do with himself. Brunetti waved him to a chair.

From the envelope Brunetti pulled out a sheet of paper folded around a few photos and one other sheet of paper, which, when opened, was revealed to be the form the police used to take a set of fingerprints. On the paper around the photos he recognized Rizzardi's handwriting.

'When I got to the operating theatre, I was told the autopsy had already been performed, but the report was not available. So I took some photos of the dead man's body: my comments on the back of each. The fingerprints on the enclosed form are his: I took them. I suggest you compare them with the ones taken during the autopsy to see if they are the same.'

A thick horizontal line served as signature. And below this was written, 'Dottor Venturi did the autopsy.'

Brunetti took the photos and dealt them out in a row on his desk. In the first of them, Brunetti recognized the man's face, eyes closed, features relaxed in what, to those who have not seen the faces of the dead, appeared to be sleep.

The next photo took a moment to interpret, for initially it looked like two speckled sculptures wearing oddly symmetrical head-dresses. As Brunetti looked, the image revealed itself as the soles of the dead man's feet, the head-dresses his toes. He bent nearer to examine the speckles, each of them circular and about the size of the tip of his finger and all of them pink in contrast to the pale soles of the man's feet. He turned the photo over and read, 'These are cigarette burns. They are fully healed, but my guess is that they are not much older than a year or two.' Brunetti flipped the photo back; knowing now, they all saw it.

The next was of the inside of the man's right thigh, where the same circular pattern ran from the knee to the point where the leg joined the trunk. There might have been twenty of them. '*Oddio*,' Pucetti whispered in horror at the terrible vulnerability revealed by the photo.

The next photo was a mirror image, this time of the inside of the left thigh. The three men stood in a silent line in front of the photos, each reluctant to speak.

The last photo showed what appeared to be another scar; the neat hole beneath it placed it at the centre of the man's stomach. Brunetti recognized the pattern: the same four triangles of the Maltese cross that was carved on the forehead of the wooden head from the man's jeans. The thin lines of the raised flesh were darker than the skin that served as smooth background to the pattern, yet the scar was utterly without menace and spoke of ritual, not pain. He turned the photo over and read, 'This scar is considerably older. Tribal scarification of some sort.'

Brunetti leaned forward and slipped the photos back into a pile. He took the fingerprint form and handed it to Pucetti, saying, 'Take this down to the lab and give it to Bocchese – but only if he's alone – and ask him to compare it to the set in the autopsy report.' He remembered the missing files and added, 'If he's still got them.'

'Do we know he was given a set of prints?' Vianello interrupted.

Brunetti, who should have checked, had not. He nodded in acknowledgement of Vianello's remark and added to Pucetti, 'Ask him. If he never received any, then ask him to see if he can get an identification.' As the young man turned away, Brunetti added, 'Discreetly.'

When Pucetti was gone, Vianello looked at the photos Brunetti still held, and asked, 'Torture?'

'Yes.'

'Why? The diamonds?'

'Yes,' Brunetti agreed, then added, 'Or whatever he was going to buy with them.'

17

Brunetti and Vianello knew that they needed to find out who the man was or at least where he came from before they could have any idea of what he was likely to have done with the money he made from the diamonds. Instinctively, they shied away from reference to the marks of torture on the man's body.

After almost twenty minutes had elapsed, Brunetti called down to the lab and asked to speak to Pucetti. 'And?' he asked when Pucetti picked up the phone.

'There was nothing to compare that sample to, sir,' Pucetti began. 'Bocchese said he was never sent anything.'

A soft 'Ah' was all Brunetti would allow himself, and then he said, 'If you've spoken to

Bocchese, you can return to your normal duties.'

'Yes, sir,' Pucetti said and hung up.

Brunetti told Vianello what Pucetti had said; the inspector echoed Brunetti's soft exclamation of surprise.

'We have to go and talk to them again,' Brunetti said without preamble, getting to his feet. Neither of them wanted to bother with the launch and thus call attention to their arrival in the neighbourhood, nor did they want there to be any possible record at the Questura of their destination. They walked quickly, unconsciously choosing the same streets and shortcuts on their way to Castello.

Brunetti let himself into the building with the keys Cuzzoni had given him. The two men paused just inside the door, listening for sounds from the apartments above. It was not yet noon, so the men were likely still to be there, waiting for the shops to close and thus signal them to set up their own transient workplaces. Together they climbed the steps and stood on either side of the door to the apartment on the first floor, silent and listening.

Nothing but silence, the sound both of them had heard outside the doors of many empty apartments but also from rooms in which waited the frightened or the dangerous. Their communication was wordless, even invisible. Brunetti moved in front of the door and slipped a key into the lock: Vianello pulled out the pistol Brunetti had not known he was carrying. He turned the key as softly as he could, but it did not move. He pulled it out, took the second pair of keys, and tried the smaller one from that set. This time he felt the key begin to move, and as he turned it, he nodded to Vianello. Brunetti turned the handle and pushed on the door; Vianello edged him aside and shoved open the door with his foot, then crouched low and moved quickly into the room.

The chaos that lay before them spoke of flight and search, but it had nothing to say of violence. The men in the apartment had decamped, done so, it seemed, suddenly and absolutely. The furniture in the living room stood upright; in the kitchen a few cooking pots and some cutlery remained, and three plates covered with some sort of red stew stood on the table. Packages of food had been removed from the cabinets and poured out on to the table amidst the plates: rice and flour overlapped in small dunes, and on the floor an empty box of tea bags sat on top of its contents.

As they moved farther back into the apartment they saw that all personal items had been removed: there was not so much as a stray sock to indicate who might once have lived here; only the camp-beds in one room indicated their number. One bed was upturned and the others shifted around, as if someone had wanted to see or retrieve what was under them. In the bathroom, a bottle of aspirin lay in the sink, its soggy contents slowly decomposing.

Abandoning any attempt at silence, they went to the apartment above, but it looked much the same as the first: all personal sign of former occupancy was gone, and what had been left behind had been roughly searched through.

After a quick look through the second apartment and without any expressed agreement to do so, they went up to the top floor. The door stood open, and here they found signs of greater wreckage, evidence of a search which the paucity of objects must have rendered short. The box of foodstuffs sat at the end of the bed, its contents spilled beside it. The peanuts and biscuits were heaped together in a small mound on the bed cover, their plastic wrappers thrown to the floor. The piece of Asiago, covered now with a thin film of white mould, lay beside the box.

'Have you got an evidence bag with you?' Brunetti asked.

'No. Maybe my handkerchief?' Vianello asked and pulled it from the side pocket of his overcoat. He spread it open on the bed and bent over to pick up the plastic wrappers, careful to lift them at the corners by the tips of his fingers. When they were wrapped in the handkerchief, Vianello pulled a plastic shopping bag from his other pocket. Yellow, it blared BILLA in red letters that would have been visible a block away; Vianello slipped the handkerchief inside.

'Bocchese?' he asked.

Brunetti nodded. 'Results to me. Privately.'

'Worth taking anything from downstairs?' Vianello asked.

'Maybe the rice and flour packages,' Brunetti suggested.

When they had done that, they left the house, having carefully locked all the doors behind them and automatically starting a conversation about the weekend's soccer results as they went out into the *calle*. A man who was walking by glanced at them, but hearing Vianello say 'Inter' gave them no further attention and turned into the bar on the corner.

By the time they got back to the Questura, they had decided how they would proceed. Vianello went down the corridor to the lab and Bocchese, and Brunetti went up to his office to phone a colleague at the San Marco sub-station, where the arrest records of the *vu cumprà* were kept, and asked if he could go over to talk to him.

Moretti, a short man with retreating hair, was waiting for him in his office. In all the years they had worked together, Brunetti had never seen him out of uniform or, for that matter, beyond the confines of this building. The desk was as Brunetti remembered it: a phone, a single open file in front of the seated sergeant, and to his left an ornate frame containing a photo of Moretti's wife, who had died three years before.

The two men shook hands and spoke of unimportant things for a moment. Brunetti declined the offer of coffee, agreed that it was indeed very cold, and then told Moretti he needed information about the *vu cumprà*.

Deadpan, giving no indication of how he viewed the issue, Moretti said, 'We've been told to refer to them as *ambulanti*.'

With equal impassivity, Brunetti said, 'About the *ambulanti*, then.'

'What would you like to know?' Moretti asked.

Brunetti took a photo from the inside pocket of his jacket and leaned forward to place it in front of Moretti. 'This is the man who was shot the other night. Do you recognize him, or do you remember ever arresting him?'

Moretti slid the photo closer and looked at it, then picked it up and angled it a bit so that more light fell on the man's features. 'I've seen him, yes,' he said, his voice pulling out the syllables. 'But I don't know that we ever arrested him.'

'Could you have seen him on the street, then?' Brunetti inquired.

'No.' Moretti's answer was so quick Brunetti was startled by it. Seeing that, Moretti explained. 'I try never to go to the places where they are. It bothers me to see them and not be able to do anything about it.'

'What do you mean, not do anything about it?' Brunetti asked, honestly puzzled.

'I can't arrest them by myself, when I'm not in uniform, and when I have no order to do so. It bothers me to see them there, breaking the law, so I avoid them if I can.' Brunetti heard the anger in the other man's voice but chose to ignore it. He waited to see if Moretti would remember where he had seen the dead man. He watched the uniformed man study the photo, watched as his eyes moved off to the middle distance, then back to the photo.

Moretti got to his feet. 'Wait here a couple of minutes, and I'll see if anyone else recognizes him.' When he got to the door, he turned and said, 'Sure you don't want a coffee, Commissario?'

'Thanks, Moretti, but no.' And the sergeant disappeared, leaving Brunetti to wait. In order to pass the time, Brunetti got to his feet and went over to the noticeboard next to the door and read the various Ministry bulletins pinned there. Opening for a job in Messina – as if anyone in their right mind would want to go there. Description of the proper way to wear the new bulletproof vests: Brunetti wondered if there could be more than one way to wear them. Duty roster for the coming Christmas holiday, which reminded him of his date with Paola at four.

He went back to his chair, curious as to what could be taking Moretti so long. He had seen only three officers downstairs when he came in: how long could it take them to look at a photo? He took out his notebook and found a blank page. At the top, he wrote 'Christmas Gifts', carefully underlined both words, and then, in small letters to the left, wrote, in a neat column, 'Paola', 'Raffi', and 'Chiara'. Then he stopped, unable to think of anything else to write.

He was still staring at the names when Moretti came back into the office and sat at his desk. He held the photo out to Brunetti and shook his head. 'No one recognizes him.'

Brunetti refused the photo with an upraised hand and said, 'Keep it. I have more in my office. I'd like you to ask anyone who's had anything to do with the *ambulanti* if they recognize him.' Moretti nodded and Brunetti, remembering the years they had worked together amicably, said, 'And I'd like you to talk only to me about this, not to anyone else.' A glance showed him that Moretti, however curious about the reason for the remark, understood its meaning.

'For whatever it's worth,' Moretti volunteered, 'we've had no encouragement to look into his murder.'

'And won't have,' Brunetti said shortly.

'Ah,' was the only comment Moretti permitted himself for a moment, and then added, 'I'm up for retirement in two years, so I have less and less patience with being told which crimes I can and cannot investigate.' He picked up the photo and looked at it again. 'I know I've seen this face somewhere . . . All I've got is a vague memory, and somehow it seems that it didn't have anything to do with this,' he said, waving the photo in a half-circle to indicate the police station.

'What do you mean?' Brunetti asked.

Moretti turned the photo to display the face to Brunetti. 'Seeing him like this, with his eyes closed and knowing that he was murdered, I'm sorry for him. He's young and he's a victim. And the last time I saw him, he was a victim too, or

218

that's the way the memory feels to me. But it was because of work I saw him; I'm sure of that.' He set the photo, face down, on the desk, looked at Brunetti and said, 'If it comes to me, or if anyone recognizes him, I'll call you.'

'Good. Thanks,' Brunetti said and got to his feet. The men shook hands and Brunetti went down the stairs and out into the Piazza.

Had he not had this mildly encouraging conversation with Moretti, Brunetti might have seen himself as a man abandoned by his wife at lunchtime, then might have added that her behaviour was even more heartless given the Christmas season. But Moretti had recognized the man, or thought he recognized him, and so Brunetti could not give himself over whole-heartedly to playing the role of the neglected spouse. He could, however, treat himself to a good lunch. Aunt Federica, apart from her temper, was known for the skill of her cook, so Paola was sure to arrive at their meeting sated not only with the latest family gossip but with the results of the recipes the Faliers had spent the last four centuries enjoying.

He took the public gondola beside the Gritti and arrived at the other side chilled to the bone and much in need of sustenance. This he found at Cantinone Storico in the form of a risotto with tiny shrimp which the waiter promised him were fresh and a grilled orata served with boiled potatoes. Asked if he'd like dessert, Brunetti thought of the heavy eating that lay ahead of him in the next weeks and, feeling quite pleased

219

with himself, said all he wanted was a grappa and a coffee.

He finished just a little after three and so decided to walk to Campo San Bortolo. As he reached the crest of the Accademia bridge, he looked down into the *campo* on the other side and was surprised to find no sign of the *vu cumprà*. That morning's *Gazzettino* had warned him how little time there remained for Christmas shopping. This made it all the stranger that the black men were not at their usual places. Like sharks in a feeding frenzy, most of the people of Italy – he among them – always seemed to use these last days to buy their gifts. If it was the busiest times for the shops, then it had to be the busiest time for the *ambulanti*, and yet there was no sign of them.

When he turned right at the church and started into Campo Santo Stefano, he did see some sheets on the ground. At first he thought they must be the forgotten groundsheets of the crime scene, but then he saw the line of wind-up toys and linked wooden train carriages, carved to look like individual letters, spelling names across the sheet. The men stationed behind the sheets were not Africans but Orientals and Tamils, and off to the left he saw a band of poncho-draped Indios and their strange musical instruments. But as for Africans, the more Brunetti looked, the more they were not there.

He walked past the various vendors but resisted the idea of speaking to any of them. Innocent curiosity about the Africans would make no sense, and police questions could provoke flight. As he studied the men and the segregation of their products, he noticed that all of the items had been mass produced, and that caused him to wonder who decided which group would sell which things. And who supplied them? Or determined the prices? And who housed them? And who got them residence and work permits, if they had such things? If the black men from Castello had disappeared, they must have gone somewhere, but where? And as a result of whose decision and with whose help?

Pondering all of these questions and again amazed that this subterranean world could exist in the city where he lived, he continued down Calle della Mandola, through Campo San Luca, and into San Bortolo.

Paola was, as she had promised, waiting for him, right where she had waited for him for decades: beneath the statue of a perpetually dapper Goldoni. He kissed her and wrapped his right arm around her shoulder. 'Tell me you ate badly and I'll get you any Christmas present you want,' he said.

'We ate gloriously well, and there's nothing I want,' Paola answered. When he failed to respond, she went on, 'Fettucine with truffles.'

'White or black?' he asked.

To goad him, she asked, 'The truffles or the fettucine?'

He ignored the question and asked, 'And what else?'

'*Stinco di maiale* with roast potatoes and a zucchini gratin.'

'If I hadn't gone to Cantinone, I'd probably have to divorce you.'

'And who would help with the Christmas shopping, then?' she asked. Into his silence, she said, as if by way of consolation, 'I didn't have dessert.'

'Good, me neither. So we can stop on the way home.'

She grabbed his arm and squeezed it and said, 'Where do we start?'

'Chiara, I think,' Brunetti answered. 'I have no idea. None at all.'

'We could get her a *telefonino*,' she suggested.

'And thus undo two years of resistance at a single stroke?' he asked.

'All her friends have them,' Paola said, sounding just like Chiara.

'You sound just like Chiara,' said Brunetti in dismissal. 'Clothes?'

'No, she's got too many already.'

Brunetti stopped in his tracks, turned to her, and said, 'I think that is the first time in my life, perhaps in recorded history, that a woman has admitted the concept of too much clothing might exist.'

'Over-reaction to the truffles,' she suggested.

'Perhaps.'

'I'll get over it.'

'Doubtless.'

Telefonino and clothes excluded, Paola suggested books, so they went down towards San

Luca, in the general area of which there were three bookstores. In the first they found nothing that Paola thought Chiara would like, but in the second she bought a complete set of the novels of Jane Austen, in English.

'But you have those,' Brunetti said.

'Everyone should have them,' Paola said. 'If I thought you'd read them, I'd get you a set, too.'

He started to protest that he had read them once, when Paola's attention swung away from him and riveted itself to the far wall. He turned, following the direction of her gaze, but all he saw was an enormous poster of a young man who looked vaguely familiar; perhaps, he found himself thinking, this was the way the black man was familiar to Moretti. So intently did Paola stare that Brunetti finally waved his hand in front of her face and said, 'Earth to Paola, Earth to Paola, can you hear me? Come in, please.'

She looked back at him for an instant and then, her eyes returning to the poster, said, 'That's it. That's perfect.'

'What's perfect?' he asked.

'The poster. She'll love it.'

'The poster?' he repeated.

'Yes.' Before he could ask who the boy was, Paola grew serious and said, 'Guido, there's something I've been meaning to tell you.'

He imagined the worst: Chiara running off to follow a rock group, joining some sort of sect. 'What?'

'Chiara is in love with the future heir to the

British throne,' she said, pointing at the poster.

'An Englishman?' Brunetti asked, shocked, remembering everything he'd ever heard about them: Battenberg, Windsor, Hanover, whatever they called themselves. 'With someone from that family?' he asked.

'Would you rather have her be in love with one of the male issue of our own dear Savoia family?' she asked sweetly.

Brunetti was too stunned to speak. He started to answer her, recalled everything he had ever heard about that family, and pursed his lips. Easily, brightly, surprising not a few people in the bookstore, Brunetti began to whistle 'Rule, Britannia!'

18

The bookseller suggested they buy a heavy cardboard tube for the poster, which turned out to be a good idea, so thick was the press of people on the streets. Three or four times, bodies bumped into Brunetti with such force that an unprotected print would surely have been crushed. After the third time, Brunetti toyed with the idea of holding the cylinder at one end and using it as a club to beat their way through the crowds, but his awareness of how much at variance this would be with the Christmas spirit, to make no mention of his position as an officer of the law, prevented him from acting on that thought.

After three hours, two coffees, and one pastry, both Brunetti's mind and his wallet were empty.

He subsequently remembered going into a CD store and marvelling as Paola reeled off a list of outlandish names, then watching, hypnotized by the colours and designs on the covers, as the clerk wrapped two separate stacks of discs. He chose a sweater for Raffi, exactly the colour of one of his that his son had taken to borrowing, and refused to listen to Paola's protest that cashmere was wasted on Raffi. His long-term plan included a casual switch of sweaters after a month or two. In a computer store, she bought two games with equally garish covers and, he was certain, equally garish contents.

After that, Paola agreed that she had had enough and turned towards home. As they were coming back towards San Bortolo and the bridge, Brunetti stopped in front of a jewellery store and studied the rings and necklaces in the window. Paola stood silent beside him.

Just as he started to speak, she said, 'Don't even think about it, Guido.'

'I'd like to give you something nice.'

'Those things are expensive. That doesn't make them nice.'

'Don't you like jewellery?'

'You know I do, but not like that, with enormous stones looking as if they've been tor-tured into place.' She pointed to a particularly infelicitous combination of minerals and said, 'It looks like something Hobbes would give to one of his wives.' When Paola had first used this name to refer to the current head of government, Brunetti's puzzled look had forced her to explain that she had chosen the name because of the English philosopher Hobbes's description of human life: 'Nasty, brutish, and short'. Brunetti had been so taken with its appropriateness that he now substituted the name, not only when reading newspaper headlines, but also in ministerial documents.

He realized that he was going to get no help from Paola in selecting her own gift, so he abandoned the attempt and went home with her to try to find a place to hide their haul from their prying children. The only thing he could think of was to put them all at the bottom of their wardrobe, but not before attaching to them carefully printed cards bearing Paola's name, her mother's, and her father's. He hoped thus to deflect the children's sorties. The thought of hiding things took his mind back to the box of salt and its strange contents.

It was too soon to call Claudio, but he did call Vianello at home, careful to use the *telefonino* registered to Roberto Rossi. Telling himself that he was a commissario of police, he refused to disguise his voice or speak in tongues, but he did confine himself to asking, when Vianello answered, 'Anything new?'

'Nothing,' came Vianello's laconic reply.

Brunetti broke the connection.

Dinner was peaceful, Raffi artlessly attempting to get his parents to say what they would like for Christmas, and Chiara asking if Muslims had Christmas, too. Paola explained that, because Muslims considered Jesus a great prophet, they probably respected the holiday, even if they didn't celebrate it officially.

When Brunetti asked why she wanted to know, Chiara answered, 'I have a new friend at school, Azir. She's Muslim.'

'Where's she from?' Brunetti asked.

'Iran. Her father's a doctor, but he isn't working.'

'Why is that?' Brunetti asked.

Helping herself to more pasta, Chiara said, 'Oh, something to do with papers. They haven't come or something, so he's working in the lab at the hospital, I think.'

'I was there once,' Brunetti surprised the children by saying. 'In Tehran. After the Revolution.'

'What for?' Chiara asked, instantly curious.

'Work,' Brunetti answered. 'Drugs.'

'And?' Raffi interrupted. 'What happened?'

'They were very helpful and polite and gave me the information I needed.' The faces which greeted this remark reminded him of a line Paola often quoted, something about sheep looking up but not being fed, so he explained, 'It was when I was working in Naples. There was someone who was bringing in drugs on trucks from Iran, and they agreed to help us arrest him.' He did not tell them that this had happened only after it was discovered that a great deal of the man's merchandise was finding its way on to the streets of Tehran, as well.

'What were they like?' Chiara asked, interested enough to stop eating.

'As I said, polite and helpful. The city was a mess, very overcrowded and polluted, but once you get behind the walls – one of the officers invited me to his home – you find lots of gardens and trees.'

'What are the people like?' Chiara asked.

'Very sophisticated and cultured, at least the ones I dealt with.'

'They've had three thousand years to become cultured,' Paola interrupted.

'What do you mean?' Chiara asked.

'That when we were still living in huts and wearing animal skins, they were building Persepolis and wearing silk.'

Ignorant of the patent exaggeration of this remark, Chiara asked only, 'What's Persepolis?'

'It's the royal city where the kings lived. Until a European burned it down. I've got a book and I'll show you after dinner, all right?' Paola asked. Then, to all of them, 'Dessert?'

Like Persepolis itself, interest in thousands of years of history fell to ruin, this time in the face of apple cake.

The next morning Brunetti's phone was ringing as he walked into his office. He answered with his name while struggling to remove his coat, the receiver pressed between ear and shoulder as he tried to pull his arms from the sleeves.

'It's me,' a man's voice said, and it took Brunetti a second to realize it was Claudio. 'I have to see you.' In the background, Brunetti heard the loud roar of what sounded like a boat's motor, so Claudio was out in the city, somewhere near the water.

Brunetti pulled his coat back on to his shoulders, took the phone with his free hand, and said, responding to the note of urgency in the old man's voice, 'I can come over right now if you want to meet at your office.' Brunetti was already plotting the course to Claudio's, deciding to have himself taken there in a launch.

'No, I think it would be better if we met at . . . at that place where your father and I always went for a drink.'

Doubly alarmed now by Claudio's use of these guarded directions, Brunetti said, 'I can be there in five minutes.'

'Good, I'll be there,' Claudio said and ended the call.

Brunetti remembered the bar, on a corner facing the pillared gates of the Arsenale: Claudio must be out on the Riva degli Schiavoni to be able to reach it in five minutes. Many times in his youth, he had sat there, listening to his father's friends talk about the war as they played endless, inconsequential games of *scopa*, sipping at small glasses of a wine so tannic it left their teeth almost blue. His father had never said much, nor had he been interested in playing cards, but he was there as a veteran and as Claudio's friend, and that had sufficed for the others.

As soon as he hung up, the phone rang again, and, thinking it might be Claudio calling back, Brunetti picked it up and held it to his ear.

'Brunetti,' barked Vice-Questore Patta. 'I want to talk to you now.' His tone matched his words, and they no doubt matched his mood. Silently, Brunetti replaced the receiver and turned to leave the office. By the time he had reached the door, the phone was already ringing again.

Brunetti barely noticed the lions when he reached the entrance to the Arsenale and walked directly into the bar, looking for the familiar face. When he saw no sign of Claudio, he checked his watch and found that it had been only six minutes since he left the Questura. He ordered a coffee and turned to face the door. After another five minutes, he saw the old man at a distance, walking with the aid of a stick, coming down the bridge that led to the Arsenale.

At the bottom of the bridge, Claudio went over and stood in front of the stone lions, studying them slowly, pausing in front of each one until he could have committed its face and form to memory. After that, he strolled back to the bottom of the bridge and looked left through the gates of the Arsenale and out towards the *laguna*. Then he turned and ambled alongside the canal in the direction of the *bacino*. To an idle spectator, the man with the cane could be a sightseer interested in the area around the Arsenale; to a policeman, he was someone checking to see if he was being followed.

Claudio turned around and came towards the bar. When he entered, Brunetti left it to him to make the first move. He came and stood next to Brunetti at the bar but gave him no greeting. When the barman approached, Claudio asked for a tea with lemon, then reached aside and pulled that day's *Gazzettino* towards him. Brunetti asked for another coffee. Claudio kept his eyes on the paper until his tea arrived, when he laid the newspaper aside, looked out the window at the empty *campo*, then at Brunetti, and said, 'I was followed yesterday afternoon.'

Brunetti spooned sugar into his coffee, and inclined his head in Claudio's direction.

'There was only one man, and it was easy to lose him. Well, I think I lost him.'

'How far did he follow you?'

'To the train station. I waited for the 82, and when it came it was crowded the way it always is. So I waited inside the *imbarcadero* until the sailor was sliding the gates closed, and then I pushed ahead and started shouting that, with all the tourists, there's no room for Venetians.' He looked at Brunetti and gave a sly smile. 'So he pulled the gate back and let me on. Only me.'

'*Complimenti*,' Brunetti said, making a note to use the tactic, should it ever be necessary.

Claudio took some artificial sweetener and poured it into his tea, stirred it round, and said, 'I spoke to a few people yesterday and sent some stones to someone I know in Antwerp.' He took a sip of tea, set his cup down, and added, 'And I took a few to show to a colleague here. It was when I was leaving his shop that I noticed this man.'

'How much did you tell these people?' Brunetti asked, wondering which one of them might have been the weak link.

'Let me finish,' Claudio said and took a sip of his tea. 'I asked someone I know in Vicenza if he had been offered any African diamonds recently. He doesn't have a shop and works the way I do, but he's the most important dealer in the North.'

When it seemed that the older man was finished, Brunetti asked, uncertain if he could inquire as to the reliability of his friends, 'Is he someone that many people know about?'

'That he buys and sells? Yes, most of the people in the North know him. He'd be the logical choice for anyone who wanted to sell a lot of stones, well, for anyone who knew anything about the market.'

'And?'

'And nothing,' Claudio said. 'No one has approached him with diamonds like these.'

Brunetti knew better than to question this. 'Where are the stones?' he finally asked.

'The ones you gave me?'

'Yes.'

'In a safe place.'

'Don't be clever, please, Claudio. Where are they?'

'In the bank.'

'Bank?'

'Yes. Ever since . . . ever since then, I've kept my best stones in a safety deposit box in the bank. I put yours there, too.'

'They aren't mine,' Brunetti corrected him.

'They're yours far more than they're mine.'

Brunetti realized there was little to be gained by arguing back and forth about this, so he asked, 'If you think no one would talk, why should anyone follow you?'

'I was awake thinking about it most of the night,' Claudio answered. 'Either the place where you got them was being watched, and you were followed until you came to see me, though I think you would have noticed had you been followed, so we can exclude that. Or the fact that I'm the best-known dealer in the city makes me an obvious person to keep an eye on, just as security. Or my friend's phone is being tapped.' He closed his eyes for a moment, then opened them and added, 'Or I'm a foolish old man who can't learn to distrust his friends. Take your pick.'

Like Claudio, he excluded the first. His love for the old man made him want to discount the last and choose one of the others, but he thought they were in fact equally likely. 'Did you learn anything about the stones?'

'I showed five stones to my friend – two of yours and three that I know are from Canada. At first he said only that he'd like to buy them.' The old man paused and then added, 'I suppose that's what I thought he'd do.' He shot a glance at Brunetti, then out of the window, then back to Brunetti. 'But when I told him they weren't for sale and I only wanted to know where he thought they came from, he said three of them were Canadian and two African. The right two.'

'Is he certain?' Brunetti asked.

Claudio gave him a long, speculative glance, as if deciding how best to explain. 'More certain than I am,' Claudio said, 'because he knows more.' When Claudio saw that Brunetti was not going to be persuaded by this appeal to authority, the old man went on, 'He didn't explain why he thought that about those specific stones. I'd be a liar if I told you he did, Guido, but he knows about these things. Other people can do it, but they need to use machines. I know you like information and facts, so I can tell you that at the chemical level, the machines measure the other minerals that are trapped along with the carbon crystals. They differ from pipe to pipe – what you'd call mine to mine. If you know enough about which minerals come from which place, then the machines let you identify stones by measuring the different colours.' Claudio paused, then added, 'But it's really a question of feeling. If you've looked at millions of stones, you just know.' He smiled and said, 'That's the way it is with this man. He just knows.'

'Do you believe him?'

'If he said they came from Mars, I'd believe him. He's the best.'

'Better than you?'

'Better than anyone, Guido; he has the gift.'

'Just Africa? Can he be more specific than that?'

'I didn't ask. All I asked him to do was to give me an estimate of their value so I could be sure the price I was asking was right. He told me he thought that they were African just as a passing comment, to show me how much more he knows about stones than I do.'

'And the value?' Brunetti asked.

'If cut well, he said the minimum would be thirty-five thousand Euros.' Seeing Brunetti's surprise, Claudio added, 'That's for each stone, Guido, and I didn't give him the best ones.'

Brunetti remembered then what he had failed so far to ask. 'How many were there altogether, after the salt was gone?'

'One hundred and sixty-four, all of them gem quality and all about the same size.' Then, before Brunetti could work it out, Claudio said, 'If you use it as an average price, that's just under six million Euros.'

The value of the stones astonished Brunetti, but it was what Claudio told him about being followed that most concerned him. 'Tell me what the man looked like,' he said.

'About as tall as you, wearing an overcoat and a hat. He could have been any one of a thousand men. And before you ask, no, I wouldn't recognize him if I saw him again. I didn't want him to know that I saw him, so once I noticed him I ignored him.' Claudio picked up his cup and took a small sip of tea.

Allowing hope to enter his voice, Brunetti asked, 'Then he might not have been following you?'

Claudio set his cup down and fixed Brunetti with a firm expression. 'He was following me, Guido. And he was very good.'

Brunetti decided not to ask how Claudio had learned to distinguish in this matter, and asked, instead, 'The men you spoke to, can you trust them?'

Claudio shrugged. 'In this business you can, and you can't, trust people.'

'Not to talk about the stones?'

Again, Claudio gave a casual shrug. 'I doubt they'd say anything unless they were asked.'

'And if they were?'

'Who knows?'

'Are they friends?' Brunetti asked.

'People who deal in diamonds don't have any friends,' Claudio answered.

'The man in Antwerp?' Brunetti asked.

'He's married to my niece.'

'Does that mean he's a friend?'

Claudio allowed himself a small smile. 'Hardly. But it does mean I can trust him.'

'And?'

'And I asked him to tell me where the stones come from, if he can.'

'When can you expect to hear from him?'

'Today.'

Brunetti could not hide his surprise. 'How did you send them?'

'Oh,' Claudio said with studied casualness, 'I have a nephew who does odd jobs for me.'

'Odd jobs like carrying diamonds to Antwerp?'

'It wouldn't be the first time,' Claudio insisted.

'How did he go?'

'On a plane. How else would you go to Antwerp? Well,' he temporized, 'on a plane to Brussels, and then by train.'

'You can't do this, Claudio.'

'I thought you were in a hurry,' the old man said, sounding almost offended.

'I am, but you can't do that for me. You have to let me pay you.'

Claudio waved this away almost angrily. 'It's good for him to travel, see how things are done there.' He looked at Brunetti with sudden affection. 'Besides you're a friend.'

'I thought you said people who deal in diamonds don't have friends,' Brunetti said, but he said it with a smile.

Claudio reached over and picked a loose thread from the seam of Brunetti's overcoat, pulled it away, and let it fall to the floor. 'Don't play the fool with me, Guido,' he said and reached for his wallet to pay for the drinks.

19

When they were ready to leave the bar, Brunetti had to fight the impulse to offer to accompany Claudio to his home. Good sense, however, intervened and made him accept that he was the one person Claudio should not be seen with, so he let the old man leave first and then spent five minutes looking at the pages of the *Gazzettino* before he himself left, consciously choosing to go back to the Questura, not because he particularly wanted to, but because Claudio had gone in the other direction.

The officer at the door saluted when he saw Brunetti and said, 'Vice-Questore Patta wants to see you, sir.'

Brunetti gestured his thanks with a wave of his hand and started up the steps. He went to his office, took off his coat, and dialled Signorina Elettra's extension. When she answered, Brunetti asked, 'What does he want?'

'Oh, Riccardo,' she said, recognizing his voice, 'I'm so glad you called back. Could you come to dinner on Thursday, instead of Tuesday? I forgot I have tickets for a concert, so I'd like to change the day, if that's possible.' Aside, he heard her say, 'One moment, please, Vice-Questore,' then she came back to him. 'Eight on Thursday, Riccardo? Fine.' Then she was gone.

Tempting as the thought was, Brunetti refused to believe that she was suggesting he leave the Questura and not return until Thursday evening, so he went back downstairs and into Signorina Elettra's office. He noticed that Patta's door was ajar, so he said as he went in, 'Good morning, Signorina. I'd like to speak to the Vice-Questore if he's free.'

She rose to her feet, went over to Patta's door, pushed it fully open, and went inside. He heard her say, 'Commissario Brunetti would like a word with you, sir.' She came out a moment later and said, 'He's free, Commissario.'

'Thank you, Signorina,' he said politely and went through the open door.

'Close it,' Patta said by way of greeting.

Brunetti did so and, uninvited, sat in one of the wooden chairs in front of Patta's desk.

'Why did you hang up on me?' Patta demanded.

Brunetti pulled his eyebrows together and gave evidence of thought. 'When, sir?'

Tiredly, Patta said, 'Entertaining as you might find it, I can't play this game with you this morning, Commissario.' Instinct warned Brunetti to say nothing, and Patta went on. 'It's this black man. I want to know what you've done.'

'Less than I want to do, sir,' Brunetti said, a remark that was both the truth and a lie.

'Do you think you could be more specific?' Patta asked.

'I've spoken to some of the men who worked with him,' Brunetti began, thinking it best to skate over the details of this meeting and the methods used to bring it about, 'and they refused to give me any information about him. I no longer know how to get in touch with them.' He thought he would suggest he believed that Patta took some interest in what was going on in the city and so said, 'You've probably noticed that they are no longer here.'

'Who, the *vu cumprà*?' Patta asked with no genuflection to politeness of phrase.

'Yes. They've disappeared from Campo Santo Stefano,' Brunetti said, making no reference to the absence of at least some of them from their homes. He had no way of knowing if it was true or not, but still he said, 'They seem to have disappeared from the city.'

'Where have they gone?' Patta asked.

'I have no idea, sir,' Brunetti admitted.

'What else have you done?'

Putting on his best voice, Brunetti lied. 'That's all I've been able to do. There was no useful information in the autopsy report.' That was certainly true enough: Rizzardi's report on the signs of torture had come after the official one, and by the time it arrived, the original report – Brunetti's thoughts turned to a phrase he had adopted from Spanish colleagues – had been disappeared. 'Everything that happened suggests that he was a Senegalese who somehow angered the wrong people and didn't have enough sense to leave the city.'

'I hope this information has been passed on to the investigators from the Ministry of the Interior,' Patta said.

Tired of lying but also aware that any more passivity would only feed Patta's suspicions, Brunetti said, 'I hardly thought that necessary, sir. They seemed quite able to get to it without my help.'

'It's their job, Brunetti. If I might remind you,' Patta said.

This was too much for Brunetti, and he shot back, 'It's my job, too.'

Patta's face flushed suddenly red, and he pointed an angry finger at Brunetti. 'Your job is to do what you're told to do and not to question your superiors' decisions.' He slapped his hand on the top of his desk for emphasis.

The sound reverberated in the office, and Patta waited for silence before he spoke again, though something in Brunetti's manner made him hesitate a second before he said, 'Does it ever occur to you that I might know more about what's really going on than you do?'

Given Patta's apparent lack of familiarity

with most of the staff at the Questura and what they did, Brunetti's first impulse was to laugh the question to scorn, but then he thought that Patta might be speaking of the powers behind the Questura, indeed, the powers behind the Ministry of the Interior, in which case he might well be right.

'Of course that's occurred to me,' Brunetti said. 'But I don't see what difference it makes.'

'It makes the difference that I know when certain cases are more in the province of other agencies,' Patta said in an entirely reasonable voice, as though he and Brunetti were old schoolfriends chatting amiably about the state of the world.

'That doesn't mean they should be allowed to have them.'

'Do you think you're a better judge of when we should and should not handle things?' Patta asked, the familiar scorn slipping back into his voice.

It was on the tip of Brunetti's tongue to say that no one should decide when the investigation of a man's murder was to be buried in sand, but this would make it clear to Patta that he had no intention of abandoning the case. He contented himself with the lie and answered with a cranky, 'No.' He put as much pained resignation as he could muster into his voice and added, 'I can't decide that.' Let Patta make of it what he would.

'I'll take that to mean you're now willing to behave reasonably in this, Brunetti, shall I?'

Patta asked, his voice giving no indication of either satisfaction or triumph.

'Yes,' Brunetti said. 'If the Ministry is going to take this over, should I continue with the university?' he asked, referring to the newly opened investigation of the Facoltà di Scienze Giuridiche, where some of the professors and assistant professors of the history of law were suspected of selling advance copies of the final exams to students.

'Yes,' Patta said, and Brunetti waited for the corollary, as certain to follow as the final section of a da capo aria. 'I'd like it to be handled discreetly,' Patta satisfied him by adding. 'Those fools at the university in Rome have a major scandal on their hands, and the Rector would like to avoid something similar here, if possible. It can only damage the reputation of the university.'

'Yes, sir,' Brunetti said and, to Patta's apparent surprise, got to his feet and left the office. His wife had taught at the university for almost two decades, so Brunetti had a pretty fair idea of how much reputation the university had to save.

Signorina Elettra was not at her desk, but she was outside in the corridor leading to the stairs. 'You had a call from Don Alvise,' she said.

'You know him?' Brunetti asked, surprised to realize she might.

'Yes, for a number of years. He sometimes asks me for information.'

Helpless to resist, Brunetti asked, 'What sort of information?'

'Nothing to do with the police, sir, or with what I do here; I can assure you of that.' And that was all she said.

'You spoke to him?'

'Yes.'

'What did he say?'

'That he spoke to a number of people, and some of them said the man you asked about was a good man, and some of them said he was bad.' Brunetti felt a sudden jolt of anger: the Cumaean Sibyl could do better than that, for God's sake.

He waited a moment for his anger to pass and asked, 'Didn't he express an opinion?'

'No,' she answered.

'Did he know him?' Brunetti asked, almost demanded.

'You'd have to ask him that, sir.'

Brunetti let his gaze wander off beyond her, to a photograph of a former Questore. 'Anything else?' he finally asked.

'I spent some time following the tracks of the person or persons who broke into my computer,' she said. 'The tracks lead back to Rome.'

'Where in Rome?' he asked peevishly. Instantly contrite, he added, 'Well done,' and smiled. He knew she would be pleased to be able to tell him it was the Ministry of the Interior, so he asked only, 'Who was it?'

'Il Ministero degli Esteri.'

'The Foreign Ministry?' he asked, unable to disguise his surprise.

'Yes.' Then, before he could ask, she added, 'I'm sure.'

Brunetti's imagination, already halfway up the steps of the Ministry of the Interior, had to hopscotch across the city to an entirely different building, and the mental list of possibilities he had prepared had to be tossed away and a new one prepared. For more than a decade, the two ministries had vied with one another in seeing who could best ignore the problem of illegal immigration, and when some disaster at sea or incident at the border made denial temporarily difficult, they switched to mutual recrimination and then to deceit. Numbers could be adjusted, nationalities altered, and the press could always be counted on to slap a photo of a bedraggled woman and child on to the front page, whereupon popular opinion would lapse into sentimentality long enough to allow the current shipload of refugees into the country, after which people lost interest in the subject, thus permitting the ministries to return to their normal policy of willed ignorance.

But that still did not explain the interference of the Foreign Ministry – if Signorina Elettra said it was they, then so it was – in a case of such apparent insignificance. He had no idea why they should choose to concern themselves with the murder of an itinerant street pedlar, though there were certainly many reasons why they might choose to concern themselves with the murder of a man in possession of six million Euros in diamonds.

'I've already started asking questions,' she said. During recent years, Brunetti's understanding of her methods had expanded sufficiently that he no longer pictured her sitting at her desk, making phone call after phone call or, like the Little Match Girl, walking from person to person in search of aid. This understanding, however, stopped far short of a firm grasp of the arcana of her contacts and of the skill with which she pilfered from the supposedly secret files of both government and private agencies. Not only government ministries were capable of willed ignorance.

'And Bocchese wants to see you,' she said.

That seemed to be all she wanted to tell him, so he thanked her and went down to Bocchese's office. On the steps, he encountered Gravini, who held up a hand both in greeting and to stop Brunetti.

'They're gone, sir, the *ambulanti*,' he said, looking concerned, as if he feared Brunetti would hold him responsible for the men's disappearance. 'I spoke to my friend Muhammad, but he hasn't seen anyone from that group for days and says that their house is empty.'

'Does he have any idea of what might have happened to them?'

'No, sir. I asked him, but all he knew was that they were gone.' Gravini raised his hand again to display his disappointment and said, 'I'm sorry, sir.'

'That's all right, Gravini,' Brunetti said. Then he added, knowing that everything that was said in the Questura was repeated, 'We've been relieved of the case, so it doesn't matter any more.' He patted Gravini on the shoulder to show his good faith and continued down the stairs.

When he entered the lab, Brunetti found the technician bent over a microscope, the fingers of one hand busy adjusting a knob on the long barrel.

Bocchese, one eye pressed to the instrument, made a noise that could have been a greeting or could just as easily have been a grunt of satisfaction at whatever he saw under the lens. Brunetti walked over and had a look at the plate of the microscope, expecting to see a glass slide. Instead, he saw a dark brown rectangle, half the size of a pack of cigarettes, that appeared to be metal of some sort.

'What's that?' he asked without thinking.

Bocchese didn't answer him. Adjusting the knob, he studied the object for a few moments more, then drew back from the eyepiece, turned to Brunetti and said, 'Take a look.'

He slid down from the stool, and Brunetti took his place. He had looked at slides in the past, usually when Bocchese or Rizzardi wanted to show him some detail of human physiology or the processes that constituted its destruction.

He placed his right eye to the sculpted eyepiece and closed the other. All he saw was what appeared to be an enormous eye, but black and metallic, with a round hole in the centre as its iris. He braced his open palms on the table, blinked once, and looked again. The image still resembled an eye, with the thinnest of lines indicating the eyelashes.

He stood upright. 'What is it?'

Bocchese moved beside him and slid the metal piece from its place under the lens. 'Here, take a look,' he said, handing it to Brunetti.

The rectangle certainly had the weight of metal; on its surface Brunetti saw a sword-wielding knight mounted on a caparisoned horse no bigger than a postage stamp. The man's armour was carved in great detail, as was that of the horse. His head and face were covered by a helmet, but the horse wore only some sort of protection on its ears, and a thin line of damask material down the front of its face. It was the horse's eye, he realized, that he had seen. Without the magnification, he had to hold the plaque to the light to be able to see the tiny hole of the iris.

'What is it?' Brunetti asked again.

'I'd say it's from the studio of Moderno, which is what my friend wanted me to tell him.'

Utterly at a loss, Brunetti asked, 'What friend and why did he want you to tell him?'

'He collects these things. So do I. So whenever he's offered a really good piece, he asks me to check it for him to see that it's what the seller says it is.'

'But here?' Brunetti asked, indicating the laboratory.

'The microscope,' Bocchese said, giving it the sort of affectionate pat one might give a favourite dog. 'It's much better than the one I have at home, so I can see every detail. It helps me be certain.'

'You collect these?' Brunetti asked, holding the rectangle up close to his face, the better to examine the scene. The horse reared up, nostrils flared in fear or anger. The knight's left hand, covered in a thick mailed glove, pulled the reins tight while his right arm poised just at the farthest point of backward extension. In less than a second, both horse and man would crash forward, and God pity anything that stood before them.

Bocchese's answer was an exercise in caution. 'I've got a few.'

'It's beautiful,' Brunetti said, handing it back carefully. 'I've seen them in museums, but if you can't get close to them, then you can't really see the detail, can you?'

'No,' Bocchese agreed. 'And you miss the patina, and the feel of it.' To display that last, he held out his hand, the bronze piece cushioned in his palm, and hefted it up and down a few times. 'I'm glad you think it's beautiful.' Bocchese's expression was as warm as his voice had suddenly become.

Brunetti held his breath at the intimacy of the moment. In the years they had worked together, he had never doubted the technician's loyalty, but this was the first time Brunetti had seen him express a feeling stronger than the detached irony with which he chronically viewed human activity. 'Thank you for showing it to me,' was all Brunetti could think of to say.

'*Niente, niente*,' Bocchese said and pulled a metal box from his pocket. When he opened it,

Brunetti saw that the inside was thickly padded, top and bottom, with some sort of soft material. Bocchese slipped the plaque inside, closed the box, and slipped it into the inside pocket of his jacket.

'She told you I wanted to see you?' the technician asked.

'Yes.'

'Come and have a look,' he said. He led Brunetti over to an examining table, where a number of photographs of fingerprints lay. Bocchese picked up one, flicked through the others with his forefinger, and pulled out another. He turned them over and checked what was written on the back, and then laid them side by side.

Brunetti saw the enlarged photographs of two single fingerprints. Like all prints, they looked identical to him. But he knew better than to say this to Bocchese.

'Do you see it?' Bocchese asked.

'See what?'

'That they're identical,' Bocchese said sharply, all trace of his former affability gone.

'Yes,' Brunetti said truthfully.

'They're both from that address in Castello,' Bocchese explained.

'Tell me more,' Brunetti said.

Bocchese turned the photos over, as if to remind himself which was which, and then put them back where they had been. 'Neither of these was in the apartment when you called and had Galli go over the first time, but both were there when he went back,' he said, tapping his own finger against the photo. He pointed to the second photo, 'And this was on the package of biscuits that Vianello brought me when you went back.'

'They're identical?' Brunetti asked.

'Same print, same hand,' Bocchese said.

'Same man, then,' Brunetti said.

'Unless he's in the habit of lending it to someone else, it is,' Bocchese said.

'Where, exactly, was this one?' Brunetti asked, tapping a finger against the first print.

Bocchese flipped it over again, studied the number and abbreviated words on the back, and said, 'In the room on the top floor.'

'Where, exactly?'

'On the handle of the door, on the bottom side. It's only a partial but it's enough for me to make a match. I assume he wiped the handle off, only he didn't wipe it all around, so he left the print,' he said, again tapping at the photo.'

He pointed to the second photo. 'As I told you, this was on the bag of biscuits. They were the only clear prints I found on the things Vianello brought me. The bag had a lot of grease on it. There were other smudges and partials, but nothing I could be sure about. Just this.' He paused, then added, 'I checked Galli's report. He wiped things clean after he checked the place, so the print went on to the bag after you were there.'

'Did you send them to Interpol?' Brunetti asked.

'Ah, Interpol,' Bocchese repeated, voice filled with the despair peculiar to those forced to deal with international bureaucracies. 'For what it's worth, even those of us down here have heard the rumours about the Ministry of the Interior, so, just to be sure, I sent them to a friend of mine who works in the lab in the Ministry, and I asked him if he could perhaps deal with it privately.' He paused a moment, then said, 'I sent him those other prints – of the dead man.'

'What does that mean, "privately"?' Brunetti asked.

'Well,' Bocchese said, leaning back against the counter and folding his arms across his chest. 'If it were an official request, it would take a week or two. But this way I should hear from my friend tomorrow or the next day. And no copy will go to anyone else at the Ministry of the Interior.'

At times Brunetti asked himself why he bothered with official police channels at all, if he had to rely almost exclusively on private connections and friendships in order to do his job. He wondered if it was like this in every country or every city. 'You think there exists a place where the police are left alone to get on with their job?' he asked Bocchese.

The technician appeared to treat this as a genuine question and gave it the consideration he thought it merited. Then he said, 'Maybe, but only in places where the government wants the police really to function, regardless of who's suspected or how important they are.' He saw

Brunetti's expression, and added, with a smile, 'But I still vote Rifondazione Comunista, so I'm bound to see it that way, I suppose.'

Brunetti thanked him for his comments and the information and went back to his office, marvelling that he had, in that brief visit, learned more about Bocchese than he had in more than a decade.

20

About an hour after Brunetti got back to his office, his phone rang. He answered with his name.

'I asked that person,' Sandrini said without introduction. 'That is, I got him talking about that subject, and he said the job was given to people from Rome, who were sent up to do it.'

'What about the guns? They have metal detectors at the airports now, you know,' Brunetti said, irritated by Sandrini's attempt to speak in code and hoping to irritate him, too. Getting a gun in Venice would be no problem to men with the right connections.

'You ever hear about the train?' Sandrini asked savagely. 'It runs on metal tracks, goes back and forth between here and Rome. Goes choo choo choo.'

Ignoring his remark, Brunetti asked, 'Is that all he said, that they were from Rome?'

'What did you expect me to do, ask for their names and addresses, and maybe a confession to make things easier for you?' Sandrini shouted, all thought of code or discretion tossed aside. 'Of course that's all he said. I'm not going to ask him about it directly, not after mentioning it once. He'd smell that a kilometre away.'

Brunetti had to admit Sandrini was right: there was no way he could ask his father-in-law about the killers without calling down suspicion on himself. He might have been able to talk his way out of the time with the prostitute: after all, some Mafiosi had survived the suspicion of adultery. But none of them, at least to Brunetti's knowledge, had survived the suspicion of disloyalty.

'Thank you,' Brunetti said.

'What?' Sandrini demanded. 'I risk my life and you say "thank you".' That was followed by a number of remarks calling into question the virtue of Brunetti's mother as well as that of the Madonna, whereupon Brunetti thought it expedient to replace the receiver.

'*Roma, Roma, Roma*,' Brunetti whispered under his breath. In the past, he would have expected killers to come from farther south, but this was a multi-cultural world now, so hit-men could come from anywhere. He thought back over what Sandrini had said: they had been sent

256

up from Rome to do the job. The fact that his father-in-law knew about it certainly implied that the killers were Mafia hit-men, but it did not necessarily mean that the Mafia had ordered the killing. He wondered if there were some pleasant freemasonry among hired killers and if, even when they were not involved, they knew what their fellow killers got up to, perhaps even sat around in small groups and speculated about how much their colleagues might have been paid for various jobs. The grotesqueness of this idea did not negate its possibility.

His phone rang again, and when he answered he was surprised to find himself speaking to his wife. 'You never call me here,' he said.

'Almost never.'

'All right, almost never. What is it?'

'The university.'

'The exams?' he asked, certain that she had come upon some information about her colleagues in the Department of the Science of Law and had not been able to wait until that evening to tell him.

'Exams?' she asked, her confusion audible.

'In the Science of Law Department,' he said.

'No, no, I don't know anything about that. It's about your black man.'

Though he was tempted to object that the black man was hardly *his* black man, Brunetti asked merely, 'What about him?'

'I did what you asked: asked my friend, and he mentioned someone he used to work with who's a specialist in this sort of thing.'

'What sort of thing?' Brunetti asked.

'Fetishes. He tells me this woman is the European expert on African fetishes.' The fact that Paola made no comment on the strangeness of this discipline suggested to Brunetti that she found it a perfectly legitimate field of expertise, and that in its turn suggested that she was spending too much time among academics.

'And?'

'And I have her number in Geneva,' Paola answered, 'and you should call her and ask.'

'Geneva?' Brunetti asked.

'Afraid of speaking French?'

'About something as complicated as all of this, yes,' he said.

'Don't worry,' Paola said. 'She's Swiss.'

'And that means?'

'They speak everything,' she said, gave him the number, and hung up.

So it turned out to be with Professor Winter: she spoke some Italian, good English and German, and, it seemed, the languages of the five African regions in which she did research. To his surprise, she displayed no curiosity about why the police were asking her to help identify a dead man, only asked Brunetti to describe the object he wanted identified.

'It's a kind of pattern, made of triangles,' he said in English. 'It's on a carved wooden head, about five centimetres tall, that looks like it was broken off something, probably a statue. And on a man's body.'

'Where?' she asked.

'On his stomach.'

'And the head: is it a man or a woman?' she asked.

'A woman, I think.'

'You say you have this object?'

'Yes,' Brunetti said. 'And there are photos,' he added. 'Of the body, as well.'

He waited for her to speak, but when she remained silent, he asked, 'Is there any information you might give me, Professor, however tentative, from what I've told you?'

After a brief hesitation, she said, 'Not until I see the photos. Anything I said now would just be speculation.'

Brunetti was struck by how much she sounded like the worst of Paola's colleagues, the ones who saw information as something to be measured out and bestowed only on the deserving.

'Excuse me,' Professor Winter said, and her voice moved away from the phone as she spoke to someone in the room with her. After a moment, she returned and said, 'Can you send me the photos?'

'Yes.'

'Good,' she answered and gave him her email address, spelling it out. 'Could they be sent to me soon?' she asked.

'I'd prefer to send you the actual photos,' Brunetti said, giving no explanation. 'If you give me the university address, I can post them to you today.' He had Rizzardi's photo of the mark on the man's body, and he had already used a police Polaroid to take a photo of the head.

'Ah,' Professor Winter said. She gave him her address at the university and then added, 'Perhaps things are done differently in Switzerland.'

'Are you familiar with police work, Professor?'

'Not particularly, no,' she said neutrally. 'I've been asked a few times to identify objects or people who have been killed, based on what I know about Africa.'

'Oh, I see,' Brunetti said, then asked, 'Often?'

'Not in Switzerland, no. By Interpol,' she answered.

'Is it common, then, that Africans are killed in Europe?' he asked, as surprised as he was curious.

'Not as often as they are in Africa,' she answered coolly.

'And why are they killed, if I might ask?'

'That's for the police,' she answered. 'My part is merely to help them in their attempt to identify the dead.'

'Men?' he asked.

'Just as often women, unfortunately,' she replied.

It was evident to Brunetti that Professor Winter was tiring of his questions, and so he said, 'I'll have the photos sent as quickly as I can, Professor. I'd appreciate it if you could tell us where you think the pattern comes from.'

'Anything I can do to help,' she said politely and hung up.

He depressed the receiver, dialled the squad room, and asked if Pucetti was there. The officer who answered said Pucetti was just leaving to answer a call and set the phone down noisily. When Pucetti picked it up a few moments later, Brunetti asked him to come up to his office. While he waited for him, Brunetti addressed an envelope to Professor Winter and enclosed photos of the wooden head and of the scar on the dead man's stomach. Just before he sealed it, Brunetti decided to slip one of the photos of the man's face inside.

Pucetti knocked and came in, and when Brunetti explained what he wanted him to do, Pucetti said he was on his way to answer a call about a burglary at a pharmacy in Santa Croce, then added that there was no real hurry to get there, so he could have the boat stop at the post office on the way.

'Fabio and Carlo?' Brunetti asked.

'Who else breaks into pharmacies?' Pucetti's question was entirely rhetorical, but his anger was real. Fabio Villatico and Carlo Renda were two local drug addicts, both in the terminal stages of AIDS and who thus could not be sent to prison. During the day they begged money from tourists and at night, if their begging failed to raise the necessary cash, they broke into pharmacies and stole drugs, mixing themselves intravenous cocktails that as often contained cold and flu remedies as anything else. The results of their experiments had landed them in the Emergency Room countless times, and each time they had survived, though the doctors at the hospital had long since declared their immune systems so fragile that the first cold or bout of flu was sure to carry them off.

In the face of Pucetti's obvious disgust at the two men, Brunetti said nothing about his own awkward sympathy for them. Neither had ever held a job, neither of them appeared to have had a lucid interval in the last decade, but still neither had ever resorted to violence, not even verbal resistance to the abuse they sometimes encountered.

'Overnight express?' Pucetti asked, recalling Brunetti's attention.

'Yes. And thank you, Pucetti.'

The officer saluted and left, leaving Brunetti faintly troubled by the difference in their response to the two drug addicts. Pucetti's was the generation that was all in favour of sentiment, sharing other people's pain, voicing compassion for the downtrodden, yet Brunetti often found in them traces of a ruthlessness that chilled his spirit and made him fearful for the future. He wondered if the cheap sentimentality of television and film had sent them into some sort of emotional insulin shock and suffocated their ability to feel empathy with the unappealing victims of the mess that real life created.

Carlo was festooned with badly drawn tattoos and moved about the city with the nervous eagerness of a crab, while Fabio often stank of urine and was a stranger to reason. In all the years he had known them, Brunetti had never given them money and longed to see them removed from the streets, but passing by them filled him with a vague unease, as though he were somehow responsible for their plight.

To distract himself from thoughts of the two doomed men, Brunetti checked the internal police phone list and dialled Moretti's number.

'Ah, Commissario,' he said when Brunetti gave his name. 'I've wanted to call you all day, but we've been invaded.'

'Tourists?' Brunetti asked, intending it as a joke.

'Gypsies. There must be a gang in town: we've had nine people in here this morning, all telling the same old story: the little kids with the newspapers.'

'I thought they used that in Rome,' Brunetti said, remembering what it was like to be surrounded by a band of small children, all waving papers in front of their faces and yelling to distract the victim long enough for another one of them to grab wallet or purse.

'They do, but they use it here now, too, it seems.'

'Have you got any of them?' Brunetti asked.

'So far, three, but they're all minors or look as though they are, so all we can do is ask their names and record them. Then they make a phone call, and soon someone with the same last name comes and picks them up and takes them away.' Moretti let out a disgusted sigh and added, 'I don't even bother any more to tell them they have to send the kids to school, just like I don't bother to tell the adults we arrest that they have to leave the country within forty-eight hours. The last time I told someone that, he laughed at me, right in my face.' Another pause. 'It's a good thing I didn't hit him.'

'No sense in that, is there?' Brunetti asked neutrally.

'Of course not. But there are times when it would feel so good to be able to do it.'

'Not worth it, though, is it?'

'Of course not. But that doesn't stop me wanting to.'

Thinking it better to change the subject, Brunetti said, 'Was it about that black man? Did you remember where you saw him?'

'No, I didn't, but Cattaneo did.' Before Brunetti could ask, he continued, 'We were out on a call one night about two months ago. Late, maybe two in the morning, and some guy came out of a bar and came running after us. He said he wanted us to come back with him because there was going to be a fight. It was over near Campo Santa Margherita. But by the time we got there, there wasn't much left of the argument.'

'And he was there?' Brunetti asked.

'Yes, and I'd say it was a good thing it was stopped before it got any worse.'

'Why?'

'The other two. Both of them were twice his size. The only thing that stopped it going any further, I think, was the other people in the bar. Well, and then we walked in, and that helped quiet things down.'

'This was at two in the morning?' Brunetti asked, making no attempt to disguise his astonishment.

'Times have changed, Commissario,' Moretti said, but then qualified that by adding, 'or maybe it's only the area around Campo Santa Margherita that's changed. All those bars, the pizzerias, the music places. It's never quiet there at night any more. Some of them are open until two or three in the morning.'

Brunetti interrupted him by asking, 'And the black man?'

'There were a couple of men in the bar, standing between him and two others, the ones I'd say he'd been arguing with, keeping them apart.' Moretti considered this, then added, 'I don't think it was much of anything, really. As I said, it looked like things had quieted down before we got there: no chairs turned over, nothing broken. Just this atmosphere in the air and three other men – might have been four of them – standing between them and sort of holding them apart.'

'Did you learn what the argument was about?'

'No. One of the others – I guess I could call him one of the peacekeepers – said the men had been sitting at a table, talking, when they started to argue. He said the black guy got up and headed for the door, and the men with him went after him and tried to pull him back to the table. That's when this guy saw us walk by and came out to get us.'

'How long before you went inside?' Brunetti asked.

'Couple of minutes, I'd say.'

'You said Cattaneo remembered him?'

'Yes. I showed him the picture, and he recognized him immediately. And then I did, too, once he reminded me. It was the same guy.'

'What did you do?' Brunetti asked.

'We asked to see their papers.'

'And.'

'And he had a *permesso di soggiorno*.'

'What did it say?' Brunetti asked.

'It gave his name and place of birth,' Moretti said, and then added, 'I suppose.'

'Why only suppose?'

'Because I don't remember any of the details.' Before Brunetti could question this, Moretti said, 'I must look at a hundred of them a week, sir. I look to see that the seal is right and the photo matches the person and hasn't been tampered with, but the names are strange, and I usually don't pay attention to the country where they're from.' Then he added, 'Cattaneo can't remember, either.' Sensing Brunetti's disappointment, the sergeant said, 'All I remember is the accent.'

'What accent?'

'When this guy spoke Italian – he spoke it pretty well – he had an accent.'

'And?' Brunetti asked, then, 'He was an African, wasn't he?'

'Yes, of course, but his accent was different. I mean the *Senegalesi* all sound pretty much the same: some French, some of their own language. We all recognize the accent by now; those of us who arrest them. But this guy's was different.'

'Different how?'

'Oh, I don't know. It just sounded strange.' Moretti hesitated, as if trying to recapture the sound, but the memory was clearly beyond his reach, and all he said was, 'No, I can't describe it better than that.'

'And Cattaneo?'

'I asked. He said he wasn't even aware of it.'

Brunetti let this go and asked, 'And the other men? Were they black, too?'

'No. Italian. Both of them had *carte d'identità*,' Moretti answered.

'Do you remember anything about them?'

'No, only that they weren't Venetian.'

'Where did they come from?'

'Rome.'

21

Like most Italians, Brunetti had mixed feelings about Rome. As a city he loved it, himself a willing victim of the excess of its beauty, in no way reluctant to admit that its majesty equalled that of his own city. As a metonym, however, he viewed it with jaundiced suspicion as the source of most of what was filthy and corrupt in his country. Power resided there, power gone mad, like a ferret at the taste of blood. Even as this exaggerated abhorrence registered, his more logical self told him how mistaken it was: surely his career had revealed to him the countless honest bureaucrats and officials who worked there; and surely there were politicians who were motivated by something other than greed and personal vanity. Surely there were.

He looked at his watch, unwilling to let himself continue along this too familiar train of thought. It was long after noon, so he called Paola and said he was just leaving, would take the vaporetto, but not to wait lunch for him. She said only that of course they would wait and hung up.

When he emerged from the Questura, it had begun to rain heavily, sheets of it skidding almost horizontally across the surface of the canal in front of the building. He noticed one of the new pilots just stepping on to the deck of his launch and called out, still huddled at the entrance, 'Foa, which way are you going?'

The man turned back towards him and looked – even at this distance – guilty. This prompted Brunetti to add, 'I don't care if you're going home to lunch, just tell me which way.'

Foa's face seemed to relax and he called back, 'Up towards Rialto, sir, so I can take you home.'

Brunetti pulled the collar of his coat over his head and made a dash for the boat. Foa had raised the canvas cover, so Brunetti chose to stay on deck with him: if they were going to abuse the power of office by using a police boat for private transportation, then they had better do it together.

Foa dropped him at the end of Calle Tiepolo, but even though the tall buildings on either side offered some protection from the rain, his coat was soaked by the time he reached the front door of the building. In the entrance hall, he took it off and shook it, spattering water all around.

As he climbed the stairs, he could feel the damp-ness seeping through the wool of his jacket, and the sound of repeated squelching told him, even before he looked, that his shoes were sodden.

He had removed his shoes and hung up his coat and jacket before he became conscious of the warmth or the scent of his home, and when both penetrated, he finally allowed himself to relax. They must have heard him come in, for Paola called out a greeting as he went down the corridor to the kitchen.

When he entered, shoeless, he found a stranger at his table: a young girl sat in Raffi's place. She got to her feet as he came into the kitchen. Chiara said, 'This is my friend, Azir Mahani.'

'Hello,' Brunetti said and put out his hand.

The girl looked at him, at his hand, and then at Chiara, who said, 'Shake his hand, silly. He's my father.'

The girl leaned forward, but she did so stiffly, and put out her hand as if suspecting Brunetti might not give it back. He took it and held it briefly, as though it were a kitten, a particularly fragile one. He was curious about her shyness but said nothing more than hello and that he was glad she could join them for lunch.

He waited for the girl to seat herself, but she seemed to be waiting for him. Chiara reached up and yanked at the bottom of the girl's sweater, saying, 'Oh, sit down, Azir. He's going to eat his lunch, not you.' The girl blushed and sat down. She looked at her plate.

270

Seeing this, Chiara got up and went over to Brunetti. 'Azir, look,' she said. As soon as she had her friend's attention, Chiara bent down and stared directly into Brunetti's eyes, saying, 'I am going to hypnotize you with the power of my gaze and put you into a deep sleep.'

Instantly, Brunetti closed his eyes.

'Are you asleep?' Chiara asked.

'Yes,' Brunetti said in a sleepy voice, letting his head fall forward on his chest. Paola, who had had no time to greet Brunetti, turned back to the stove and continued filling four dishes with pasta.

Before she spoke again, Chiara made a business of waving her open hand back and forth in front of Brunetti's eyes, to show Azir that he was really asleep. She leaned down and spoke into his left ear, dragging out the final syllable in every word. 'Who is the most wonderful daughter in the whole world?'

Brunetti, keeping his eyes closed, mumbled something.

Chiara gave him an irritated glance, bent even closer and asked, 'Who is the most wonderful daughter in the whole world?'

Brunetti fluttered his eyelids, indicating that the question had finally registered. In a voice he made intentionally indistinct, he began, speaking as slowly as had Chiara, 'The most wonderful daughter in the world is . . .'

Chiara, triumph at hand, stepped back to hear the magic name.

Brunetti raised his head, opened his eyes, and

said, 'Is Azir,' but as a consolation prize, he grabbed Chiara and pulled her close, kissing her on the ear. Paola chose this moment to turn from the stove and say, 'Chiara, would you be a wonderful daughter and help serve?'

As Chiara set a dish of pappardelle with porcini in front of Brunetti, he sneaked a glance across the table at Azir, relieved to see she had survived the ordeal of being mentioned by name.

Chiara took her place and picked up her fork. Suddenly she looked suspiciously at her pasta and said, 'There isn't any ham in this, is there, Mamma?'

Surprised, Paola said, 'Of course not. Never, with porcini.' Then, 'Why do you ask?'

'Because Azir can't eat it.' Hearing this, Brunetti consciously kept his eyes on his own daughter and did not glance at the most wonderful one in the whole world.

'Of course she can't, Chiara. I know that.' Then, to Azir, 'I hope you like lamb, Azir. I thought we'd have broiled lamb chops.'

'Yes, Signora,' Azir said, the first words she had spoken since what Brunetti had come to think of as her ordeal began. There was a trace of an accent, but only a trace.

'I was going to try to make *fessenjoon*,' Paola said, 'but then I thought your mother probably makes it much better than I could, so I decided to stick with the chops.'

'You know about *fessenjoon*?' Azir asked, her face brightening.

Paola smiled around a mouthful of pappardelle. 'Well, I've made it once or twice, but it's hard to find the right spices here, and especially the pomegranate juice.'

'Oh, my mother has some bottles my aunt brought her. I'm sure she'd give you one,' Azir said, and as her face took on animation, Brunetti saw how lovely she was: sharp nose, almond eyes, and two wings of the blackest hair he had ever seen swinging down alongside her jaw.

'Oh, that would be lovely. Then maybe you could come and help me cook it,' Paola said.

'I'd like that,' Azir said. 'I'll ask my mother to write it down, the recipe.'

'I can't read Farsi, I'm afraid,' Paola said in what sounded very much like an apologetic tone.

'Would English be all right?' Azir asked.

'Of course,' Paola said, then looked around the table. 'Would anyone like more pasta?'

When no one volunteered, she started to reach for the plates, but Azir got to her feet and cleared the table without being asked. She attached herself to Paola at the counter and happily carried the platter of lamb to the table, then a large bowl of rice and after that a platter of grilled radicchio.

'How is it that your mother speaks English?' Paola asked.

'She taught it at the university in Esfahan,' Azir said. 'Until we left.'

Though the word hung in the air, no one

asked Azir why her family had decided to leave or if, in fact, it had been their decision.

The girl had eaten very little of her pasta, but she dug into the lamb and rice with a vigour that even Chiara found hard to match. Brunetti watched the tiny curved bones pile up on the sides of the plates of the two girls, marvelled at the mounds of rice that seemingly evaporated as soon as they got within a centimetre of their forks.

After a time, Paola took both the platter and the bowl back to the sink and refilled them, leaving Brunetti impressed at how she had foreseen this adolescent plague of locusts. Azir, after saying that she had never eaten radicchio and had no idea what it was, allowed Paola to pile some on her plate. While no one was watching, it disappeared.

When offers of more food met with honest protests, Paola and Azir cleared the table, and Paola handed the girl smaller plates and fruit dishes. Then she opened the refrigerator and pulled out a large bowl of chopped fruit.

Paola asked who wanted *macedonia*, and Azir asked, 'Why is it called that, Dottoressa?'

'I think because of the country, Macedonia, which is made up of small groups of people who have been all cut up and segmented. But I'm not sure.' She turned to Chiara and, as was usual in such situations, said, 'Get the Zanichelli, Chiara.'

Because the dictionary was now kept in Chiara's room, she disappeared and returned with the heavy volume. She opened the book and started flipping pages, muttering under her breath as she went: *'macchia'*, *'macchiare'*, *'macedone'*, until she finally found the right place and read out, 'Macedonia', and the origin, proving Paola's guess correct. After that her voice dropped into the mumble of a person reading to herself. She slid her plate to one side and replaced it with the open book. Then, as if the other people at the table had evaporated along with the rice, she began to read the other entries on the page.

Azir finished her fruit, refused a second helping, and got to her feet saying, 'May I help you with the dishes, Signora?'

Brunetti pushed back his chair and went into the living room, thinking that perhaps he had been mistaken about Chiara all these years and Azir really was the most wonderful daughter in the whole world.

When Paola came in about half an hour later, Brunetti asked, 'Do you want to say it or shall I?'

'What, that she can say, "only a *vu cumprà*", at the same time she can be concerned that her Muslim friend isn't served pork?' Paola asked as she sat down beside him. She set a book and her glasses to one side of the low table in front of them.

Brunetti might not have phrased it this way, but nevertheless he answered, 'Yes, I suppose so.'

'She's an adolescent, Guido.'

'And that means?'

Absently, Paola pulled a cushion from behind her and tossed it on to the table, then kicked off her shoes and put up her feet. 'It means that the only constant in her life is that she's inconsistent. If enough people approve of an idea or an opinion, then she's likely to think it's a reasonable proposition; if enough people object, then she'll probably reconsider it and perhaps change her mind. And because of her age, there's all that adolescent static flying around in her head, so it's difficult for her to think straight for a long time without worrying what her friends will think of her for saying or doing what she does.' She paused, then said, 'Or, for that matter, for wearing or eating or drinking or liking or listening to or watching what she does.'

'But isn't she aware of the inconsistency?' he asked doggedly.

'Between attending to one foreigner's needs and casually dismissing the death of another?' Paola inquired, again phrasing it bluntly.

'Yes.'

Adjusting to a more comfortable position, Paola leaned her shoulder up against his chest. 'She knows Azir, likes her, so she's real to Chiara: the black man was a faceless stranger,' Paola said, then added, 'And she's probably still too young to be affected by how beautiful they are.'

'By what?' asked Brunetti.

'By how beautiful they are,' Paola repeated.

'The *vu cumprà*?' Brunetti asked with open surprise.

'Beautiful,' Paola repeated. She watched Brunetti's face and then asked, 'Have you ever looked at them, Guido? Really looked? They're beautiful men: tall and straight and in perfect shape, and many of them have the sort of faces you see on carvings.' When he still looked unpersuaded, she asked, 'Would you prefer to look at fat tourists in shorts?'

Accepting that he was not going to answer, she went back to the original subject. 'It's also about class, I think, much as I don't like to say it.'

'Class?' he asked, still puzzling over the idea of the beauty of the Africans.

'Azir's parents are professionals. The black man was a street pedlar.'

'Is it better or worse if that's the reason she said it?' asked a genuinely confused Brunetti.

Paola gave this a great deal of thought and finally answered. 'I'd say it's better, in a perverse sort of way.'

'Why?'

'Because it's more easily corrected.'

'I'm lost,' Brunetti confessed, which was often the case when Paola's mind moved to consideration of the abstract.

'Think of it this way, Guido: if it's based on the difference in race, thinking that one race is superior, then it's lodged in some inner space in her mind, some atavistic place where sweet reason is unlikely to penetrate. But if it's based on the belief that people are better than others because they have more money or are better educated, then she's bound sooner or later to encounter enough counter-examples of this to see how ridiculous the idea is.'

'Should we point it out to her?' he asked, dreading her answer.

'No,' Paola's response was instant. 'She's intelligent, so she'll figure this one out by herself.' When Brunetti said nothing, Paola added, 'If we're lucky, and she is, too, then she'll figure both out.'

'Because you did?' Brunetti had never been satisfied with any explanation she had ever given him of how a person from a family as limitlessly wealthy as hers could have ended up with social and economic ideas so different from those of her class and most of her relatives.

'It was easier for me, I think,' Paola said. 'Because I never actually believed it. There was never any suggestion, when I was growing up, that we were better than other people. Different, for sure: it would have been hard to disguise that, with all that money washing around.' She turned to him and tilted her head to one side, the way she did when new ideas sneaked up on her. 'You know, Guido, hard as this will be for you to believe, I think it never occurred to me – at least when I was young – that we really were rich. After all, my father went off to work every day, just like everybody else's: we didn't have a car; we didn't go on expensive vacations. But it was more than that, I think,' she said, and he turned to watch the play of thought on her face as she worked this out.

'It was more a question of what was approved

of or disapproved of, sort of without saying. At home, I mean. What I learned to be important about people.'

'Give me an example,' he said.

'The worst, I think – the worst disapproval, that is – was of people who didn't work. It didn't much matter to my parents what work a person did, whether they ran a bank or a workshop: the important thing was that they worked and that they thought their work was important.'

Paola pulled away and turned to face him. 'I think that's why my father has always liked you so much, Guido, because your work is so important to you.'

Discussion of Paola's father, his likes and dislikes, always made Brunetti faintly edgy, so he turned back to the matter at hand. 'And Chiara?'

'She'll be all right,' Paola said with what Brunetti suspected she forced to sound like certainty. Then, after a long pause, she added, 'At first, I thought I'd reacted too strongly to what she said about him, but now I think I was right.'

'Better than hitting her, at any rate,' Brunetti said.

'And probably more effective,' Paola added. She leaned back against him and said, 'We'll just have to wait and see.'

'See what?'

'How she turns out,' Paola said and reached forward to pick up her glasses and her book.

22

When he left the house soon afterwards, Brunetti felt no regret that he had escaped a longer discussion of the vagaries of the adolescent female psyche. The decades had eased his own memory of adolescence, removing the visceral fear of not fitting in or not being accepted by his companions. He knew these uncertainties beset his daughter, but he no longer felt their power; thus he was uncomfortable at the ease with which he had forgiven her.

He remembered enough of his study of logic to recognize a slippery slope when he saw it, even in his own thinking, but still it felt right to suspect that Chiara's failure to give sympathy might somehow lead to a refusal to give aid. He was in a hurry to get back to his office, so he stifled the voice asking him if, for example, his own habitual suspicions of southerners would, in comparable fashion, affect his treatment of them.

There was a message on his desk, asking him to call Signor Claudio at home. He did so immediately, using Signor Rossi's *telefonino*, and was relieved to hear the old man give his name.

'It's me, Claudio,' Brunetti said. 'I got your message.'

'Good, I'm glad you called; I spoke to my friend, and I thought you'd want to know what he told me.'

'The one in Antwerp?' Brunetti asked.

'Yes.'

'And?'

'I spoke to him twice, actually,' the old man clarified. 'The first time he told me they were from Africa, but I told him I already knew that much, so he said he'd call back. When he did, he said he'd shown them to someone else.'

Brunetti could not stop himself from asking, 'Someone discreet, I hope?'

Claudio's voice was cool when he said, 'Guido, no one's more discreet than an Antwerp diamond merchant. They make Swiss bankers seem like blabbermouths.'

'All right,' said a relieved Brunetti. 'I'm sorry I interrupted. What did he say?'

'That they're from the Kansai. My friend says he agrees.'

'What's that?' Brunetti asked, never having heard the word.

'A region of West Africa. It's in the Congo, but some of the pipes cross over into eastern Angola, and so both countries lay claim to the diamonds. It's pretty much a war zone, and the border doesn't mean much to anyone any more.'

'And he's sure?' Brunetti asked. He had no idea whether this mattered, but he was tired of almosts and guesses and uncertainty and longed to have definite information, regardless of whether he knew what importance it might have.

After a pause, Claudio said, 'Not entirely,' and, with greater patience, added, 'The other man kept them long enough to check where they come on the colour spectrum,' as if this should be enough to convince anyone, then went on: 'You'd understand it if you knew the technology, but you can believe him: it's a ninety per cent probability that that's where they come from.' At Brunetti's answering silence, Claudio said, 'No one can make it more certain than that, Guido.'

'All right,' Brunetti said. 'Please thank him for me.' He let a moment pass and then asked, 'Anything else?'

'A friend of mine said he was approached by an African about a week ago.'

'A friend where?'

'Here. A jeweller.'

'Approached with diamonds?'

'Yes.'

282

'Could they have been the same diamonds?' Brunetti asked.

'I have no way to know that, Guido. All I know is that the man was African and he had diamonds he wanted to sell.'

'And?'

'And my friend looked at them and declined the opportunity to buy them.'

'Why? Too expensive.'

'No. The opposite.'

'What?'

'They were cheap. The man was asking about half their value. My friend didn't tell me how many stones were involved, but he did tell me that the man who tried to sell them let it be known that there were more than a hundred of them.' Before Brunetti could ask, he said, 'It was a situation where I couldn't really ask him, not for anything more than he told me.'

'Did he tell the man he didn't want to buy them?'

'Yes.'

'And?'

'And he seemed surprised, which my friend thought meant he knew how good the price was.'

'Why did he?' Brunetti asked. 'Your friend. Turn them down, I mean.'

Claudio's answer took a moment to come. 'Some of us won't deal in conflict diamonds or stones that we think are: there's too much blood on them. It's as simple as that. And my friend said it was pretty clear that's what these were.'

'He wouldn't buy them even at that price?' Brunetti asked.

'No,' Claudio said, then added, by way of explanation, 'We all make enough money with our business. We don't need this on our consciences.'

'How many of you feel this way?' Brunetti asked.

'Ah,' Claudio began, 'not a lot.'

'Then why bother?'

'I told you: there's too much blood on them,' Claudio said. 'I know people who do buy them. They say it's not their business where the stones come from or what happens with the money that they pay for them, who gets killed with the weapons that are usually bought with it. They buy the stones and that's the end of it.'

'You don't agree?'

'I've asked you not to play the fool, Guido,' Claudio said with uncommon heat. Brunetti heard the other man take a deep breath, and then Claudio said, 'Don't provoke me. I'm an old man, and I want to live in peace.'

'I think you do, Claudio,' Brunetti said, regretting that he had, indeed, provoked him. He asked, 'Did your friend say what he looked like, the man selling the diamonds?'

'No. Only that he was African.' Before Brunetti could respond, Claudio said, 'I know, I know: they all look the same.'

'Did he say what language they spoke?' Brunetti asked, recalling that Angola had once belonged to Portugal.

'Italian, and he said the man spoke it reasonably well,' Claudio answered without hesitation.

'Did he say anything about an accent?'

'No, but if he was from Africa, he'd have an accent, wouldn't he?' Claudio asked.

'Yes, of course,' Brunetti said, deciding not to pursue this. Instead, he asked, 'Do you have any idea where he would be likely to go after your friend turned him down?' Then without allowing Claudio to speak, Brunetti asked, 'When did this happen?'

'Last week some time. Let me think,' Claudio said and then went silent. Brunetti waited as the older man searched his memory and then said, 'Last Friday.' He paused again. 'That's two days before the man was killed, isn't it?'

'Yes. So maybe he didn't have enough time to talk to anyone else. But if he did, who would he have gone to?' Brunetti asked.

There was a long pause, so long it grew awkward. Finally Claudio said, 'The only one I can think of is Guelfi. He has a shop in San Lio, but there's no sense talking to him. He won't tell you anything, not if he bought them, and not if he didn't buy them, either.'

'Any reason?' Brunetti asked, idly paging through the map of his memory to see if he could recall a jewellery shop anywhere near San Lio.

'No,' Claudio answered. 'It's a sort of principle with him. He never gives anyone anything, even information. Trust me and don't waste your time trying to talk to him.'

'I will,' Brunetti said, and then as quickly, 'I mean I won't. Anyone else?'

'No, not really. Not here, at least. My friends and I are the only other people in the city who would buy in that quantity, and the man I told you about is the only one who was asked. I'm sure about this.'

'Sure sure or just semi-sure?' Brunetti asked.

'Sure sure,' Claudio answered. 'Trust me,' he said again and hung up.

Angola. Was that the country where the old government was taken down to the beach and slaughtered by the men leading the coup? Or was it the one where the old government simply disappeared? Brunetti had once come across the term 'compassion fatigue', but thought that the oh-so-clever press had got it wrong, and the term should really be, 'horror fatigue'. He had a friend in Rome, a former camerawoman for RAI, who had been to most of the world's trouble spots during her career. Some years ago, when she returned to Rome from Rwanda, she submitted a one-sentence letter of resignation: 'I cannot film any more piles of bodies.'

Brunetti read widely, as did Paola, but neither of them could keep up with the succession of misfortunes to afflict that desperate continent. Mineral wealth to make the West salivate with desire and villains at every turn ready to sell it to them. Maybe Mr Kurtz was right, and all there was was horror.

If the man had succeeded in selling the diamonds, what would he have done with the money? If this were a case of private theft, he would most likely have spent it on himself, but private theft hardly seemed on the cards, not in a scenario where the Ministries of the Interior and of Foreign Affairs were to be heard shuffling their feet somewhere offstage. It was the duty of the Ministry of the Interior to control the flux of foreigners into the country, so they would have had a legitimate interest in the dead man. But why take over the investigation of the death of this one foreigner without offering any explanation?

As to the Ministry of Foreign Affairs, their involvement could have been just about anything: keeping an eye on a known or suspected criminal or, because it had become so much easier to justify arresting them, keeping an eye on someone they defined – or had decided to define – as a terrorist. Or, and Brunetti had to admit the possibility, keeping an eye on him because they had been asked to do so by the people who had tortured him and because it served their political interests to do those people a favour.

When he was new to the police, thoughts of this kind would never have come to Brunetti, regardless of all the political talk of the Left, regardless of his bride's political convictions. Now, after decades of involvement with the forces of order, Brunetti had to admit that no possibility, no matter how vile or incredible, was to be excluded.

He sat at his desk, studying the opposite wall,

and continued to invent reasons why the offices of government might want to impede the investigation into the murder of a foreigner. Not for an instant did it occur to Brunetti that either of the two ministries might have had any interest in simply apprehending the man's killers. Had that been the case, they would have left the job to the police.

Why had they not found the diamonds? And why had they delayed in coming to search for them? The likely solution was that the killers, or whoever had sent them, did not know where the victim lived and had taken days to find out. Either the other black men had left before the apartments were searched, or they had panicked and fled when they discovered that their homes had been searched.

He pulled the phone book from his bottom drawer and took from it the photos that had been taken of the dead man's body. He studied the face, peaceful in death, stared long at the handsome symmetry of his features. 'Were you a good guy or a bad guy?' Brunetti asked the photo. He stuck them back inside the phone book and tossed it into his drawer. He picked up the phone and called his father-in-law.

Conte Orazio Falier, when his secretary passed the call to him, told Brunetti that he was about to leave for the airport. When Brunetti said he would like to speak to him now, if possible, the Count offered to have his boat stop at the Danieli dock and pick him up. They could talk on the way to the airport, and then Massimo could bring him back. Brunetti said he'd be there in ten minutes, and hung up.

He looked out of the window: it was still raining, so he took an umbrella from the back of his closet, put on his overcoat, and went downstairs. He found the glass doors of the Questura open and no guard in sight. He glanced into the small guardroom and saw that it was empty. On the desk lay an officer's peaked blue cap, and over the back of the chair was draped a belt and holster, presumably containing a service pistol. For a moment, Brunetti was tempted to take the gun and toss it into the canal in front of the door: he was stopped only by the thought of the wave of paperwork that would then wash through his own office. Instead, he pulled the door to the office shut and, as he left, that to the building.

When he emerged on to the Riva degli Schiavoni, huddled behind his umbrella, the wind coming off the *bacino* yanked the umbrella over his head and behind him, then ripped the material free of the thin struts and left it hanging shredded in his hands. Brunetti grabbed at it, gathering it up into a bulky, prickly lump, and made his way through the driving rain to the dock. The Count's boat was there, Massimo draped in a yellow slicker, waiting for him on deck. The pilot extended his hand and half pulled Brunetti forward, against the force of the wind, on to the boat. His foot slipped on the top step and he bounced down the other two, landing beside Massimo, who steadied him with both hands.

'*Buona sera, Commissario*,' the pilot said and relieved him of the umbrella.

Brunetti thanked him, but did not linger over it. He pushed open the double doors and went down, more carefully this time, the two steps that led to the cabin. The Count was seated at the back, talking on his *telefonino*, but as Brunetti came in, the Count said, 'I'll call later,' and slipped the phone into the pocket of his jacket.

He smiled at Brunetti, and as the Count's face softened, Brunetti saw a hint of the age he knew must lie behind the deeply tanned skin. But it was gone as quickly as it came, that flash of mortality, leaving behind the clear blue eyes, the thick white hair, and the general impression of effortless well-being. Suddenly Brunetti felt the heat of the cabin caress his face and hands.

Stooping forward, he shook the Count's extended hand and sank into one of the long benches running down the sides of the cabin. 'God, it's cold out there,' Brunetti said, rubbing his hands together, as much to dry as to warm them.

'Would you like me to tell Massimo to turn the heat up?' the Count asked, half rising.

'No, no,' Brunetti said, placing a hand on his father-in-law's shoulder and gently pushing him back into his seat. 'I feel it already.' He unbuttoned his overcoat and struggled out of it without getting to his feet. He laid it beside him and looked down at his feet: another pair of shoes soaked through. 'We need the rain,' was all he could think of to say.

'The defining statement of modern life,' the Count said, confusing Brunetti entirely.

The sound of the motor deepened, and a quick glance out of the window opposite showed Brunetti that they were backing away from the dock and into the *bacino*. 'I'm glad you have the time,' Brunetti said. 'Where are you going, by the way?'

'London,' the Count answered, offering no explanation.

'Will you be back for Christmas?' Brunetti asked, alarmed at the possibility that his children would be deprived of what remained one of the highlights of their year.

'I'll be back tonight,' the Count answered.

The younger Brunetti, the less worldly Brunetti, would have asked if it were really possible to get there and back on the available flights, but the Brunetti who had for more than twenty years been a member of the Falier family did not ask such a question.

'I'd like to be direct and save time,' Brunetti said without further preamble.

'By all means,' the Count said, then added, 'A pleasant change from the way the people I deal with generally do business.'

'Last Sunday,' Brunetti began, 'an African was shot in Campo Santo Stefano.' The Count nodded but said nothing. 'I later searched the place where he was living and found what has been estimated as six million Euros in uncut diamonds – diamonds that are thought to be from Africa, specifically from a region near the border between the Congo and Angola – hidden there. Some time later, the apartment was searched again, presumably by his killers or by someone who knew of and wanted the diamonds. Two days before the murder, an African tried to sell a large number of diamonds to a merchant here, who refused to buy them.'

Brunetti stopped, curious to see how the Count would respond to this. The man's face was impassive. As Brunetti's silence lengthened, the Count said, 'I'm waiting for you to ask me for information. With this little, Guido, I can't tell you anything. I'm waiting for the plot to grow more complicated.'

'It does,' Brunetti said. 'Since the investigation was opened, both the Ministry of the Interior and the Foreign Ministry have displayed interest in the case.'

'Together?' the Count asked with open surprise.

'I think not. They appear to be working separately. The Ministry of the Interior has taken over the case officially, with a request to Patta. The Foreign Ministry broke into the computer where the records were kept and erased them.'

'I will not ask how you found that out,' the Count remarked.

'Better not,' Brunetti said.

The Count crossed his legs and pressed both palms on to the seat to push himself upright. He turned to look out of the window. Brunetti's eyes followed his, and through the water-speckled glass he saw the metal light stanchions of the stadium and the odd collection of decom-missioned vaporetti stations that the ACTV stored down here at the end of Sant'Elena.

The heat, the dampness of his clothing, the constant thud of the motors, all lulled him into dullness. Still the Count said nothing. Suddenly the boat lurched to one side as the open waters of the *laguna* hit them.

'Six million Euros is a relative sum,' the Count said. Brunetti turned his attention to him. 'That is, to most people it is a fortune, undreamed-of wealth. But to many others it is a relatively insignificant sum.' Brunetti wondered where the Count stood on this spectrum.

'To an African, well, to most people in Africa, the sum is even more monumentally grand, perhaps so grand as to lose all meaning and be nothing more than a sum.' He paused again, and Brunetti could almost hear the Count's brain humming as it worked through this problem.

'Then we must consider what an African would want to do with the money to be had from selling diamonds. If it were for his own use, he would be likely to try to sell them one at a time, perhaps going to private jewellers, perhaps even to their shops, to try to sell a stone or two, though few jewellers would be interested in uncut gems, I suspect. If he did succeed in selling them separately, he would have a steady source of money, at least until the diamonds were gone, but it would leave him with the problem of having to find a safe place where he could keep the diamonds.' The Count glanced in Brunetti's direction to see if he was following. 'But you say this man tried to sell many of them at one time?'

Brunetti nodded.

The Count rested his head on the cushions behind him and closed his eyes. 'If he tried to sell them all, then there was something he needed a lot of money in order to buy.' He opened his eyes, turned his head, and gave Brunetti a sharp look. 'You've got this far already?' he asked.

'To arms and guns, yes,' Brunetti said. 'I wanted to ask you who the likely seller would be so I can begin to have some idea of what's been going on.'

The Count closed his eyes again. 'Ah, you never disappoint me, Guido.' He smiled and shook his head in amused distress. 'But, in future, I would be very grateful if you would not indulge me by letting me show off how clever I am when you've already reached the conclusion.'

'Of course,' Brunetti said.

Both men gazed out of the windows, watching the wooden channel markers march past them. 'Once he, or they, arrange to buy the weapons,' the Count said, 'which I think would be the easy part, they would have to transport them. That's where things would become complicated.'

Brunetti had no idea what sort of weapons, or how many, could be bought for six million Euros, assuming this to be the minimum raised by the sale of the diamonds. Television movies had, over the years, turned Uzi and Kalashnikov into household words; Brunetti tried to calculate the volume of the disassembled machine-guns that could be bought for that sum, but he made a hopeless muddle of it.

The Count continued, 'They would have to get to a port: easily enough done in trucks. Then there would be the false bills of lading, the Customs inspectors to be paid, the shipping company persuaded to be accommodating. And then the unloading at whatever port of entry was used, where it would all be put on trucks.' He paused to give Brunetti an idea of the possible complications here. 'So whoever was arranging this would need a great deal more money for these – what shall I call them? – incidental expenses, and then he would need someone at the other end to collect and, er, distribute whatever weapons he managed to acquire.' He placed a hand on Brunetti's arm and said, 'It would require an efficient organization, at least there. Here, you'd need someone to sell the diamonds and buy the arms. Presumably your dead man.' The Count raised a hand and wiped at the condensation on the window, then took out a handkerchief and dried his hand. The clean window showed them little more than the wet one had.

'What I don't understand,' the Count said, 'is

the attempt to sell the diamonds privately. These things are generally taken care of beforehand.'

'I beg your pardon,' Brunetti said.

'Usually, the deal is arranged before the diamonds are brought here, to Europe, and often at the governmental level. Very often it's a simple barter arrangement: stones for guns, so the complication of moving large amounts of money is avoided,' the Count said, increasing Brunetti's uneasiness by saying, 'and the transport can usually be arranged by the addition of a percentage charge.'

Brunetti wondered what the phrase 'governmental level' might mean, but before he could ask, he felt the slowing of the engine as the boat approached the narrow channel leading to the airport dock. He looked at his watch. 'What time does your plane leave?' he asked.

'Don't worry,' the Count said. 'It will wait.' The boat pulled up to a dock and Massimo glanced into the cabin, but when he saw that the Count did not get to his feet, he backed out into the channel and set the motor to idling. Brunetti glanced outside, at the abandoned airport terminal, and saw that it had stopped raining.

'The question you haven't asked, Guido, is why someone would kill him.'

'To steal the diamonds?'

'Possibly,' the Count answered. 'But I doubt that either one of us believes that.'

'Then to prevent their sale,' Brunetti countered.

'Their sale or the purchases that would be made with the money?'

'That, I think,' Brunetti agreed.

'And that's why you want to know who the likely arms seller would be? To lead you to your dead black man?' the Count asked, bringing the conversation back to its point of origin.

'Yes. It's the only place I can think of to start at.'

'If I might comment on this, Guido,' the Count said deferentially, 'it sounds as if the arms dealer would be the least likely to kill him. It would stop the sale, and the people who sell weapons aren't usually in the business of killing.'

Brunetti let that one lie.

'It is the involvement of those two agencies of our government,' the Count said, 'that puzzles me.' He looked down and flicked a speck of dust from his trousers, then back at Brunetti. 'It is not unusual for sales of weapons – after all, they are one of our most successful industries – to be, well, to be accommodated by the government. But they usually do that when the purchaser is known to them.'

'You mean another government?' Brunetti asked.

'Yes. Or, just as easily, some group eager to replace an existing government.' His smile was wolfish. 'The Americans are not the only people who welcome the removal of inconvenient politicians and their replacement by those better disposed towards their business methods.'

Again, that smile. 'Even better, at least from an economic point of view, is to see that hostilities continue more or less indefinitely so that the process of replacement can be prolonged for as long as there are natural resources that can be sold to pay for new weapons. Ideally, by both sides.'

The Count gave Brunetti a long look, raised a hand as if to reach across and touch his shoulder, but did not; he pressed his palm back on the seat beside him. 'It is the involvement of either one of these ministries that makes me think – I might even say fear – that this could be a very dangerous situation.'

Before Brunetti could answer, the Count went on, 'No, don't tell me that it has already been shown to be dangerous because that man is dead. I mean for you, Guido, for you and for anyone they perceive as being in their way.'

A taxi passed them going faster than it should and slammed its motor into reverse just metres from the dock. Its wake caught them broadside, flinging Brunetti forward so that he had to brace himself on the edge of the seat opposite him.

'Come, it's impossible to stay here,' the Count said. He went forward, stooping, and tapped on the glass of the door. Massimo engaged the motor and slid the boat alongside the dock, grabbed a rope and jumped ashore. He held the boat tight to the side while the Count stepped up on to the dock. Leaning back down, he said, 'No, Guido, don't bother. Massimo will take you back.'

As Brunetti waited, the Count said, 'I'll make some calls and let you know whatever I can.'

A sudden wave slapped the side of the boat, and Brunetti looked down to check where he had placed his feet. When he looked back up at the Count, a man in a chauffeur's uniform was standing next to him, and at the kerb stood a dark grey Lancia, its back door open and its motor running.

Massimo jumped back into the boat and backed quickly away from the dock. 'Shall I take you to the Questura, Dottore, or would you like to go home?'

'Take me home, please, Massimo,' he said. When he looked back at the land, the car was pulling slowly away from the kerb to take the Count the three minutes to the terminal.

As Massimo took him back towards the city, Brunetti recalled the Count's precise words. He had not said that he would make calls and tell Brunetti whatever he learned, but that he would tell him whatever he could. Brunetti felt suddenly uneasy and wondered if, like Claudio, he was a man who put too much trust in his friends.

23

The next morning, as Brunetti stood alone in the living room, drinking his second coffee, the brightness of the day lured him out on to the terrace. Though it was hardly springlike, it was easily warm enough to allow him to stand there for a few minutes and watch the light reflected on the wet tiles of the roofs around and below him. There was no sign of a cloud; in fact, the light hurt his eyes, even at this hour. Much as he had welcomed the rain, he prayed that this brilliant day would last and give them all a chance to shake off the gloom of the previous days.

When he felt the cold begin to penetrate his jacket, he went back inside, set his cup and saucer on the table in the living room, then thought better of it and took it into the kitchen and put it in the sink. He considered taking scarf and gloves, but he decided to invest in hope for the day and so left them and put on only his overcoat before he let himself out of the apartment.

The weather seemed to have infected people on the street; even the newsagent, whose face was usually as grim as the headlines, managed a gruff '*grazie*' as he gave Brunetti his change. Brunetti decided to walk: if this was the global warming that Vianello was always banging on about, then surely there were worse things facing the world.

He turned right along the Canale di San Lorenzo and paused to study the scaffolding on the old men's home, searching for signs of progress. It appeared that the windows were finally in place on the third floor: Brunetti could not remember having seen them before. A workman climbed down the scaffolding and walked across the *campo* and Brunetti, his mind idling, followed him with his eyes. As the workman let himself into a wooden shack, Brunetti noticed two men sitting on one of the benches in the *campo*, two black men. The bench was set parallel to the canal and thus permitted the men to look across at the façade of the Questura.

It was too far for him to be sure, but he thought the men were the one he had defined as the leader and the very thin young man who had raised his hand to Brunetti. Brunetti continued towards the bridge. He stopped there and gazed across the canal. He was sure the two men recognized him. Their heads moved closer together, and he watched them talk, saw their hands move as first one, then the other, gestured across the canal, either at him or at the Questura. The young man used his left hand to point; his right hand sat useless in his lap. No sound of voices came across the canal, and so it was rather like watching a television with the volume turned down. The older man turned away from the other and raised a hand in Brunetti's direction, then waved his fingers quickly down towards the ground and then again, signalling Brunetti to come and join them. The man then turned back to the other, placed his hand on his knee, and spoke to him.

The younger man nodded, either in agreement or resignation.

A noise to his right caught Brunetti's attention and he turned towards it. Beyond the other bridge, a police launch was turning into the canal, its blue light flashing. Heedless of the waves it created on either side, it came towards him, shot under the first bridge, and pulled noisily up to the Questura.

The pilot, the one who had taken him home for lunch, jumped on to the dock and secured the rope to a hawser, then stood back and saluted. First to step up on to the dock were two guards, both wearing bulletproof vests, machine-guns held across their chests. Then in quick succession came the Questore and then

Vice-Questore Giuseppe Patta. A moment later a man in a business suit whose face was vaguely familiar to Brunetti emerged from the cabin and followed the others. The guards seemed to pay scant attention to the men alighting from the boat, their eyes busy roaming up and down the *calle* and then across to the *campo* on the other side of the canal. Brunetti allowed his eyes to follow theirs and was not at all surprised to see that the two black men had disappeared.

He did not recognize either of the guards with the machine-guns and so remained where he was, making no attempt to approach the door of the Questura. The two guards went to the building, and one of them held open the door. When the three civilians were inside, the guards followed them. The door closed.

Brunetti went over to the pilot, who was securing the stern of the boat with a second rope. He noticed Brunetti approaching and saluted.

'What's that all about, Foa?' Brunetti asked, hands in his pockets, tilting his head back towards the Questura.

'I'm not sure, sir. I had to pick up the Vice-Questore at home at eight-thirty, and then we went to the home of the Questore and got him.'

'And the guys with the guns?' Brunetti asked.

'They were with the one who gave me the order, sir, the civilian. He showed up here at about eight and handed me a letter.'

'You still have it?' Brunetti asked.

'No, he took it back right after I read it.'

'Who was it from?'

'I didn't recognize the signature, or even the title: it was some sort of under-secretary to a secretary of a committee. But I certainly understood the letterhead: it was from the Ministry of the Interior.'

'Ah,' Brunetti sighed, but softly, more to himself than to Foa. 'What did it tell you to do?'

'To follow the orders of the person who gave me the letter. And he told me who to pick up, and in what order.'

'I see,' Brunetti said, doing his best to make it sound as though the news Foa gave him was of no particular interest to him. He thanked the young man and went back to the Questura and, once inside, up to Signorina Elettra's office. When he went in, she looked up and asked, 'You weren't invited to the party?'

'Hardly. Only the grown-ups.' Then, after a pause, 'You got any idea?'

'None. The Vice-Questore called me from the launch and told me he'd be in a meeting with the Questore for a good part of the morning and to explain that to anyone who phoned for him.'

'Did he mention anyone else?' Brunetti asked, sure that Patta would not have missed the opportunity to drop the name, or at least the title, of any important person he had a meeting with.

'No, sir, he didn't.'

Brunetti thought for a moment, then asked, 'Will you call me when it finishes?'

'Do you want to see him?'

'No. But I'd like to know how long their meeting lasts.'

'I'll call,' she said, and Brunetti went up to his office.

He spent the next hour alternately reading the paper, which he opened across his desk, making no attempt to hide it, and walking to the window to stare for long minutes down into Campo San Lorenzo. The black men reappeared in neither place. Restless, he opened first one drawer of his desk and then the others and pulled out any object or paper he could justify throwing away. Within half an hour, his wastepaper basket was full and the open newspaper was covered with an assortment of objects he either could not identify or lacked the will to throw away.

His phone rang. Thinking it was Signorina Elettra, he answered by saying, 'Are they gone?'

'It's Bocchese, sir,' the technician said. 'I think you better come down here,' he added, and hung up.

Brunetti picked up the newspaper by its corners and dumped the objects back into his bottom drawer, kicked it shut, and went downstairs.

When Brunetti entered the laboratory, Bocchese was sitting at his desk, a place where Brunetti seldom saw him. The technician was always so caught up in cleaning, measuring, weighing things that it had never occurred to Brunetti that there might come a time when he simply sat and did nothing. 'What is it?' Brunetti asked. 'Those fingerprints?'

'Yes,' Bocchese said. 'There's no match in the Interpol files for the dead man. Nowhere – neither in personnel files nor among people with a criminal record.' He waited for Brunetti to digest this and then added, 'But . . .' When he saw Brunetti's eyes flash towards him, he continued, 'a flag went up when his prints were submitted, saying all requests for information should immediately be forwarded to our Ministry of the Interior.'

'Did that happen?' Brunetti asked, worried about the consequences.

Bocchese gave a small cough of audibly false modesty. 'My friend thought it kinder not to burden them with his request.'

'Ah, I see,' Brunetti said, and he did.

'He did say, though, that he had one other place he would try to look, but it might take some time.' Before Brunetti could speak, the technician said, 'No, I didn't ask.'

Bocchese waved a hand in what might have been a comment on the reliability of friends and then said, 'He also gave me a very strange answer about the print that was found at that house.'

'What did your friend say?' Brunetti asked, coming closer to the desk but not sitting.

'The print is a match for one that belonged to Michele Paci, who was an officer with the DIGOS until three years ago.'

'Belonged?' Brunetti asked.

'Yes. He died.'

Bocchese gave this time to sink in and then

said, 'When he told me, I asked him if it was possible that there had been a mix-up. But he told me he'd had the same reaction, so he'd checked it again. It's a perfect match, probably because the DIGOS are so careful about taking prints when they set up files on their employees.'

'Died how?'

'The record doesn't say. The entry says' – and here Bocchese looked down at some papers on his desk – ' "killed in the course of duty".'

'Then what's his fingerprint doing on the door? And on that bag?'

The best Bocchese could do was shrug. 'I checked it myself when his answer came in. The match is perfect. If the one in the Ministry files is his real print, then so are the other two.'

'And that means he's not dead?'

With not much of a smile, Bocchese said, 'Unless he really did lend his hand to someone.'

'You ever come across something like this?' Brunetti asked.

'No.'

'Would it be possible for someone to have left it there deliberately? Someone else, that is?' Brunetti asked, though it made no sense.

Bocchese dismissed the possibility.

'So he's alive?' Brunetti asked.

'I'd say so.'

'And Interpol? Any results from them?'

'They have no match for the print.'

'Don't they have the prints of other member police forces on file?'

'I'd always thought so,' Bocchese said. 'But perhaps not DIGOS because they're not exactly police.'

After a long silence, Brunetti asked, 'You trust your friend?'

'Not to tell anyone?'

'Yes.'

'As much as I trust anyone,' Bocchese answered, adding, 'which isn't very much.' When he saw Brunetti's pained response to this, he added, 'He won't tell anyone. Besides, it's illegal, what he did.'

Brunetti walked slowly back to his office, trying to make some sense of what Bocchese had told him. If the fingerprints had indeed been left there by an agent of the Italian Secret Service, Brunetti was into an investigation that could lead anywhere. He considered this for a moment, and then quickly realized how much more likely it was that the investigation would lead nowhere. Recent history was filled with examples of *insabbiatura*, the burying of an inconvenient case in the sand. He had worked on some in the past, and they always forced him to confront the extent of his own cowardice. Or his despair.

It nagged at Brunetti: if the man was not dead, then who had faked his death, his employer or himself? Or both? In any case, what sort of retirement had the man gone to? He'd been in the apartment of the dead man, perhaps both before and after his death. Brunetti forced himself to stop speculating about what else the man might have done.

On an impulse, ignoring the fact that he had asked Signorina Elettra to phone him, he left the Questura and walked down towards Castello. Perhaps the black men had gone to earth in their apartment. He tried to concentrate on what he saw as he walked, intentionally chose an indirect route in the hope that it would divert him from the thought of the dead man and the man who was not dead.

As he knew was likely to be the case, the shutters were closed on the windows of the house, and a padlock hung from the door. He had nothing to lose, so he went down to the bar on the corner and asked for a coffee. The same card game was in progress, though the players had shifted it to a table nearer the back of the bar.

'You were in here before,' the barman said, 'Filippo's friend.' He said it with a certain amusement.

Brunetti thanked him for the coffee. 'I really am, you know,' he said. 'But I'm also with the police.'

'I thought so,' the barman said, obviously pleased with himself. 'We all did.'

Brunetti grinned and shrugged, downed his coffee and put a five-Euro note on the bar.

As the other man looked for change, he said, 'You wanted to know about the Africans, didn't you?'

'Yes. I'm trying to find out who killed that man last week.'

'That poor devil in Santo Stefano?' the

barman asked, as though he had Venice confused with some more wildly violent place, where it was necessary to specify the location of a recent murder.

'Yes.'

'Lot of people want to know about them, it seems,' the barman said, making himself sound like someone in a film who expected the detective to do a double-take.

Much as he would have liked to please him, Brunetti said only, 'Such as?'

'There was a man in here asking about them a couple of days before he was killed.'

'But you didn't tell me about this then.'

'You didn't ask,' the barman said, 'and you didn't say you were a cop.'

Brunetti nodded to acknowledge the man's point. 'Would you tell me about him?' he asked in a perfectly conversational voice.

'He wasn't from here,' the barman began. 'Let me ask,' he said and turned to the card players. 'Luca, that guy who asked about the *vu cumprà*? Where was he from, do you think?' Then, before the other man answered, the barman added, nodding towards Brunetti, 'No, not this one. The other one.'

'*Romano*,' the man named Luca called back, laying a card on the table.

Brunetti had forgotten to ask Bocchese if the report said where Paci was from. 'What did he want to know?'

'If any of them lived around here.'

'What did you tell him?'

310

'When I heard he wasn't from here, I told him that none of them did and they wouldn't try to, not if they knew what was good for them.' In answer to Brunetti's unspoken question, he added, 'I figured that would convince him we didn't want them here. Besides, the ones who came in here were always polite and quiet, paid for their coffee, said thank you. No reason to tell some stranger where they were.'

'But you're telling me.'

'You're not a stranger.'

'Because I'm Venetian?'

'No, because I asked Filippo about you, and he said you're all right.'

'Can you describe this man?'

'Big. Little taller than you, but bigger, probably ten kilos heavier. Big head.' He stopped.

'Anything else you remember about him?' Brunetti asked, wondering if there were some way Signorina Elettra could get into the personnel file of a deceased employee of the DIGOS.

'No, just that he was big.'

From the card players, a voice called out, 'Tell him about the guy's hands, Giorgio.'

'Yes, I forgot. Strange. The guy had hands just like a monkey's, all covered with hair.'

24

And then it was Christmas. As it happened every year, most people added Christmas Eve and the day after Santo Stefano to their holiday, to make a long bridge of the weekend, so there was a period of five days when nothing much got done, not only at the Questura, but in most of the country. The only activity, it seemed, was in the shops, which were open longer than usual, attempting to lure customers into that year-end buying frenzy which statisticians employed to make the economy look better than it was.

Brunetti got through it all: the last purchases of gifts, the visits and the toasts, the endless dinners, gift-giving and receiving, more dinners. He had with Paola's family, and when he managed to have a word alone with his father-in-law, the Count told him that he had asked certain friends to let him know if they came to learn of anything relating to the death of the African in Venice or perhaps of any connection there might be between his death and an attempt to buy arms. After five days, all Brunetti had to show was a new green sweater from Paola, a lifetime membership in a badger protection society from Chiara, from Raffi a parallel text edition of Pliny's letters, and the conviction that he would be more comfortable if he had the shoemaker cut another hole in his belt.

When he returned to the Questura, he found the general mood oppressive, as if everyone there were suffering the after-effects, both physical and moral, of prolonged overeating. Further, someone appeared to have forgotten to turn the heating down while the offices were closed, and the rising temperature had sunk into the walls, which were warm to the touch. The first day back was bright and unseasonably warm, so opening the windows helped very little: the heat seeped from the walls, and people had no choice but to work in their shirtsleeves.

There were the usual reports of break-ins and burglaries from people returning from vacations; these kept the crime squads in and out all day. It soon began to appear that there had been two gangs at work: professionals who went after only the most expensive pieces, and what must have been drug addicts, who took only the quickly resaleable. The rich suffered most at the hands of the first gang; the less wealthy suffered at the hands of the other. Two bizarre reports at least relieved Brunetti's mood: the professionals had offended an ageing film star who lived on the Giudecca by going through her house and scorning her paste jewellery, leaving her home without taking anything, while the addicts had walked past a de Chirico and a Klimt as they left an apartment carrying a five-year-old laptop and a portable CD player.

Because it was soon to be a new year, time for resolute behaviour, Brunetti went downstairs after lunch and, seeing that Signorina Elettra was not at her desk, knocked at Patta's door.

'*Avanti*,' Patta called out, and Brunetti entered.

'Ah, Brunetti,' he said, 'I hope you had a happy Christmas and that it will be a successful new year.'

'Thank you, sir,' Brunetti answered, not a little taken aback, 'and the same to you.'

'Yes, let's hope it will be,' Patta said. He waved Brunetti to a chair and pushed himself back in his own. Brunetti, as he seated himself, glanced at his superior and was surprised to see that he had not brought his usual vacation tan back with him this year. Nor, he noticed, the usual supplement to his embonpoint. In fact, the collar of Patta's shirt looked a bit loose, or else he had not knotted his tie tightly enough.

'Did you have a pleasant vacation?' Brunetti asked, hoping to get Patta to talk and thus provide him with more opportunity to observe his superior's state of being.

'No, we decided not to go away this season,' Patta said, then hastened to explain, as though such dereliction of consumption needed an excuse, 'Both of the boys were home, so we decided to enjoy the time with them.'

'I see,' Brunetti said. Having met Patta's sons, Brunetti was doubtful as to the joy to be had from their company, but still he added, 'That must have made your wife happy.'

'Yes, yes,' Patta said and adjusted one of his cufflinks. 'What can I do for you, Brunetti?'

'I'd like to know if we should think about clearing up some of last year's cases, sir,' he began. As a ruse, it was pathetically transparent, but Brunetti was dulled by the heat and could think of nothing better.

Patta looked at him for a long time before saying, 'It's not like you to think so much like a bookkeeper, Brunetti. Cases sometimes do run over from year to year.'

Brunetti stopped himself from saying that most criminal cases ran over far longer than that and contented himself with answering, 'I'd still like to see if we could get some of the out-standing cases settled.'

'That's not going to be so easy,' Patta said, 'not now, while we're short-staffed.'

'Are we, sir?' Brunetti asked. This was news to him.

'Lieutenant Scarpa,' Patta explained. 'He'll be away until the end of January, and there's no one to cover his workload while he's away.'

'I see, sir,' Brunetti said, thinking it better not to ask. 'But we should still try to settle some things,' he insisted.

'For instance?' Patta answered, leaning the least bit forward.

There was no sense in flirting with it or flirting with Patta. 'The murder in Campo Santo Stefano. It's the only outstanding murder case we have.'

'It's not,' Patta said instantly.

'What?' Brunetti asked shortly, then thought to add, 'sir.'

'It's not our case, Brunetti, as I made clear to you. The case has been handed over to the Ministry of the Interior for investigation.'

'With no explanation?'

'I am not in the habit of questioning the decisions of my superiors,' Patta said. Only with difficulty did Brunetti prevent himself from gasping outright or from making a sarcastic response.

Forcing himself to remain calm, he said, 'I'm hardly questioning their decisions, sir. But I would like to know if the case has been solved. If so, we can close it here.'

'That's already been done, Commissario,' Patta said calmly.

'Closed?'

'Closed. All copies of documents have been forwarded to the Ministry of the Interior.'

'And the records on the computer?' Brunetti asked, immediately regretting it.

'They have been forwarded, as well.'

'Vice-Questore,' Brunetti said with a voice he forced to remain amiable and calm, 'I don't know much about computers, but I do know that working with them is different from working with actual pieces of paper. When something like an email is forwarded, the original remains on the computer.'

Patta smiled, as if to compliment and applaud this very bright student. 'That corresponds with my own understanding of the process, Commissario.'

'But is it the case here?'

'I beg your pardon?'

'Are the originals of the documents still on our computer?'

'Ah, I don't think I can answer that for you, Commissario.'

'Who could?'

'The computer people from the Ministry who were in here during the holidays. They came here on the order of the Minister.' The heat. The heat. He should have known.

Brunetti could think of nothing to say. He got to his feet, asked if he should start interviewing the people whose homes had been robbed, and when Patta said he thought that would be an excellent use of his time, Brunetti excused himself and left the office.

Signorina Elettra was at her desk. She looked up at Brunetti, saw his expression, and stopped herself from saying whatever it was she was about to say.

Speaking in a conspiratorially low voice, Brunetti said, 'The Vice-Questore just told me that some people, computer people, from the Ministry of the Interior were in here during the vacation. He said that they were,' he continued, emphasis on the next word, '*forwarding* the files about the murder of the man in Campo Santo Stefano to their office, which is now in charge of the case.' As he said the last phrase, he realized how close he was to losing control even of this soft voice he was using. He forced himself to relax and said, 'Could you have a look?'

She pulled her lips tight, something she did when stressed or angry. 'I've already done that, sir. In fact, that's what I wanted to tell you, just now. It's all gone.' He had to lean forward to hear her.

'All? Aren't there things like backup and . . . other things?' he asked.

'There are. And they're all gone from there, too. It's been wiped clean.'

'Is that possible? I thought you were . . .' He didn't know the words to express what he thought she was.

'I am,' she said. 'Usually. But these people, from what you tell me, had almost a week in here. They could have found anything.'

'Did they?'

She shook her head. 'No. Luckily, the only things I keep on here are the current cases, and that was the only one I had.'

'Really the only one?' he asked, utterly confused. 'But the, what's it called, hard disc or hard drive,' he said, waving a hand at her computer. 'Aren't there traces of other things in there?'

'There would be. Ordinarily. But this is a new computer. I had to get it before Christmas, so the only . . . the only delicate information on there was about the man in Campo Santo Stefano, and not even all of that.'

He thought of all the things she had used her computer to help him with in the past, all the codes she had broken, to make no mention of the laws, and he closed his eyes in a relief he could not fully comprehend. But then he asked, 'Had to?'

'In my capacity as the Vice-Questore's administrative assistant,' she said with overweening humility.

'The old one?'

'Vianello has it.'

'In his office?' Brunetti asked in a voice close to panic.

'No, at home.'

'Just like that?' he asked. Was this a confession of abuse of office or merely of simple theft?

'No, he had to pay the Questura for it. There's a procedure for the transfer of office supplies to private persons, so long as they are not employees of a government agency.'

'Aren't the police a government agency?' he asked.

'Yes, of course. But his mother-in-law isn't on the police force.'

He had to know. 'How much did he – she – have to pay for it?'

'Ten Euros.'

'Planned obsolescence?' he asked.

'Hardly, sir. It developed a problem with the hard drive, and the technician I called said it could not be repaired and should be sold for scrap.'

'Presumably he wrote this out for you?'

'Of course.'

'And then?'

'And then Vianello's mother-in-law offered to buy it, to save us having to pay for someone to come and take it away.'

He waited for her to continue, but she did not. As if her story were a loose tooth, he prodded at it: 'And?'

'And then I just happened to be there one evening and Nadia asked me to have a look at it, to see if I could think of anything, and, well, I saw what the problem was and got it working again.' She smiled happily at the memory of this triumph.

'I'm sure you were all surprised.'

'Simply astounded, sir.'

25

The near-miss with the Ministry of the Interior, even though Brunetti had no idea what might have been discovered among Signorina Elettra's records if they had found her old computer, left Brunetti shaken. At any time, they had just been shown, the information she stored could be unearthed and looted by some other agency of the government. His mind shied away from the risks he had taken in the last years and from the realization that proof of all of it lay in the hard disc of the computer now in Vianello's possession. His career would not last a day, nor would Vianello's, nor would Signorina Elettra's, if the wrong people at the Questura came to learn what information the three of them had accumulated over the years and the means they had used to acquire it.

His memory went to the rich garment that Medea had sent to Jason's bride: no matter what she or her father did, no matter how they tried, they could not put out the flames that burst from it the instant she put it on. Similarly, once information was stored in a computer, it seemed that nothing except complete destruction could reliably extinguish it.

He told himself not to exaggerate the dangers and that he really did not know enough about computers to be sure that this was true; further, the only information that had been detected concerned a crime which he had every reason to be investigating. Rizzardi's addendum with its terrible photos was safely lodged in his phone book. When he got to his office, he hung up his coat the way he always did, checked the surface of his desk for messages or post, and with the strange sensation that unseen viewers could see what he was doing, opened his bottom drawer and pulled out the phone book. Lodged in the Ps he found the photos. He removed them and folded them into three before slipping them into the inside pocket of his jacket. As he did so, he was swept by a wave of relief so strong he felt his shirt grow damp under his arms.

The photos, however, had reminded him that Professor Winter had never got back to him. The *telefonino* he thought of as belonging to Signor Rossi had spent the holiday on the top of his dresser, despised and rejected of men, but as he dressed that morning for his return to the Questura, Brunetti had slipped it into his pocket.

When he took it out, he saw that its battery was running low but that the memory still stored her number. He started to key it in but then changed his mind and wrote it down on a piece of paper. He put the phone back in his pocket and left the Questura, heading up towards the public phones on the Riva degli Schiavoni.

'Ah, Commissario,' Professor Winter said, when he identified himself, 'I hope you had a happy Christmas.'

'Yes, I did. Thank you. And you?'

'Very. I was in Mali, you see. Didn't you get my message?'

'Message?' he asked, sounding stupid.

'Yes. I called to tell you I would be away, and your assistant said he'd tell you I called.'

Brunetti loosened his hold on the receiver, saw that the money on his phone card was fast disappearing, and said, struggling to sound calm, 'He must have forgotten to tell me, or he wrote it down and it's got lost in all the mail that's come in. Could you tell me again what you told him?' He tried a quiet little laugh and found it sounded quite convincing, so he asked, 'Did you tell him what it was about?'

'No, only that I'd be away.'

'Ah, but now you're back,' he said, forcing pleasure into his voice but fearing he managed only to sound foolish. 'And the photos? Did they get to you?'

'Yes. But I'm afraid they came at Italian speed,' she said with a little – slightly superior – laugh. 'So I didn't see them until I got back. In fact,' she said, 'when I didn't hear from you, I assumed you'd simply found it out yourself. It would be in any book about African art, of course.'

'No, nothing like that, Professor,' Brunetti said, forcing *bonhomie* into his voice and suppressing his growing anger. 'Just bureaucratic delay,' he said, trying, and failing, to fake the easy laugh he thought might be appropriate here. 'Could you tell me about the design, then?'

'Of course. One moment while I get it,' she said. 'I had one of my assistants put it on my computer.' As he waited, he watched the *centesimi* running out until he had little more than one Euro left.

'Ah, here it is,' she said. 'Yes, that's what I thought I remembered. The photo you sent is of the top part of what is called a diviner's or healer's power stick.' She paused, then asked, 'You said the head was about five centimetres high, didn't you?'

'Yes.'

'Then my guess is that the stick was about a metre long, but I've no idea how the head could have been broken off,' she said.

If that was meant to be a question, Brunetti had no answer, so he said, 'I don't know, either.'

'I suppose it doesn't matter,' she said, and Brunetti noticed that he had seventy *centesimi* left on his phone card.

'The sign on the forehead is called a *calige*,' she went on, 'the sign of life. The other figures on the staff would be animals or other figures that represent the attributes of the magician.' She stopped, as if waiting for Brunetti to speak. When he remained silent, she added, 'It's the same sign that's used in the scar. Is that what you wanted to know?'

'Certainly, Professor, it's all very interesting, but could you tell me where this sign is from?'

'Oh, didn't I tell you? It's Chokwe. No question about it. They're among the finest wood carvers in . . .' she began, but Brunetti cut her off.

'Where are they from, geographically, Professor?'

If she seemed surprised by his abruptness, she gave no sign and answered, 'Along the Zambezi River.'

Brunetti took a long breath and whispered his mother's favourite prayer for patience in times of adversity, then said, 'And where would that be politically, if I might put it that way?'

'Ah, sorry,' she said. 'I'm afraid I didn't understand your question. Angola. Or parts of western Congo. Maybe even Zambia, but it's not likely that the sub-tribes there would produce an object like that or use that sort of scarring. No, I'd say Angola.'

'I see,' Brunetti said, watching the sum on the phone reach ten *centesimi*. 'Thank you for your help, Professor; you've been very generous with your knowledge.'

325

'That's what it's for, Commissario. Will it help you, what I told you?'

The units ran out. Seeing the double zero on the phone counter, Brunetti knew he had only a few seconds to answer. 'I certainly hope so, Professor Winter,' he began, but then the line clicked and went dead. Into the dull hiss of a lost connection, Brunetti added, 'But I doubt it.'

He took the used phone card from the phone and turned back towards the Questura. Was Angola where bands of children went on drug-induced killing sprees? He stopped, looked across the *bacino* to the cupola of San Giorgio, then to the sweep of cupolas running up the *riva* of the Giudecca. There crazed children hack and chop and maim, and here the ferry boat passes in the direction of the Lido just on time.

Brunetti put out a hand and braced it against the wall of the *calle*, waiting for this strange dislocation to pass. He had read that people who thought they were going to faint should lower their heads below their knees, but he could hardly do that here. He did, however, close his eyes and lower his head.

'You all right, Signore?' he heard a man's voice ask in Veneziano.

He opened his eyes and saw a short, roly-poly man in a dark jacket, wearing a green plaid tam on what appeared to be a bald head.

'Yes. Fine. Thank you. Too much Christmas, I think,' Brunetti said and tried to smile. 'Or maybe it's these changes of temperature.'

The man smiled, relieved to hear Brunetti was

all right. 'That's probably it,' he said, 'too much Christmas.' Then, cheerfully, 'Time for us all to get back to work, isn't it?'

'Yes,' Brunetti said, 'I think it is.'

As he continued towards the Questura, he considered how he *could* get back to work. The files were gone, the case had been 'removed', not only from him, but from the Venice police force as a whole. Brunetti had no idea who the victim was or why he had been in Venice, nor had he any idea of why the man was so important that the Ministry of the Interior and the Foreign Ministry should busy themselves investigating his death or suppressing any investigation of his death. Brunetti had to confront the fact that he had no clues and no evidence. No, that was not entirely true: he still had the diamonds, or Claudio's bank did, and he still had the man's body – or assumed he did.

At that thought, he turned back towards the embankment and returned to the public phone. All he had were some Euro coins, and he put one into the phone, then dialled Rizzardi's number from memory.

When the doctor answered, Brunetti said, without introduction, 'That person we were talking about before Christmas, is he still there?'

There was a long pause, during which Brunetti could imagine Rizzardi recognizing his voice and then deciphering the question. Finally the pathologist asked, 'You mean that man from the Christmas fair?'

'Yes.'

'No, he's not,' Rizzardi said. 'I thought you knew.'

'No. Nothing. Tell me.'

Rizzardi's voice tightened, as if he found this speaking in code to be a game more fit for adolescents than for grown men. But he continued, nevertheless. 'Some people – I thought you must know about it because they work for the same company you do – they came to get him and decided they'd give him a great send-off.' Rizzardi paused, perhaps waiting to see if Brunetti was following. When Brunetti asked no questions, the pathologist added, 'Just like your friend Hector.'

Now the doctor was being too clever by half. Whatever code Rizzardi was trying to use, Brunetti was completely lost. 'Ah, Hector. Which one was that, which Hector, I mean?'

'The one in that book you're always reading, the one about the war.'

That could only be the *Iliad*, which ends with the death of Hector. And his funeral pyre.

'Ah, I see. Well, thanks, Lorenzo. I'm sorry I missed him.'

'I imagine you are,' Rizzardi said and hung up.

Something close to panic gripped at Brunetti's throat. He could not have answered if someone had asked him a question. He had lost his coin when Rizzardi hung up; he dug out another one and found he had trouble putting it in the phone. Brunetti had never had much faith in the divine; if he had, he probably would have tried to make some sort of deal: Claudio's safety for just about anything: the diamonds, the entire case of the African and his death, Brunetti's job.

He dialled Claudio's number. It rang four, five, six times, and then a woman answered.

'*Ciao*, Elsa. It's Guido. How are you?'

'Ah, Guido, how good to hear your voice. I wanted to call Paola over the holidays, but I was always so busy here, with the boys and the grandkids; I never found the time. Is she all right? Did you have a nice Christmas?'

'Yes, the kids, too. And all of you?'

'No reason to complain. We go on.' Then her voice changed and she said, 'I suppose you want to talk to Claudio.'

'Oh, is he there?'

'Yes, he's helping Riccardo's youngest with a jigsaw puzzle. We have the kids today.'

'Ah, then don't bother him, Elsa. Really, I just wanted to know how you and everyone were. Just tell him I called, and give him my love. And to all of you, as well.'

'I will, Guido. And the same to Paola and the kids. From all of us.'

He thanked her and hung up, folded his arms on the top of the telephone and rested his head on them.

After a few minutes, someone banged roughly on the door to the phone booth. It was one of the vendors from the stalls of tourist junk that lined the *riva*, a much-tattooed man with long hair, a man known to Brunetti in his professional capacity.

He apparently failed to recognize Brunetti and said, 'You all right, Signore?'

Brunetti stood up straight and let his arms drop to his sides. 'Yes,' he said, pushing open the door. 'I just had some good news.'

The man gave him a peculiar look and said, 'Strange way to react to it.'

'Yes, yes, it is,' Brunetti said. He thanked the man for his concern, words that the man shrugged off as he turned back to his stall. Brunetti started back to the Questura.

On the way he decided to tell no one. Signorina Elettra's computer had been wiped clean: let it stay that way. Vianello's was gone from the Questura: let it stay where it was. The body was gone, but Claudio was safe. If the powers that ruled them wanted to investigate the death on their own, then let them do it. They'd get no more of him. All the way back, he washed his hands of the case, raged at what he referred to as his former, unreformed self for daring to put his friend in jeopardy and for having risked the jobs and, for all he knew, the safety of the two people he loved at the Questura.

Part of his mind had moved on before the other part registered what it had heard. His steps slowed. He shoved his hands into his pockets and looked at his shoes, almost surprised to see that he was wearing shoes that were not soaked. 'The two people I love at the Questura.'

'*Maria Santissima*,' he said, echoing the exclamation with which his mother had always recognized happy surprises.

26

During the next few days, Brunetti fell into a torpor in which he failed to find the will or the energy either to work or to care that he was not working. He interviewed various professors and students at the university and judged them all to be lying, but he could not bring himself to care overmuch that they were. If anything, he took a grim delight in the fact that corruption and dishonesty should manifest themselves in the Department of the Science of Law.

The children sensed that something was wrong: Raffi occasionally asked him for help with his homework, and Chiara insisted on having him read her essays for Italian class, then asked his opinion of what she had written. Paola stopped complaining about school; in fact, she stopped complaining about everything, to such a point that Brunetti began to suspect that his wife had been the victim of alien abduction and a replicant left in her place.

One night at two in the morning, the drug addicts who had committed the rash of burglaries were discovered in the home of a notary, found there by the owner's son, who had just come back from a party at a friend's home. The boy had had too much to drink, made a great deal of noise entering the apartment, and when he saw the two men in his parents' living room, rashly attacked one of them. The father, awakened by the noise, came into the living room carrying a gun, and when the thieves saw him, one of them raised a hand. The notary shot him in the face and killed him. The other one panicked and tried to flee, but when he broke loose from the son, the notary shot him in the chest, also killing him instantly. He put the gun down and called the police.

Brunetti, reading the reports the following morning, was appalled by the waste and stupidity. They might have taken a radio, a television at worst, maybe some jewellery. The notary was the sort of person who would have insurance; nothing would be lost. And now these two poor devils were dead. The uncle of one of them was a tailor at the shop where Brunetti bought his suits and came to the Questura to ask him if anything would happen to the notary. Brunetti had to tell him that there was every likelihood that it would be declared a case of *legittima difesa*, in which case no blame would fall upon the killer.

'But is that right?' the man demanded. 'He shoots Mirko in the face like he was a dog and nothing happens to him?'

'Legally he did nothing we can charge him with, Signor Buffetti. He had a permit for the gun. His son says your nephew tried to attack him.'

'Of course he'd say that,' the man shouted. 'He's his son.'

'I know how it must seem to you,' Brunetti said. 'But there's no legal case that can be brought against him.'

The tailor tried to control his anger. Accepting the validity of Brunetti's judgement, he got to his feet and went to the door. Before he left, he turned and said, 'I can't argue with you, not in a legal way, Dottore. But I know that the police shouldn't let a man be shot and do nothing about it.' He closed the door quietly as he left.

Brunetti was not a man given to belief in signs and portents: the real had always seemed sufficiently marvellous to him. But he could recognize the truth when someone presented it to him.

Signorina Elettra, perhaps sobered by the ease with which her computer had been violated, had not asked about the case and had made no suggestion that she resume making inquiries. Vianello had taken his family to the mountains for two weeks. When Buffetti had gone, Brunetti used Signor Rossi's *telefonino* to call Vianello on his.

'Lorenzo,' Brunetti said when the inspector answered, 'when you get back, I think we have to attend to some unfinished business.'

'That's not going to make some people happy,' Vianello answered laconically.

'Probably not.'

'I've still got all the information,' Vianello said.

'Good.'

'I'm very glad you called,' Vianello said and broke the connection.

Two nights later the phone rang just before eleven. Paola answered with the cool, impersonal curiosity she directed at anyone who called after ten. A moment later, her tone changed, and she spoke to the person using the familiar *'tu'*. Brunetti listened, wondering which of her friends it might be, but then she turned to him and said, 'It's for you. It's my father.'

'Good evening, Guido,' the Count said when Brunetti took the phone.

'Good evening,' answered Brunetti, doing his best to sound normal.

The Count surprised him by asking, 'Do you get CNN?'

'What?'

'The television, CNN?'

'Yes. The kids watch it for their English,' he answered.

'I think you should turn on their news at midnight.'

Brunetti glanced at his watch and saw that it was only a few minutes after eleven. 'Not until then?'

'It won't be on until then, what I want you to see. I've just had a phone call from a friend.'

'But why CNN?' Brunetti asked. He thought RAI had a midnight newscast, but he wasn't sure.

'You'll understand when you see it. It'll be in the papers tomorrow, but I think you'd better see the way it's going to be presented.'

'I don't know what you're talking about,' Brunetti said.

'You will,' the Count said and hung up.

He told Paola about the conversation, but she could make no sense of it, either. Together they went into the living room and turned on the television. Paola took the remote and switched from channel to channel. They flicked past people trying to sell mattresses, women reading tarot cards, an old film, another old film, two people of indeterminate gender engaged in an activity that was perhaps meant to be sexual, another fortune teller, until finally they came upon the faintly alien face of the CNN news-reader.

'They never have two matching eyes,' Paola remarked as she sat on the sofa. 'And I think they all wear wigs.'

'You mean you watch this?' asked an astonished Brunetti.

'Sometimes, with the kids,' she said defensively.

'He said midnight,' Brunetti reminded her and took the remote control from her hand. He pushed the mute button.

'There's time for something to drink, then,' Paola said and got to her feet. She disappeared towards the kitchen, leaving Brunetti to wonder whether she would emerge with something real to drink or a cup of tisane.

His eyes turned to the screen and he watched what appeared to be a programme about the stock market: a man and a woman, equally other-worldly in appearance, chatted amiably, occasionally reducing each other to peals of not very convincing silent laughter, while below the picture scrolled stock prices that would reduce any thinking person to tears.

After about ten minutes Paola came back with two mugs, saying: 'The best of both worlds: hot water, lemon, honey, and whiskey.'

She handed him one, then joined him on the sofa to observe the two not-talking heads. Soon she too registered the disparity between the hilarity of the presenters and the misery of the numbers that continued their tidal flow below them. 'It's like watching Nero playing the lyre while Rome burns,' she observed.

'That's not a true story,' the historian in Brunetti declared.

At five to midnight he restored the sound but quickly adjusted it to a barely audible minimum. With a final cheery smile, the two presenters disappeared, to be replaced by a rapid series of views of some Gulf state eager for foreign investment or tourism.

A globe, the throb of portentous music, and then the face of another presenter. Brunetti increased the sound and together they listened to a report on the latest suicidal attack in the Middle East, then one by an F16 with an equal number of victims. There followed a report from Delhi about another failed attempt to restore peace in Kashmir.

And then the presenter's face took on an expression of learned seriousness. Brunetti increased the volume again. 'And now, breaking news from Italy. We pass you to our local correspondent, Arnoldo Vitale, with a live report of a terrorist attempt that has been foiled by the Italian police. Arnoldo, are you there?'

'Yes, Jim,' said a lightly accented voice in English. There was a slight pause and crackle as the image changed and the voice line switched over. In the top left corner of the screen appeared a talking head, behind him the dome of St Peter's Basilica.

The rest of the screen showed the grey stucco façade of an apartment building. In front of it were parked the black Jeeps and cars of the *Carabinieri* as well as four unmarked dark sedans. Men in helmets and flak jackets with CARABINIERI written across the back, all carrying machine-guns, milled around with evident lack of purpose. To the left of them stood a group of four or five men in combat gear, all wearing ski masks.

The voice continued. 'This evening, Italian police raided an apartment in Vigonza, a generally peaceful suburb of the northern Italian city of Padova, not far from Venice. This in response to a report that members of an Islamic fundamentalist sect had been using one of the apartments in the building as a centre for meetings and training sessions. Italian security experts linking the group to the Al Qaeda terrorist organization and its attacks against American interests.

'First reports that the police attempted to get the two men in the apartment to give themselves up. Response from the terrorist suspects violent, leaving the police no choice but to storm the apartment. In the ensuing gun battle, one police officer wounded and both of the terrorists in the apartment killed.'

'Arnoldo,' asked the unaccented voice, 'how strong is this link to international terrorism?'

'Yes, Jim, the police here say they have been aware of this group for some time. As you know, arrests have been made all over Italy this year of suspected terrorists. A government spokesperson reporting that this is the most violent confrontation so far and hopes it is not a sign of things to come.'

'Arnoldo, is there any perceived threat to Americans travelling in Italy?'

'No, none at all, Jim. The same spokesman said that any connection to US interests would be to US base in Vicenza, about twenty miles from here. Authorities examining that possibility, but believe no danger to the civilian population.'

As the two men spoke, the *Carabinieri* continued to wander about in front of the building. Finally the door opened inward and a man carrying the front of a stretcher emerged, then a second man. A long shape covered with a sheet lay on it. A second stretcher emerged, but the *Carabinieri* ignored both, turning to face the crowd that stood behind a hastily erected row of barriers.

'Once again, Jim: terrorist network broken up by intervention by Italian police. No threat to Americans on vacation in the country.' Voice sinking into inflated portentiousness, he concluded, 'But it looks like Italy is now home to something other than la dolce vita.'

The picture returned to the news-reader. He gave a serious smile and said, 'That was our Italian correspondent, Arnoldo Vitale, speaking from Rome. Italian police reporting break-up of terrorist ring based near Padova, Italy. No threat to Americans in the area.'

The camera panned to the woman sitting beside him. She turned to Jim, saying, 'We've got more news from Italy, Jim, but of a different sort.' There was a pause, one no doubt deemed long enough to erase the thought of the death of two men, and she went on, 'In news that has stunned the fashion industry, one of Italy's most famous fashion designers says he will not use leather or any animal products in his spring collection.'

Brunetti switched the channel to RAI, but the same old movie was still playing. He tried all of the channels in turn, but there was no report of the incident, not even on the local stations.

He turned the television off. 'Did your father say where he was calling from?'

Surprised by the question, Paola said, 'No, he didn't.'

Brunetti looked at his watch. 'If I call now and he's not there, I'll wake your mother, won't I?'

'Yes.'

'Then it will have to wait,' he said, picking up his cup. But the drink was cold and he set it down untasted.

Brunetti slept little and was outside by six-thirty, walking in rain he barely noticed towards Sant'Aponal and the *edicola* there. He saw the shouting headlines and bought four papers. As he handed Brunetti his change, the news dealer said, with a return to his normal tone, 'Lousy rain. It'll never stop.'

Brunetti ignored him and went back home, not bothering to stop to get brioche on the way. In the kitchen, he made himself a pot of coffee and set some milk on to heat. Then he mixed them in a mug and sat in front of the papers, which he had arranged in a neat pile with his glasses folded on top.

Paola came in half an hour later and found him still reading, newspapers open across the entire surface of the table. Though he had read all of the accounts carefully, he still had no idea why his father-in-law had told him to watch the news.

She poured what remained of the coffee into a cup, stirred in sugar, and came to stand behind him. Placing her hand on his shoulder, she asked, 'And?'

'And it's pretty much what they said last night: two men in an apartment near Padova. The *Carabinieri* received a phone call saying they were members of a terrorist group that was preparing attacks against American interests.'

'What interests?' Paola asked.

'That wasn't explained. At least not in the papers,' he said, pushing the one he was reading aside.

'And then?' she asked, her coffee forgotten, hand still on his shoulder.

'And they went. You saw the way they were last night, cars and Jeeps and trucks, and God knows how many of them.' Brunetti pulled one of the papers towards him and flipped back to the front page, where they could both see a photo of the same apartment, the same stretcher bearers, the same apparently purposeless *Carabinieri*.

'The *Carabinieri* hoped to catch them unawares, the article says,' Brunetti reported.

Paola bent forward and jabbed a finger at the photo, 'With half an armoured division at the front door?' she demanded.

'The men in the apartment,' Brunetti began

and then bowed his head to hunt for the account. '". . . responded with violence, leaving the forces of order no choice but to defend themselves. In the resulting exchange of fire, one policeman was shot in the arm, but the two terrorists were fatally wounded."' He read another paragraph silently and then again out loud. '"Among the documents found in the apartment were hand-drawn maps of the American embassy in Rome and what is believed to be the water system of the US base in Vicenza."'

Brunetti removed his glasses and tossed them on to the papers. 'There is a statement from someone who is listed as "a member of the special anti-terrorism unit", who says that the police responded bravely and well and that it is hoped that an investigation will reveal the full extent of the links between this group and international terrorism.'

Paola moved over to the sink and poured her cold coffee into it. She opened and cleaned the pot, started to fill it with water. 'More?' she asked.

'No,' Brunetti said. 'I've had too much already.'

When the pot was on the stove, Paola sat down opposite him. Gesturing at the papers on the table, she asked, 'But why did my father call you? What does it mean?'

Brunetti shrugged. 'Just about anything, I suppose. It could mean that it is exactly what they say it is, a terrorist cell. But it could mean other things.'

'You've had coffee, so you tell me what the possibilities are. My political imagination isn't awake yet.'

'The first thing that is strange is that they don't give the nationality of the suspects, nor do they give their names. Nor do they give any idea of what larger terrorist group they're linked to.'

'The Americans said Islamic fundamentalists.'

'The Americans say that if someone double parks,' Brunetti answered angrily. Then, in a cooler voice, he went on, 'Your father called me and told me to watch this, but the original call came from a friend of his. But your father wouldn't call unless it were related to the black man's death. But I have no idea how.'

The coffee bubbled up, and Paola went to take it off the stove. 'Then go to work and see what they tell you there.'

At the Questura, where he arrived a little after eight, things seemed as quiet and restrained as they generally did at that hour. He went up to his office, but since he had already read the newspapers, he had no choice but to read through the documents and files that had been accumulating on his desk for more than a month. He found himself thinking that, if the people from the Ministry of the Interior had seen fit to answer his phone for him while they were there, the least they could have done was read and process all of these papers.

He kept at it doggedly until about eleven, when his phone rang. He answered on the sixth ring, reluctant to be taken from the mindless rhythm of his paperwork. 'Yes?' he answered gruffly.

'Good morning, Commissario,' Signorina Elettra said.

'Sorry,' he said automatically. 'I've had too much coffee.'

'Apparently so has the Vice-Questore.'

'Excuse me?'

'He's quite ebullient, if that's the proper word to describe his behaviour. And he wants to see you.'

'I'll come down,' Brunetti said, entranced by the idea of what form an ebullient Patta would take.

It took the form, he saw when he entered Patta's office a few minutes later, of a broad smile in which Brunetti noticed a considerable proportion of self-satisfaction. 'Ah, Brunetti,' Patta fairly chirped when he saw him. 'I'm glad you came down. There are a number of things I want to tell you.'

'Yes, sir?' Brunetti asked, coming forward.

'Sit down, sit down,' Patta said, pointing Brunetti to a chair just in front of him.

Brunetti took his place but said nothing.

'I know we're all busy, so I won't take up too much of your time,' Patta began, which told Brunetti that he must have plans for an early lunch or for one out of town.

'Yes, sir?'

'It's about this black man who was killed,' he began, but then, slipping a note of camaraderie into his voice, 'or, if I must say it, about your refusal to trust me when I said it was being handled by higher authorities.' Brunetti asked for no explanation, so Patta continued. 'I told you they knew what was going on with these men.'

When he saw Brunetti react to that last word, Patta said, 'Yes. Men. There were a number of them, and the man who was killed was a member of their group.'

Here Brunetti interrupted the flow to ask, 'Are you speaking about the incident in Vigonza last night, sir?'

'Yes, I am. I've spent the morning with my counterpart' – ah, how Patta loved the rhetoric – 'at the Ministry of the Interior. He came here to share with me their intelligence on the men who were killed in that gun battle last night.'

'And that was?' Brunetti inquired.

'The news reports have it right, at least in essence. They were members of a terrorist organization: there's no question of that. But they aren't certain yet which larger group they were linked to.'

'No doubt they'll discover that,' said a diffident Brunetti.

Missing his tone, Patta smiled at his words. 'Of course they will. I'm glad you can see it that way.'

'And the phone call?' Brunetti prodded.

'An anonymous call, apparently made from a public phone. It told the police where to go.'

'The police? I thought I saw pictures in the

paper of *Carabinieri* vehicles.' He remembered, but did not mention, the unmarked cars.

'It was a mixed operation,' Patta answered smoothly.

Brunetti thought of the men in ski masks but said only, 'I see.'

'They wanted to get into the apartment before the men realized they were there. But they must have been on guard, or perhaps they heard them.'

'Or saw them from the window?' Brunetti suggested.

'I don't know about that,' Patta said with the first signs of irritation. 'But what I do know is that, when the men went in, the terrorists opened fire. There was no choice but to fire back, and in the confusion, both of them were killed. Luckily, only one of us was hit, and not badly.'

Brunetti resisted the impulse to give voice to an exclamation of prayerful thanksgiving.

'When it was over, they searched the place and found weapons and documents. False passports, an arsenal.' When Brunetti did not comment or question, Patta added, 'One of the guns they used is the same calibre as the one that killed the man in Campo Santo Stefano. The first hypothesis is that there was some sort of falling out between them, and they decided to eliminate him,' Patta concluded. The statements describing the killers as white were among those things disappeared from Signorina Elettra's computer, and he had never bothered to get the addresses of the American witnesses. Patta pointed at a folder that lay on the desk between them and said, 'My counterpart brought me copies of the police photos.'

'Will they be in the papers?' Brunetti asked.

'Perhaps, in days to come,' Patta answered, then added, 'but perhaps some of them are too graphic to be given to the press.' He opened the folder and turned the photos around, then pushed them across the desk to Brunetti.

Brunetti knew he would recognize them even before he saw them, so he gave no indication of surprise when the first photo revealed a close-up of two of the black men he had spoken to in the apartment in Castello. The gentle eyes of the older one were open in death, gentle no longer. Nor was he unprepared to see the profile of the very thin young man, who succeeded in looking just as angry in death as he had in life. It was the later photos, taken from farther away so as to give a full view of the room, that did succeed in surprising Brunetti. The older man lay on his back, a machine-gun across his chest, one hand gripped around the stock. The younger man lay on his left side, his right arm thrust out, fingers wrapped around the butt of a pistol.

'I see,' Brunetti said, sliding the photos back across the desk.

'I hope the sight of these will be enough to convince you that they knew what they were doing, the men from the Ministry of the Interior.'

'There's no doubt of that,' Brunetti said, getting to his feet.

27

As he walked up the stairs to his office, Brunetti realized the low humming sound he heard was one he was making himself. He forced himself to stop, hoping that the pressure he felt as a physical force in his head and chest would ebb away if he did. It seemed to help, and by the time he was back in his office, his rage had diminished sufficiently to allow thought.

The set-up was easily understood: arrive with enough firepower, blow the men away, and then provide an explanation likely to be believed. What more fashionable than terrorism these days? It was entirely likely that the *Carabinieri* who were called in had no idea of what was really going on, were there like extras in a production of *Aida*, useful to cross the stage once or twice to provide verisimilitude in what might otherwise be revealed as a shabby, ill-rehearsed spectacle.

Brunetti thought back to the scene the cameras had revealed: the blue cars had no markings, and the uniforms of the men in the ski masks bore no insignia. By calling in some favours, he could probably see the *Carabinieri* report on the incident, but there was no guarantee that it would reveal the identity of the masked men, nor was it likely to specify which corps had been the first to enter the apartment.

He tried to recall the appearance of the room in which the two men were photographed, for it suddenly occurred to him that they might just as easily have been executed somewhere else. The shapes on the stretchers were merely shapes, and it was easy enough to spill blood on a floor, any floor. He stopped himself there, realizing that he was entering the land of paranoia: it would, after all, have been far easier for them to track down the two men and follow them to where they were hiding. It required far less scene-setting than the other scenario. Besides, only those who broke into the apartment need know what had happened there.

Inside his office, Brunetti went to the battered wardrobe against the far wall and pulled down the metal box in which he kept his service revolver. He placed it on his desk and unlocked it, then took out the cloth-covered wooden head.

He unwrapped it and set it upright on his desk, but the splintered pieces of the neck caused it to fall over and roll to one side. He took it in his hand and studied the face. Though there was no trace of a smile, the head nevertheless gave a sense of peace and well-being. The smooth finish reflected the light. He placed a finger on the pattern carved into the forehead and followed the zigzag until it returned, unbroken, to the point where it had begun.

'Chokwe,' Brunetti said, trying to pronounce the word as Professoressa Winter had.

After some time, he replaced the figure in its cloth, slipped it back in the box, and put the box back on to the top shelf of the closet. Then he went home.

For two days, Brunetti neither discussed the case, nor allowed himself to think about it at any conscious level. To his colleagues, he seemed abstracted, but they paid little attention.

On the morning of the third day, a Saturday, his father-in-law called him at home early enough to wake him up.

'Guido,' the Count began, 'have you been out to get the papers yet?'

'No,' said a befuddled Brunetti.

'Then I suggest you do so. Get *Il Sole 24 Ore* and look at the short piece at the bottom of page eleven. It might answer some questions for you.' Before Brunetti could ask for any explanation, the Count was gone.

Paola remained inert beneath the covers. Brunetti got up and did as he was told, but on the way back from the news-stand he stopped and bought a package of pastries and took them home with him. He put them on the counter in the kitchen and made coffee, perversely delaying the process of opening the paper and reading whatever it was the Count wanted him to see. When his coffee was ready, he sat at the table, glanced at the black headlines against the orange, and opened the newspaper to page eleven.

Two single-column articles, each of about fifteen centimetres, stood among the ads at the bottom of the page. The first carried the headline, UBS LAYS OFF SIX HUNDRED EMPLOYEES IN RESTRUCTURING: Brunetti did not bother to read any further.

The second read, MILAN CONSORTIUM SIGNS AFRICAN MINERAL RIGHTS AGREEMENT. Brunetti set down his coffee and pulled the paper closer. The article reported that a group of Milanese mineral and oil exploration companies had signed a ten-year contract with the government of Angola, which granted them exclusive rights to all exploration and future mining of 'extractive materials and products' in the eastern part of the former Portuguese colony. This agreement was made possible, the article explained, by the recent sweeping victories of government forces in the decades-old civil war against insurgents of the Lunda and Chokwe tribes. It was hoped that the disappearance of the leader of the rebel movement, presumably in recent fighting, would contribute to the restoration of peace in the region, which had for more than a decade been the scene of rebel massacres.

Giorgio Mufatti, senior Vice-President of the conglomerate, said in an interview that the contract would create at least five hundred jobs for European employees of the contract-winning companies and at least twice that many for the local population. 'These jobs will help restore peace to this war-ravaged nation,' said Mufatti.

Dottor Mufatti praised the aid and encouragement given the project by the Ministry of Foreign Affairs, whose 'assistance to and close ties with the legitimate government of Angola have been instrumental in winning this contract for an Italian company'.

Details of the terms of the deal were not yet available, but it was hoped that exploration would begin with the end of the spring rains.

He looked up as Paola came into the kitchen, still drugged with sleep. She wiped her face with both hands and looked across the room at him. 'Did the phone ring earlier?' she asked, moving to the sink to make fresh coffee.

'Yes,' he said.

'Who was it?' she asked.

'Oh, nothing,' he answered. 'A wrong number.'

She moved much in the manner of a robot, filling the pot with water, spooning in the coffee, screwing the top back on. While she moved about, he closed the newspaper and set it aside, then opened the *Gazzettino*. She came and stood behind him, resting her elbows on his shoulders. 'Why are you up so early?'

'I don't know. Couldn't sleep.'

She saw the package on the counter and went over and opened it. 'Guido,' she said, 'you are a saint.'

The coffee boiled up, and she poured it into a cup, then added some of the hot milk he had left on the back of the stove. She came and sat beside him.

She sipped at her coffee, sipped again, then asked, 'Who was it that called?'

'Your father,' he answered, wondering why he was, after all these years, still such a transparent liar.

'What for, so early?'

'To give me some information about the black man.'

'Ah. Did it help?'

'I think so, yes.'

'How?'

'It showed me who he might have been and why he was killed.'

She sipped again. 'And?' she asked.

'And Patta was right: there's nothing to be done about it.'

'Nothing?' she asked in honest surprise.

He shook his head.

After a long time, Paola asked, 'What about the diamonds?'

Her question startled Brunetti, who had forgotten about them entirely. 'They're in a bank,' he said.

'I should hope so. But what will you do with them?'

He picked up his cup and found it empty, but he didn't want to go to the bother of making more coffee. The man who had had the stones was dead, and it seemed the cause they were perhaps meant to aid was lost. They lay in a bank, inert, without real value until someone placed it on them. 'I don't know,' he admitted.

'What do you want to do?' Paola asked.

'About the diamonds?'

'No, about today.'

When she spoke, Brunetti realized that, though he had walked down to Sant'Aponal an hour ago, he had paid no attention to the day. He looked out of the window, towards the mountains, and when he saw them in the distance, he realized the day was clear. 'I'd like to walk down to Sant'Elena and then go out to Lido and take a walk on the beach,' he said.

'A purification ritual?' she asked with her first smile.

He shrugged. They remained silent for some time until Brunetti said, 'If Claudio sold them, Don Alvise could see that the money got to people who need help.'

'It's better than keeping them in the bank,' Paola said.

'And it's better than what the money was supposed to be used for,' Brunetti said, but instantly added, 'I think.'

His mood suddenly lightened and he got to his feet to make more coffee. He paused and looked out of the window again, at the distant mountains, covered with snow now: pure, aloof, eternally unconcerned with the lusts and desires of men. 'I'll wait for you to get dressed,' he said. 'And then we'll go for a walk.'

Suffer the Little Children

Donna Leon

When Commissario Brunetti is summoned to the hospital bedside of a senior pediatrician whose skull has been fractured, he is confronted with more questions than answers. Three men – a Carabinieri captain and two privates from out of town – have burst into the doctor's apartment in the middle of the night, attacked him and taken away his eighteen-month old baby. What can have motivated such a violent assault by the police?

But then Brunetti begins to uncover a story of infertility, desperation, and an underworld in which babies can be bought for cash, at the same time as Inspector Vianello uncovers a money-making scam between pharmacists and doctors in the city. But one of the pharmacists is motivated by more than thoughts of gain – the power of knowledge and delusions of moral rectitude can be as destructive and powerful as love of money. And the uses of information about one's neighbours can lead to all kinds of corruption and all sorts of pain . . .

Praise for Donna Leon:

'*Through A Glass, Darkly*, like all her work, has the exuberance of a Puccini opera.' *Independent*

'A joy from start to finish.'
Evening Standard

ALSO AVAILABLE IN ARROW

Friends in High Places
Donna Leon

When Commissario Guido Brunetti is visited by a young bureau-crat investigating the lack of official approval for the building of his apartment years earlier, his first reaction, like any other Venetian, is to think of whom he knows who might bring pressure to bear on the relevant government department. But when the bureaucrat rings Brunetti at work, clearly scared, and is then found dead after a fall from scaffolding; something is obviously going on that has implications greater than the fate of Brunetti's apartment . . .

'Leon tells the story as if she loves Venice as much as her detective does, warts and all. The plot and subplots unfold elegantly; beauty and the beast march hand in hand, and the result is rich entertainment.'
Sunday Times

'All Donna Leon's novels are excellent in their evocation of place, whilst in Brunetti she has created a character, who becomes more real in each book . . . However, *Friends in High Places* is by far the best and makes a quantum leap forward.'
Evening Standard

arrow books

THE POWER OF READING

Visit the Random House website and get connected with information on all our books and authors

EXTRACTS from our recently published books and selected backlist titles

COMPETITIONS AND PRIZE DRAWS Win signed books, audiobooks and more

AUTHOR EVENTS Find out which of our authors are on tour and where you can meet them

LATEST NEWS on bestsellers, awards and new publications

MINISITES with exclusive special features dedicated to our authors and their titles

READING GROUPS Reading guides, special features and all the information you need for your reading group

LISTEN to extracts from the latest audiobook publications

WATCH video clips of interviews and readings with our authors

RANDOM HOUSE INFORMATION including advice for writers, job vacancies and all your general queries answered

Come home to Random House

www.randomhouse.co.uk